Churchill's
Secret
Spy

Raymond Buckland

QVP
Queen Victoria Press
P.O. Box 892, Wooster, OH 44691-0892

CHURCHILL'S SECRET SPY

ISBN 978-0-9794560-7-7

Queen Victoria Press
P.O. Box 892, Wooster, OH 44691-0892

www.raymondbucklandbooks.com

CHURCHILL'S SECRET SPY

CHURCHILL'S SECRET SPY

1: NEW ACQUAINTANCES

Afterwards she claimed that it wasn't bravery. "I just did what I had to do at the time," she said. But the newspapers reported it differently.

At the height of yesterday's air raid, Kirsteen Craig, a nurse employed at London's Queen Charlotte's Hospital, ran into a blazing building, set on fire by falling incendiary bombs, and rescued two young children trapped in their bedroom.

Kirsteen lived in a small flat on Duke Street, off Oxford Street. She had taken the tube across town and had just emerged at Marylebone Station when the air raid started. She stayed underground for a while but finally decided that she had to get on to work; the nurses on duty had been there for well over eighteen hours and desperately needed to be relieved. So she came up out of the station and headed for the hospital. As she turned a corner she saw a tenement building burst into flames; an incendiary bomb had made a direct hit. A hysterical woman was dragged out of the front door by an elderly man.

"My babies! My babies! They're still in there!" the woman screamed.

"You can't help them!" the man said, keeping a firm grip on her. "Don't you see that? We were lucky to get out ourselves. You can't help the poor things."

Kirsteen saw they were both in tears. She ran up to the woman.

"Where are they?" she asked.

"What?" The woman seemed to be in shock.

"In the back. Ground-floor bedroom," the man said. "But you can't ..."

Kirsteen didn't stop to hear what she couldn't do. She ran into the smoke-filled hallway and headed toward the back of the house. The staircase was blazing and she had to duck down and press against the side wall to get past the flames, thankful the children were not upstairs. The passageway was filled with smoke and, despite holding up the collar of her coat over her mouth, she had difficulty breathing. She paused for a moment, listening, then made out the sounds of crying and whimpering coming from behind a closed door. She ran to it and turned the handle. It wouldn't open.

Kirsteen didn't know if it was locked or just stuck. She didn't wait to find out. Raising her leg, and giving thanks that she was wearing her low-heeled hospital shoes rather than high heels, she slammed her foot against the door by the handle. With a bang it flew open. Flames sprang up from the carpet inside. Through them she could just make out two small dark forms huddled together on the bed in the far corner of the room. She leapt through the flames and landed on the bed beside them. Immediately the two little girls clung to her, crying loudly.

"Hold on, sweeties," she cried. "You're going to be all right. Just wait one minute and then we'll be out of here." To herself she thought "This isn't going to be easy!"

She pulled free of the girls and quickly grabbed a blanket off the bed and wrapped it around them. Then she ran to where the curtains at the window were starting to burn. Grabbing up a small chair, Kirsteen smashed it through the window, curtains and all. She ran back to the bed, scooped up the children and, holding them tightly in her arms, jumped out of the window. She knew they were on the ground floor but other than that she didn't know what might be outside; she just took her chance. As she hit the ground she fell but had the presence of mind to try to turn so that the children would fall on top of her. Next thing she knew the firemen were there and helping her and the two little girls away from the now blazing house.

"No, I didn't stop to think about my own danger," Kirsteen said, matter-of-factly, to the interviewer. "You don't in a situation like that. You see what has to be done and you just go and do it." She looked about her at the questioning faces. She was standing in the Matron's office at the hospital. Reporters had caught up with her and wanted a full report. "It's not like I'm the only one who's done something like this," she added. "With all the bombing that's going on, this is hardly an isolated event, I'd think."

One or two of the reporters smiled and shook their heads. "It's still not what you might call your everyday occurrence," one of them said.

Kirsteen shrugged and, after fielding a few more questions, got Matron's permission to return to her duties. By the end of the long shift she had almost forgotten the way her day had started.

Like so many other Londoners, Kirsteen had lived through the German *Blitzkreig* of 1940; eighteen months before. At that time over a period of fifty-seven days, from September 7 to November 13, between one hundred fifty and three hundred Luftwaffe bombers had flown over and dropped at least one hundred tons of explosives on London each and every night. About a million incendiary bombs had also fallen in that period. By the end of the blitz Kirsteen, along with others, had become hardened to the air raids.

The telephone rang and woke Kirsteen. Through sleepy eyes she looked at the luminous hands of her alarm clock. Seven thirty in the morning. She had hoped to sleep till at least eight.

"Hello?"

"Miss Kirsteen Craig?" The voice sounded educated and polite.

"Yes." She struggled up into a sitting position.

"I'm awfully sorry if I woke you. I know what long hours you've been working," the voice said.

"Who is this?" She ran her hand back through her long brown hair then leaned across to snap on the bedside light. Daylight was sneaking in around the blackout curtains over the window but not enough to really allow her to see anything.

"Oh! Sorry again! My name's Simpson. Nigel Simpson. War Ministry. I'd like to speak with you, if I may?"

"I thought we were speaking," she said.

"Oh! Oh, yes." Her caller gave a high-pitched laugh. "Jolly good! No, what I meant was, I'd like to get together and talk with you, in person. Not just over the telephone," he spelled it out.

"Who are you?" she asked again.

"I told you. Nigel . . ."

"No! Not your name. I mean, what do you want with me? Why should I meet with you?"

She heard a sigh.

"I'm afraid all I can say right now is that I'm with the War Office. It's <u>very</u> important that I speak with you, but I'm afraid I can't go into any details over the telephone." He paused, then: "Careless talk costs lives, y'know."

She had seen the many posters up all over London, especially on the underground trains and in the Post Offices, with a variety of cartoons by the popular Fougasse emphasizing those same words *CARELESS TALK COSTS LIVES*. But she had never expected to hear them used directly to her, with any deep meaning. She had no idea what this was all about.

"All right," Kirsteen said. "I don't have to be at the hospital till two this afternoon."

"I know," Nigel said.

She ignored it. "So when and where do we meet? And do I have to wear a long black cloak?"

Nigel laughed his high-pitched laugh again. "Very good! Yes; cloak-and-dagger. I got it! No, just your usual attire will do fine. I suggest the foyer of the Regent's Hotel. At nine-thirty? I'll be wearing a red carnation in my buttonhole, so you'll spot me."

It was Kirsteen's turn to laugh out loud. "Of course!" She chuckled. "That's the least I'd expect!"

Nigel Simpson was a thin, stoop-shouldered young man, not much older than Kirsteen. She judged him to be in his late twenties. He had a nervous little giggle and would run his finger quickly around his collar when he was uncomfortable.

"Now what's this all about?" she demanded.

Kirsteen's girlfriend, Isobel, had told her many times that she was too direct.

"You'll never get a boy-friend if you're that direct all the time," she'd said.

"I don't know that I want a boy-friend," Kirsteen had responded. "And if I do, I'd rather have one that doesn't beat around the bush anyway. I don't like playing games. I like to know what's going on."

And that's what she said to Nigel. "What's going on? How do you know all about me; about where I work and what hours I'm there?"

Nigel looked pleased with himself.

"You might say that's all part of my job," he said. He ran a finger quickly around his collar and glanced over his shoulder to make sure no one was anywhere near the banquette on which they sat in the hotel lobby. He leaned a little closer to her. "I'm with MI-6."

Kirsteen was impressed. MI-6 was part of the British Secret Service. She had heard of it, of course, though actually knew few details concerning it. It was something to do with spies and, obviously, was very active during the war.

"MI-6?" she said. Nigel looked pleased at her response. "You mean, you're a spy?"

Again he looked quickly over his shoulder.

"Sssh! No, not exactly . . . Actually, not at all. I'm *with* MI-6, but just in the office. I type up a lot of reports and arrange meetings and things. Not very exciting." He sounded deflated after his initial enthusiasm.

"Still, it is with MI-6," she said, and he perked up. "That would be exciting enough for me. Now, Nigel, where do I come in? What does MI-6 want with me?"

"Actually I don't know," he admitted. "Not exactly, anyway. I was told to contact you and to set up a meeting for you."

"I see." Kirsteen thought for a moment. "A meeting with whom?"

"I - I don't know. But I know it's very important," he added hastily.

They arranged a time that was convenient for her and then Nigel left, first glancing dramatically around the lobby before jumping into the revolving doors. Kirsteen laughed to herself, feeling sure he had exited that way solely to impress her.

The meeting was to take place in the evening, in two days time.

Kirsteen felt she was perhaps being unnecessarily extravagant, but she took a taxi to the appointed place. She had a sense that something very important was about to take place. Added to that was the fact that she wasn't too sure of the exact location of Storey's Gate, the rendez-vous address Nigel had given her. Happily, as she had hoped, the taxi driver knew right away where it was. As they sped along she peeped out at the darkened streets thinking, as she so often did, how strange it was to see so few cars in the big city these days. Those that were to be seen had, like her taxi, fitted covers over their headlights; slotted flaps directing the light downward so that no enemy aircraft could catch sight of the light.

The cab pulled into the curb and the driver turned back to her.

"Storey's Gate, Miss."

They were in Whitehall, though at which building she was unsure. She presumed it was the War Office. As she paid off the taxi a tall, middle-aged man in the uniform of an army Major, came forward and saluted her.

"Miss Craig?"

"Yes."

"Follow me, please."

She went past the sand-bagged entrance into the building, noticing an assortment of uniforms; all the services seemed to be represented there. People hurried back and forth, coming and going through a number of different doors that led off from the main lobby. The Major had her sign her name in a book at a desk near the door, and pinned a TEMPORARY VISITOR'S PASS to her coat.

"If you'll be seated here, Miss," he said, "I'll let Mr. Rance know you're here."

She sat on the wooden chair by the desk and he disappeared. She hadn't long to wait.

"Miss Craig?" An elderly man in a gray suit came out of a door and beckoned her. "This way, please."

She got up and followed. He led her along a narrow passageway to another door at the far end. Through that was a small vestibule with an elevator door. It was already open, as though waiting for them. They stepped inside and the door shut. Kirsteen noticed that the elderly gentleman did not touch any buttons. Indeed, there were no buttons. The elevator descended, without her knowing how far it went down, and the doors opened again. They stepped out.

"Here we are," he said.

Kirsteen couldn't keep quiet any longer.

"Where?" she asked. "Mister . . . ?"

"Rance. George Rance. I'm sorry for all the cloak and dagger stuff, Miss Craig. Really I am. But in just a moment all will be made clear, I promise you."

He led her along another narrow corridor and stopped outside a wooden door.

"Come!" A voice called from inside when George Rance knocked. They went in.

Kirsteen's heart nearly missed a beat when she saw, sitting looking at her, the Prime Minister, Winston Churchill.

2: NEW DIRECTIONS

Winston Churchill was wearing what was known as a "siren suit" -- a two piece battle-dress-style outfit that actually made Kirsteen think of a baby's rompers! In the War Room, the underground command post where they were, the Prime Minister spent so much time -- even sleeping there many nights -- that he needed to be completely comfortable, so this was his adopted style of dress. He peered at her over the tops of his half-glasses.

"Won't you sit down, Miss Craig?"

The room was small, with several solid pillars and sloping roof supports. The Prime Minister sat behind a wooden desk that was well covered with assorted piles of official papers. Kirsteen noted a whole nest of telephones: black, white, red and green in color. Filing cabinets lined two walls and large-scale maps of Europe and of the world covered another. There was another chair beside the Prime Minister's desk -- a comfortable, padded one -- and Kirsteen sat down, well forward on the edge of it, her feet planted together and her hands tightly gripping her leatherette-covered gas-mask case. All Britons carried a gas-mask at all times and had done since they were issued at the outbreak of the war. Most used the basic-issue cardboard box-cum-carrying case but some adopted more stylish containers. As she sat there Kirsteen hardly dared meet the great man's gaze.

He had a newspaper open in front of him and, looking down, started to read aloud from it. It was a report on Kirsteen's rescue of the two children.

"You seem to have little regard for your personal safety," was Churchill's comment, when he stopped reading and looked up.

Although it wasn't a direct question, she took it as one. "I care about my own life as much as anyone, sir," she said. "It just seemed that there was something more important to concentrate on at the time."

He nodded, silently, and looked down again at the paper. "You made a statement to the press that you are doing your part in the war effort but that you wish you could do more." He looked up again, looking her straight in the eyes. "Did you mean that?"

"Of course!" The answer came automatically.

"Hmm!" Churchill carefully folded up the newspaper and placed it to one side, on top of a pile of similarly folded newspapers. He sat back, his lower lip jutting out and the fingers of his hands steepled together, as he became lost in thought. Kirsteen sat quietly. Suddenly realizing that she was holding her breath, she let it out slowly and, she hoped, quietly. After a moment Churchill looked up at her.

"Miss Craig, I think we might be able to use you to greater advantage. I -- we; the country -- have a problem that you might be able to help us solve."

Her heart beat so loudly she was sure he would hear it. Did he really mean it? Was this really Winston Churchill telling her that he needed her help? She slipped one hand along her other arm and gave herself a pinch, just to make sure she wasn't dreaming.

"Yes, sir?"

"I have taken the liberty of checking your background," he continued. "Your father, as I understand it, is retired Brigadier Donald Campbell Craig."

"Yes, sir." She nodded. "Daddy was severely shell-shocked in World War I. He's now down in Torquay."

The Prime Minister opened a file folder and glanced at the papers inside it. "Right! At the

Channelview Rest Home, I see. He's a well-decorated veteran. War Medal; DSM and bar. Such a shame about his condition. How badly off is he?"

Kirsteen swallowed before answering. "He doesn't really know anyone any more," she said. "He has to have complete rest and absolute quiet."

Churchill nodded sympathetically. "And your mother died when you were quite young."

"Yes, sir. When I was fifteen. Pneumonia."

"You have no brothers or sisters?"

"No, sir."

"Hmm." He seemed to be thinking it all through though Kirsteen was sure he had long since gone over these details and knew exactly what he wanted.

"So, Kirsteen, you are all alone?" It was the first time he had used her first name and it surprised her.

"Yes, sir. Is that a problem?"

He smiled. "Quite the contrary. Kirsteen, what I am about to tell you is top secret. It must never be discussed with anyone outside this room, do you understand?"

She nodded. "Yes, sir. Of course." She settled back a little more comfortably in the chair.

"As I'm sure you're aware, we have a number of secret agents who have infiltrated enemy lines and are active in occupied territories." She nodded. He continued. "We created a new ministry, the Ministry of Economic Warfare, and under its broad umbrella comes the Special Operations Executive, along with the Theatre Intelligence Service and various others you have no need to know about. S.O.E. is pretty much a saboteur force. T.I.S. works with the receipt and interpretation of intelligence reports coming in from abroad. MI-5, MI-6, MI-9 and others have, of course, been long established."

She knew there were spies behind enemy lines. It would seem the sensible thing to do, to try to gain information about the enemy's intentions. She didn't know the extent of the networks or the actual duties of the many departments. She'd had no reason to consider it before. Now she realized that, of course, there would be different types of operators in enemy territory. Some would be destructive; disrupting troop movements and sabotaging factories. Others must be involved in collecting information and still others in helping captured men and downed airmen escape. She wondered what Churchill had in mind for her. She hoped it was nothing involving explosives or killing.

"One of our operators," continued the Prime Minister, "in fact our top agent, is missing. We've had no word from him in ten days. That's not like him. Not a good sign.'

"Do you think he's been captured?"

Again his lower lip was thrust out. Then he continued. "It's one of the possibilities. Another is that he has been killed. I hope that's not the case."

"He was important to you?" As she said it she thought it was a dumb question. Of course the man was important! Hadn't Churchill just said he was the top operator? She felt herself blush. Churchill seemed not to notice.

"Very important. But there's more to this than just his disappearance. We think there's a good chance he was betrayed. All indicators seem to point to there being a double agent at work. You know what a double agent is, Kirsteen?"

"Someone who is believed to be working for one side but in fact is actually working for the other?"

"Correct. We may believe we have someone spying for us but he or she may, in fact, be giving us false information working for the benefit of the enemy. Yes. Not an unusual situation and not one that's easy to discover."

"So you think this man, your top agent, may have been turned in to the Germans by someone the agent thought was on his own side?"

"Exactly. Turned in, as you put it, or even killed by the other man."

"Where do I fit in?" she asked. "How can I help?"

Churchill referred again to the file in front of him.

"I see you did very well at school in French and German."

"French, yes," she agreed. "I enjoyed it. And I managed to get across the Channel quite a bit before the war, for odd weekends in Paris and around the country. For a couple of summers I even lived over there with a French family. But no, I wouldn't say I was good at German. I could struggle through but I wasn't fluent by any means."

"And today?"

"Today?" She laughed. "I don't know! It's been some time since I used either. I'm sure the French would come back pretty quickly but I'd really have to work on my German to be even mediocre."

He nodded. "Then you will start working on both, my dear." He took one of his famous cigars from a humidor and pushed his chair back a little from the desk. He busied himself with lighting the cigar as he spoke.

"With double agents at work, of course, it's not easy to know whom one can trust. Some people in surprisingly high offices have been found to have, shall we say, misplaced loyalties. For this reason I did establish, right at the very beginning of the war, my own special circle of people. My own little group of those about whom I had no doubts whatsoever. I call them my Secret Circle."

"Spies?" Kirsteen asked.

Churchill puffed blue smoke into the air. She became aware of his eyes gleaming through it, looking at her.

"Spies, yes," he said. "My own personal spies, answerable only to myself. And now I'm asking you if you will join my Circle?"

That night Kirsteen couldn't sleep. She lay in bed going over and over again her meeting with the Prime Minister. He wanted her to be one of his top secret agents; a member of his Secret Circle. She would be known only to him.

"No one else will receive your reports. No one else will know what your assignments are. You will report directly to me," he had said. "On the reverse side, you will receive no recognition of any sort for whatever you are able to achieve. I can promise you no medals or honors, since you are here in an unofficial capacity. All must be of the highest secrecy. But know that you are working for the good of your country, towards our eventual victory in this horrendous conflict. And, of course, you will have my personal undying gratitude."

She was to go into training immediately. Excuses would be given to Queen Charlotte's Hospital; they would be told she had been transferred down to the West Country so that she could be closer to her father. But in fact she was off, in two days time, to start training at an address in Cheshire, close to the Welsh border. Nigel Simpson was to contact her with travel details and papers. She could hardly wait.

Next morning she was up early and started on her first task. She went through her entire wardrobe, as Churchill had suggested, removing labels identifying her clothes as having been made in England. She was delighted to find that she still had a number of items that she had bought in France. On these she left the labels. She packed a small suitcase with such "cleansed and checked" clothes and also made sure she had no identification papers of any sort in her handbag. She then sat down and had a cup of tea and went over in her mind, once again, Winston Churchill's last words to her.

"You will need a code name. Let me see. Kirsteen Craig. Initials K.C. . . K.C. -- Of course! We'll call you 'Casey'! My mother -- she was an American, you know -- when I was a child she used to sing me a song about a Casey Jones, a railway man. Yes! From now on you will be Casey."

Casey! Just the thought of having a code name, known only to the Prime Minister of England, made her whole body tingle. But she soon came back down to earth. What she had agreed to do was ridiculously dangerous! Was she out of her mind? She had agreed to be put into occupied France, alone, and to not only find out what had happened to 'Stonehenge" -- the code name of the missing agent -- but also to discover the man who had betrayed him. If Stonehenge himself, who was considered by Churchill to be the *crème de la crème* of spies, a man fluent in four languages, had been captured or killed, what chance did she think she stood?

But Winston Churchill seemed to think she did stand a chance, and that was good enough for Kirsteen Mary Craig! She drank her tea and felt like a new woman. Suddenly life was worth living again.

3: TRAINING

Kirsteen was met at Wrexham railway station, in Cheshire, by a silent young man in a black Austin car. He wore the uniform of an army Captain, though Kirsteen noticed that there was no regimental flash of any sort on his shoulder. After verifying who she was -- not that anyone else got off the train at that small station -- he saw her and her suitcase into the car then drove her, without speaking a word, down winding lanes and through small villages until she had lost all sense of direction. Several times she tried to initiate conversation but was rewarded only with grunts and shrugs till she gave up. She settled back and tried to enjoy the passing scenery. It was late March and spring had not yet broken through. There was a chill wind blowing and what few people they passed were bundled up against the weather.

The car eventually turned into a driveway between two tall stone gateposts. Their heavy black, wrought-iron gates were open. Kirsteen noticed a small gatehouse but the car didn't stop there. The tree-lined driveway curved around so that the main house was out of sight of the road. When it did come into view she saw that it was a red brick, eighteenth century, manor house similar to many others scattered across England. The type of house usually lived in by generations of local Squires; landowners who oversaw the welfare of the local populace.

Her silent driver took her suitcase and led the way past the solid, iron-studded, oak front door and into the entrance hall. Kirsteen was aware of Persian carpets, rich, dark wainscoting, oil paintings, and a wide curving staircase disappearing up to the upper floors. The driver put down her bag and, still without a word, went back outside again. She heard the car drive away.

"Well, now! You must be Christine Craig?"

She turned to face a distinguished looking gentleman who had come out of a door to the right of the stairway.

"Kirsteen," she said. "It's the Scottish version of Christine. Kirsteen Craig."

"My apologies."

He came forward and shook her hand. He was about six feet tall, she guessed -- a good eight inches taller than herself. He looked the epitome of an English country Squire, with silver hair noticeably thinning, a fine waxed moustache, and wearing a tailored tweed suit and regimental tie.

"Colonel Sandringham," he continued, introducing himself. "I'm the C.O. here."

Kirsteen was surprised. "Commanding Officer? Is this a military establishment, then?"

The colonel put a fatherly arm around her shoulder and led her back into the room from which he'd emerged.

"Not exactly," he chuckled. "Leastways, not like any other military establishment I've ever encountered. You must excuse me my terminology. Everyone seems to refer to me as the C.O. and I've come to think that way. No, you'll find we're much more relaxed here -- in some ways -- though I must warn you that you're going to be doing some pretty intensive training; physical as well as mental. But more on that later."

Kirsteen found herself in what was obviously the library. Every inch of wall space was covered with built-in bookshelves, reaching from floor to ceiling, filled with old leather-bound books. The only respite, other than the door, was a cosy fireplace which had a fire burning in it. In the center of the room was a polished, mahogany desk. The Colonel led Kirsteen to a chair facing it then went around behind the desk and sat down. He opened a folder and looked at it.

"Ah, yes! Kirsteen. Kirsteen Mary Craig. Again my apologies."

She smiled at his old-fashioned courtesy.

"Now," he continued. "I have no idea why you are here, in the sense of what your final mission might be. I just know that you are to undergo the *intensive* course." He stressed the word and glanced up at her very briefly before looking back down at the folder. "You must be out of here in no more than three weeks, it seems."

"Do you know who sent me here?" Kirsteen couldn't resist asking. Just how secret was the Prime Minister's Secret Circle, she wondered?

"I've no idea! People are sent here from the Army, Navy, Air Force, the Marines, SIS, MI-5, MI-6, even Scotland Yard. We are just interested in doing the training, not in *who* it is we are training." Colonel Sandringham sat back in his chair and pulled a pipe out of his pocket. "D'you mind if I smoke?"

She shook her head.

"No, I never know from whence my charges come, nor where they go. I am given certain basic information but on a 'need to know' basis only. In fact," he said, filling the pipe and lighting it, "I am the only person here who will know your true name. To everyone else you will simply be," he glanced again at the folder, "Casey." He puffed clouds of blue smoke into the air and then wafted it away with a wave of his hand. He settled back to enjoy his pipe.

"What sort of things am I going to be learning, Colonel?" Kirsteen was intrigued by his earlier reference to 'physical as well as mental' training.

"Survival, in all senses of the word. The language or languages in which you will be working -- and I don't know whether that's French, German, Italian, Spanish, Russian or what -- that's up to you to work on and bring up to snuff. We do have language aids here in the form of books and records and, if you need them and let me know, we can bring in personal teachers. But that homework you are going to have to do on your own time."

"Will there be much of that?"

"Not a lot, I must admit. Now, in classroom style you'll be learning codes and cryptography, passwords, disguises, invisible inks and all that good old Boy Scout stuff!" He chuckled at his own little joke and pulled on his pipe. "You'll become proficient in the use of short-wave radio, and learn enough about demolition to be able to use it if necessary. You'll be taught all about surveillance, avoiding surveillance by others, about 'safe houses' and when you need to change addresses. You'll learn some basic lock-picking and safe-cracking and do a lot of handgun shooting. You'll also run an abbreviated Commando course."

"How abbreviated?" she couldn't help asking.

Again he chuckled. "Not by much! You'll see. How athletic are you, Casey?"

"A little above average, I think," she said. "I play a lot of tennis, I swim and enjoy hiking. I bicycle and I've had lessons in ju-jitsu."

She saw his head nodding through the pipe smoke.

"We'll be supplementing your ju-jitsu with some Soft-Karate," he said. "Though don't let the word 'soft' fool you. This is the killing art of the Samurai. It will enable you to kill with your bare hands, should you have to."

"I hope it doesn't ever come to that," Kirsteen couldn't help saying.

"I know. And don't think I don't agree."

"Anything else I'll learn, Colonel?"

"Oh, yes. There is one thing that's rather essential," he said, a wicked gleam in his eye. "You'll be taught to jump out of an aeroplane without a parachute!"

Kirsteen was exhausted. She fell back on top of her bed without even taking off her boots. The front of her coveralls was muddy and stained and her fingernails were black. Her face was scratched and her hair had broken out from under the old RAF beret she had taken to wearing for the obstacle course. Six times that morning she and four others had gone over the course. By the end of the second time through she had felt she could hardly put one foot in front of another but there was to be no rest.

"That's okay for a warm-up, now let's do it properly!"

Their instructor was a short, round, totally bald individual named Sergeant-Major Parker. "Sandpaper" Parker, he was known as, because he could wear you down to nothing. Kirsteen quickly found that her sex did nothing to save her from the scathing sarcasm of the Sergeant-Major. He treated her just like any one of the four men.

"All right, Casey! You're not strolling through the bleedin' park! Get that rear end down and keep it down! 'Ow'd you like a Jerry machine-gun to trim it off for you, eh?"

She'd hug the ground closer than a snake and wriggle across the dirt field, beneath the stretched-out strands of barbed wire, as though her life depended on it. Which it did the last time they made the journey, for their instructor actually started shooting live rounds across the top of the wires, to "give them the feel" of what it would be like in action.

After that the five ran a course which included scaling high wooden fences and brick walls, climbing trees, and swinging across wide streams on ropes. If their technique was all right, they took too long in doing it to satisfy the Sergeant-Major. If they did it quickly, he found something wrong with the way they went about it. Kirsteen quickly came to the conclusion that there was no satisfying the man.

She rolled off the bed, stripped off and headed for the bathroom. She just had time to get cleaned up before lunch, then she had to be in the classroom for a lesson in lock-picking and pocket-picking. She couldn't help smiling to herself when she thought back to her old days at Queen Charlotte's.

"If Matron could see me now!" she said aloud.

Kirsteen had her heart in her mouth for several days before she found out what the Colonel had meant when he said she'd have to jump out of an airplane without a parachute. It turned out that she would have to jump but the plane would only be about four feet off the ground at the time. She breathed a sigh of relief. The relief was short-lived.

"When you are taken into enemy territory," said the young RAF Flight-Lieutenant who was responsible for this part of her training, "there is not always an opportunity for the aeroplane to land and let you out in a civilized manner. More often than not it will have to do a long, sweeping pass at low level and you'll have to jump. Here we're going to teach you how to judge that jump, and how to land without breaking a leg or snapping an ankle."

The five of them were loaded onto the back of an open truck and driven out to the center of a large grass field. Kirsteen looked uncertainly at her companions. She had grown close to them in a very short time, though details of exactly who they were, or what their missions might be, she had no idea. There was "Dumbo", a short, overweight man with a perpetual red face, who had a lot of difficulty with the physical aspects of the training but was a whiz when it came to codes and cyphers. He was in his mid-thirties and had let slip that he was married. His accent gave him away as a Yorkshireman. Then there was "Doc". He was tall and thin, with a drooping moustache. He wore steel-framed spectacles and Kirsteen sensed that he had been a college professor before the war. Like Dumbo, he had difficulty with the physical aspects.

Not so, "Sampson". Looking at his bulging biceps Kirsteen thought he was very appropriately named. Every spare minute he seemed to spend doing push-ups and sit-ups, knee-bends and stretches. She guessed his physique was tied-in with the mission he had ahead of him and she wished him well on it. Lastly there was "Greyhound". Again the name seemed appropriate. He was a small, dark, wiry young man with prominent cheekbones and a sharp nose. Doc had told her he was a Gypsy. He could run like the wind and could disappear from view even in the middle of a bare field, it seemed. Kirsteen envied him his ability to blend with nature. He seemed quite at home out in the woods and had shared with her many little tips on how to survive in the wild. Now they were all together in the back of the truck, which came to a stop in the middle of the field.

"All right!" The Flight Lieutenant got out of the cab, where he'd been riding beside the driver, and climbed in the back with them. "Now we're going to start slowly. The bed of this lorry is about the same height off the ground that you'll be in the Lysander, or whatever you're dropping from. We're going to drive across the field at about fifteen miles an hour and I want each of you to jump off. Remember what I've told you about landing on the balls of your feet, dropping and rolling. You can't hurt yourself if you do it properly."

"Isn't fifteen miles an hour a bit slow for an aeroplane?" Doc asked. "I would think it would stall long before that."

The RAF officer smiled. "We're just starting you off on your practice jumps at this speed," he said. "Don't worry -- we'll be getting faster and faster until you can jump off at two or three times that speed!"

They all winced. Thirty miles an hour or more, Kirsteen thought? She could never do it! But she did.

They got up to twenty-five miles an hour before they had their first mishap. At that speed Dumbo was loathe to jump but was talked into it. He dropped off the truck and landed badly, crying out in pain. He had broken his ankle. It was a lesson from which the rest of them learned.

"He was too rigid," said the Flight Lieutenant, as the unfortunate was driven away in an ambulance. "He didn't allow his foot to relax and flex. At this speed, you can't get away with trying to stay on your feet. As soon as you touch, let yourself fall into a ball, head down to your stomach, knees drawn up and arms wrapped around your knees. You'll roll but you won't get hurt."

It was Kirsteen's turn right after the unfortunate Dumbo. She let herself fall from the truck, rather than forcefully jumping, and tucked herself up into a ball as soon as she touched the ground. She was surprised to find a certain exhilaration in the exercise. When they had all done a number of successful drops, and worked up to nearly forty miles an hour, they were told that the following day they would be jumping from an actual airplane.

Kirsteen had only once been up in an airplane. Eight years ago, when she was seventeen, she had been to an air show at Croydon Aerodrome and had gone up for a ten-shilling fifteen-minute trip in a De Havilland Tiger Moth. The bright yellow, open-cockpit biplane had looked somewhat ungainly and difficult to manage on the ground but once it was airborne it had become a thing of beauty and as graceful as any soaring bird. She had fallen in love with it and had promised herself that one day she would learn to fly. But the war had put a stop to that.

Now Kirsteen climbed into the cockpit of the big, bulky-looking Westland Lysander and strapped herself in behind the Flying Officer pilot. The obvious difference from the Tiger Moth was that she was sitting behind the pilot rather than in front of him -- in fact separated from him by the fuel tank -- and it was an enclosed cabin not an open cockpit. The massive cockpit cover reminded Kirsteen of an enormous greenhouse. The plane had a seemingly monstrous fifty foot wingspan.

She later learned that this particular aircraft was from No. 138 Squadron, based at Tempsford, in Bedfordshire. The Squadron had been established first as No. 419 Flight -- Special Duties, at RAF North Weald, with just one Whitley bomber. They had subsequently changed airfields, and number. Now they possessed several Mk. III Westland Lysanders, all painted matte black and slightly modified for their mission of dropping agents into enemy territory. Kirsteen knew that each carried an extra 150-gallon fuel tank between the fixed main gear legs, which gave the plane a total endurance of eight hours flying time. The legs themselves had bulky fairings over the wheels. The fairings each contained a 0.303" Browning machine gun. She looked at the metal ladder that had been attached to the left side of the fuselage, to expedite the embarking and disembarking of "Joes", as the pilots called the agents they carried.

"All set?" the Flying Officer asked over the intercom.

The big plane's Bristol Mercury-XX, 870hp, 9-cylinder radial engine roared and the aircraft lumbered forward. Before she knew it they were in the air.

"That was quick," she said.

She saw the pilot's head nod. His voice came back: "That's why they use these Lysanders for dropping off and picking up Joes in occupied territory. They can fly low and slow -- as slow as thirty-five miles an hour actually, if you hit it right. And with the flaps you can get off in just a few hundred feet and clear a fifty foot obstacle, like a line of trees or telephone wires. Pretty amazing."

She had little time to enjoy and appreciate the airplane.

"Get ready," the pilot said. "We're coming around now."

Kirsteen unfastened her seat belt, took off her helmet and slid back the canopy. The wind whipped at her as she clambered over the side and clung to the ladder. Her heart seemed to be beating so loudly she was aware of it over the sound of the engine and her mouth became so dry it felt as though it had suddenly filled with sand. She squeezed her eyes tightly closed for a moment, bracing herself against the tug of the slipstream. The pilot swooped down and ran across the field into the wind as low and as slowly as he could.

"Now!" he shouted and, leaning out, thumped the side of the fuselage.

She launched herself off the ladder and, almost immediately it seemed, hit the ground. She was surprised to find it no more forceful than the drop from the truck. She rolled for a moment, came to a stop and got to her feet. She felt great!

4: CALL TO ARMS

"Will we have to do parachute jumping?" Kirsteen asked. She strolled with the Colonel around the perimeter of the huge lawn in front of the house. The driveway arced around the lawn on one side; a copse of trees edged it on the other. Time had passed quickly and Kirsteen was already into her final week of training.

Colonel Sandringham puffed on his pipe and strolled, hands clasped behind his back, obviously enjoying the crisp morning air. "Not here, Casey. If there's a need then you'll get special training, but I've been advised that wherever you're going you'll be taken in at night by Westland Lysander." He took the pipe from his mouth. "How'd you enjoy jumping from that, by the way?"

"Very much!" She was surprised at how exhilarating she had found the jumps. "How's poor Dumbo getting on?" She hadn't been able to forget the large, worried figure who'd been so loath to leap from the moving truck. "I keep catching glimpses of him hobbling around on crutches but he doesn't train with us anymore."

"Oh, he's all right. Surviving." The pipe went back into the mouth. "He'll go through worse than that before he's finished, I'm sure."

"He is still continuing then?"

The Colonel nodded. "Oh, yes. I probably shouldn't tell you but it seems he's going to be going somewhere where he can be landed from a boat!"

They both laughed, and then walked on in silence for a while. A group of about eight men and three women appeared from the area of the stables and trotted around part of the driveway to turn off and disappear again into the trees.

"How many people are training here, Colonel?" Kirsteen asked.

"That I'm afraid I can't tell you, my dear. However, I can say that there are quite a few little groups like yours doing . . . various things, all around the place."

She nodded understandingly then looked at her watch.

"Oh, well! That's it for the morning stroll, I think, Colonel. Time for me to get to class."

With a wave of her hand she left the C.O. and jogged off toward the manor house. Ten minutes later she was in a small room at the back of the mansion, sitting at a wooden table, the only audience watching a movie projected onto a small portable screen. An elderly, bespectacled woman stood behind the projector. She had her hair pulled back in a tight bun and wore a severe gray suit with a plain white blouse buttoned up to the neck. When Kirsteen had first met Miss Rinehart she had immediately placed her as an ex- school teacher.

The movie, a documentary covering the progress of the war in France up to the present, came to an end. Miss Reinhart turned off the projector and pulled open the curtains. Sunlight streamed into the room once more.

"Questions?" The older woman didn't waste any words.

"Yes," Kirsteen said, blinking in the light. "I see there's the Occupied Zone and the so-called Free Zone. There's also the Forbidden Zone. Can you enlarge more on those?"

A brief smile flickered across Miss Reinhart's face. It was there for so short an instant that Kirsteen wondered if she had imagined it. The woman's face was set and serious once again.

"Of course. The Occupied Zone is in the north of France and extends down to a rough line from Nantes across to Lyon and on to just above Grenoble." She walked across to a large map of Western Europe on the wall and pointed with her finger. "The Occupied Zone is also generally referred to as 'The North'. Immediately south of that line, is the so-called 'Free Zone'. It's comprised of what's known as 'Midi' -- the middle area of France -- and 'The South', south of Bordeax and Valence."

"Both Midi and the South are in the Free Zone then?"

"Correct. And all around the whole country runs the narrow band known as the Forbidden Zone. That includes the Pyrenees, of course, between France and Spain. It's to keep the French in and outsiders out. You need certain special papers to be in the Occupied Zone but you need even more documentation to ever be found in the Forbidden Zone."

"The French government is at Vichy, just south of the line, in the free Zone, right?" Kirsteen asked.

"The *puppet* government!" Miss Reinhart's voice, for a brief moment, was bitter. Kirsteen wondered what the story was behind her prim exterior and dedicated work for the British government.

For the next hour the two of them went over the current segmentation of France together with what documentation was needed to be in what place. Miss Reinhart, despite her forbidding appearance, possessed a great deal of knowledge and was adept at presenting it to Kirsteen.

"We'll continue with this tomorrow morning," Miss Reinhart said, at the end of the hour. "I'd suggest you thoroughly familiarize yourself with the boundaries we've talked about. Also, be sure you know exactly which necessary documents you would have to present for wherever you happen to be."

"Right! Thanks, Miss Reinhart." Kirsteen beamed at her. The older woman nodded curtly and swept out of the room. "Thank God I'm thick skinned," Kirsteen muttered to herself, as she gathered up her notes. "I could easily get a complex from that lady!"

After lunch Kirsteen made her way into the ballroom -- the largest room in the manor and one which had been turned into a lecture hall. There were about thirty people in the room, sitting in scattered groups, keeping to their respective cliques. She noticed three or four other women amongst all the men. Dumbo was there and came eagerly across, on his crutches, to sit between Kirsteen and Doc. They all greeted him like a long lost brother.

The lecture -- illustrated with colored slides -- was given by a famous London fashion

designer whom Kirsteen recognized immediately. He spoke for nearly two hours on the
various uniforms of the Germans: the Wermacht
and their officers, the Gestapo, Himmler's SS, the
Waffen SS, and even the French Militia -- the
corps of Frenchmen who aided the Germans in
their occupation. He dealt with all the uniforms
that might be encountered in France plus those
found in Germany itself.

"It probably wouldn't matter if you
couldn't tell an *Obersturmführer* from an
Untersturmführer," he said, waving his hands in
mock bewilderment, "but you do need to know
that, for example, a Wehrmacht *Oberst* is not
necessarily a Nazi while an *SS-Standartenführer*
definitely is."

Kirsteen found the lecture extremely
interesting and made copious notes. There was a
handout showing some of the finer details of
rank insignia, and this she tucked into her
notebook. After the lecture she went up to her
room for a short break then on to the butts for
some handgun practice.

Over more than two weeks she had tried
several different guns -- an Enfield No. 2 Mk 1, a
Webley .38mm Mk 4, American Smith and
Wesson Revolver .38/200, Tokarev TT33,
Beretta Model 34 9mm Short, even a German
Walther 9mm PPK and a Luger P-08. Finally she

had settled on the Walther PPK as her favorite. It was about three ounces lighter than the Beretta, which she also liked, fractionally shorter in length and had a slightly higher muzzle velocity. She felt quietly confident that, should she ever have to defend herself with a handgun, she could do a competent job with the Walther.

As she had been doing for several days, Kirsteen sat on the floor in the office at the firing range, blindfolded, with a Mark II Sten gun dismantled and scattered all around her. She groped about to find the many pieces and slowly but surely put them back together again, knowing that should she ever have to she could assemble such a submachine-gun in the dark. She had just completed the assembly, slid a 32-round box magazine of 9mm bullets into the left side and put on the safety catch, when she heard someone come into the room.

"Do you spend much time sitting on the floor blindfolded?"

She recognized the voice of Winifred, the Colonel's aide.

"Just note the fact that I have a loaded automatic weapon in my hands before you go making smart remarks," Kirsteen said. Then, laughing, she took off the blindfold. "What's happening, Winnie? Is it me you're looking for?"

"Yes. The Colonel would like to see you right away."

Colonel Sandringham looked up from a bulky file folder when she entered his office. He closed it and waved her to a seat beside the desk.

"Casey, it's time for you to move on," he said.

She was surprised. "But - but I haven't completed the three weeks you said I was to do."

"Well, technically I said you would be here *no more than* three weeks." He smiled, a little grimly she thought, then continued. "I've had a top priority message asking that I ensure you report immediately to 'your superior'." He looked at her intently through lowered eyebrows. "You know who that refers to, I take it?"

Kirsteen nodded. "Oh, yes."

"Fine!" The Colonel got to his feet and stretched out a hand to her. "Good luck, Casey! You won't actually need luck, I'm sure. You strike me as a particularly competent young woman. You've done extremely well here. Much better than expected, I might add. I'm sorry to see you go."

She shook his hand warmly and, in a slight daze, went to her room to pack her few belongings. Within the hour she was on her way back to London and another meeting with the Prime Minister.

"I've had excellent reports on your progress at the training facility."

Sometimes even when praising Churchill sounded as though he was admonishing, thought Kirsteen. She looked at his bulk huddled down in the seat, pouring over her folder. He looked tired, she thought. God knows, he had the weight of the Empire on his shoulders.

"Don't you ever get any rest, sir?" she blurted out, almost before she knew what she was doing.

He looked up, surprised. Slowly a smile spread across his face. "Thank you," he said. Then he sighed. "Not as much as this old body would like, I must admit. But then, how many of us do these days?" He waved a hand at a pile of signals on the desk. "The gallant island of Malta has just experienced its two thousandth air raid alert. In the East, Bataan has just fallen to the Japanese. I understand approximately thirty-five thousand of our American and Filipino friends have been started on a forced march from Balanga towards San Fernando. Japanese naval aircraft have attacked the Ceylonese port of Trincomalee. Happily we had anticipated this and cleared the harbour, but our carrier *Hermes* was sunk, together with a destroyer, a corvette and two tankers."

"Is there any good news?" Kirsteen asked hopefully.

Again the smile. "Yes -- a little. An RAF Halifax bomber, just last night, dropped an 8,000-pound bomb for the first time, in a raid on Essen. That's the home of the German Krupp factory. That is definitely good news." Again he sighed. "Thank you for your solicitude, my dear. War is never easy. Let's just hope we can do everything possible to bring it to an end."

"I'm all for that," Kirsteen said.

"Then, to that end, I must tell you that we have had a contact purportedly from our friend Stonehenge."

"You have?" She sat forward on the edge of her seat. "Then he's alive after all?"

"Not necessarily." A pause. "I did say 'purportedly' from Stonehenge. As you now know from your training, when an agent sends a radio message he always includes one or two recognized errors in it. Recognized by us, that is. This message did not have those errors."

"So it looks as though someone else has got hold of his code book and is sending messages, pretending to be him?"

"Precisely, my dear."

Kirsteen sat back in her chair and thought hard. If Stonehenge's radio and code book had been taken by the enemy they would transmit from the book hoping to fool those in London that it was Stonehenge himself there. But, of course, they wouldn't know of the 'code within the code' as it were; the trademark of that particular agent. This confirmed that Stonehenge had indeed been either captured or killed. He wasn't just missing and in hiding.

"So you see, Casey, we need you now. In fact more than ever," Churchill said. "MI-6 has got other agents over there who are trying to find out what is happening but, as I told you originally, we must ask ourselves 'whom do we trust'? No! I want to know what's happening? I want *you* over there, Casey, reporting back directly to me."

"Yes, sir."

5: INTO THE FRAY

Her first impression was that Paris looked the same. The same, that is, except for the addition of German flags, fluttering in the gentle breeze from almost every large building. Four swastika pennants hung from the *Arc de Triomphe.*

Kirsteen strolled casually along the avenue des Champs-Elysée to the place Clemenceau, trying to look as though she was just out enjoying the early spring sunshine. Her eyes darted back and forth, taking in all that she could.

She was surprised to see that most of the people looked reasonably well fed and that many of the women were even wearing make-up -- without which, in pre-war times, no Parisian woman would have felt complete! There were businessmen hurrying along, carrying bulging briefcases. Grey-green German uniforms were everywhere; many of the soldiers carrying cameras, like tourists. A newspaper seller was at his stand, selling both French and German newspapers and magazines.

Kirsteen sat down at a table on the sidewalk, outside the café on the corner of rue du Marignan, and watched the passing scene. There were old-fashioned carriages and horse-drawn cabs, brought out of retirement, moving along the avenue. Most of the old horses moved very slowly and the cabs seemed to have few customers. By contrast there were innumerable bicycle- and tandem-pulled box-carts painted in bright colors. They were known as "vélo-taxis". Muscular young men and women pedaled furiously, taking a wide assortment of passengers through the streets at a good pace. Well-to-do women sat in the little wooden boxes behind the bicyclists, clutching their shopping bags to them; German officers rode by, sometimes two or three of them crammed onto the tiny seats, looking about like the tourists that many of them were. Regular bicycles, old and not so old, seemed to be everywhere, pointing up the shortage of gasoline. People of all ages and social classes rode them. Many of the machines were supplemented with baskets, boxes, and panniers for carrying luggage.

Kirsteen had been landed in France just outside the small town of Le Mans, west of Paris. The Westland Lysander, piloted by Wing Commander "Mouse" Fielden -- King George's personal pilot -- had flown low across the

English Channel, only a few feet above the waves the whole way. It finally touched down in a field surrounded on three sides by woods. As they came in over the trees, she climbed out of the cockpit. She clung to the ladder as the airplane wheels gently made contact with the grass and rolled to a near stop. As she dropped off onto the ground the big Bristol Mercury engine roared up to full rpm and the black-painted airplane gathered speed and disappeared once more into the dark night sky. Kirsteen looked about her, clutching a brown-paper shopping bag containing her few clothes and other items, thankful that on this her first "drop" she had not had to jump off without the airplane landing.

It was after three o'clock in the morning. Pulling herself together, Kirsteen wasted no time getting away from the landing area, in case any German patrols might have heard the airplane come in.

Within an hour she was at the railway station at Le Mans, waiting for the first train to Paris. There were half a dozen other people, all sleeping in the small waiting room, so she didn't feel at all conspicuous. Obviously they had spent the night there. When the *guichet* finally opened up she was ready to show her fake papers, but there was no need; the agent sold her a ticket with no questions asked.

It was seven o'clock before the first train steamed slowly into the station. By that time the platform held over thirty people of all sorts, all heading for the capital city. She tried not to look at the few German soldiers who jostled along with the other passengers, cramming into the tiny compartments on the two-carriage train. She found herself wedged between a plump, elderly, peasant woman and a white-faced young curé.

Just outside Paris the train stopped and Kirsteen wondered what it was waiting for. Suddenly the carriage door slid back. An SS-Haupsturmführer stood outside in the corridor, looking in. None of the passengers looked up; not even the two German soldiers in the carriage -- an Unteroffizier, or Sergeant, and a Mannschaften, or Private. All seemed to be avoiding the Gestapo officer's eyes. Kirsteen did likewise. After standing surveying them for a long moment the German slid the door closed and moved on. Kirsteen breathed a sigh of relief. Ten minutes later the train began to move again.

Paris had been declared an "open city" on capitulation and consequently had avoided any great bomb damage. Kirsteen found the station busy with many people; German uniforms were in evidence everywhere. As she passed through the barrier she was asked, along with all the other passengers, to show her papers. The young Leutnant glanced at them while Kirsteen held her breath. She had been given the name Marie Nègre and described as a schoolmistress. The officer seemed satisfied and, to Kirsteen's relief, handed back the papers and turned to the next in line.

"*Café?*"

Kirsteen jumped.

"I'm sorry, Mademoiselle. I didn't mean to startle you." It was the café waiter.

She smiled. "It's all right," she said. "I was miles away, thinking."

"Ah, yes!" He was a short, tubby, middle-aged man with his thin, black hair plastered down across his balding head. His besmirched white apron had obviously not seen the washtub in several days. "We all have much to think about these days, *n'est pas*?"

She ordered coffee and received a murky, yellow-colored, almost unpalatable concoction made from chicory and dandelion roots. Other choices on the menu were *viandox*, a meat extract; *tilleul*, lime tea; *verveine*, verbena tea; and, three times a week when alcohol was banned, another ersatz coffee called *café national*, made from acorns and chick-peas.

Kirsteen took a few sips of the liquid then pushed it away. She had to plan her day. Her first task was to find somewhere to stay. She had been given the address of where to contact a Resistance group. It wasn't far from where she was so she decided to go there first, from the café, and then from there start trying to track down the missing Stonehenge. She knew his last known whereabouts and had the name of a woman he had mentioned in his last transmission, before the long silence.

The building on avenue de Villars, that was supposed to be home for the Resistance group, turned out to be a rundown boarding house right next door to a *Soldatenheim*; a home for occupying German soldiers. Kirsteen paused before climbing the steps to the front door. It would certainly be audacious for the Resistants to operate right next door to the Germans. She smiled . . . she liked the idea.

An elderly, emaciated, stern-faced woman with tired eyes answered the door on the third knock.

"I'm looking for the offices of the Notre Dame Friends of Charity," Kirsteen said.

"Then you've come to the wrong place," came the reply.

"Are you sure?" Kirsteen was momentarily taken aback.

"This is a rooming house. There's no offices here." The woman made to close the door. Kirsteen quickly put up her hand to hold it open.

"Wh-what about Gaston Dissart? Does he live here, by any chance?"

The woman's face changed. A smile cracked its previously cement-like passivity.

"Gaston? You're a friend of Gaston's?"

"Yes!" Kirsteen nodded enthusiastically. "Well, not a friend, exactly. I mean . . . is he home?"

"Come!" The woman turned away from the door and led the way inwards. Kirsteen followed.

They climbed slowly and, for the woman, laboriously to the third floor. Kirsteen couldn't help but notice the peeling paper on the walls and the dirty, stained, threadbare carpeting on the stairs. There was a faint smell of urine only briefly overpowered by the odor of boiling cabbage coming from one of the doors they passed on the second floor. Finally, on the floor above, the woman stopped in front of a door bearing the number '3C'. She knocked.

"Gaston! Gaston! You have a visitor."

Kirsteen heard a murmur of voices behind the door followed by the scraping of chairs. After a moment the door was opened a crack and a small man with bright brown eyes peered out.

"Qu'est que c'est?"

Kirsteen leaned around the woman and smiled at the face.

"Bon jour," she said. "I was asked to give you a message about the Notre Dame Charities Fund Drive."

She thought she saw a moment of panic flash across the otherwise round and friendly face. Then the man stepped back and opened the door wide enough for her to enter.

"Thank you, Madame Delestraint!" Gaston beamed at the old woman then firmly closed the door on her.

Kirsteen looked around the room. It was small, furnished only with a table and four chairs, a chest of drawers with an old *bière* radio and a gas ring sitting on its top, a battered old wardrobe and a single bed that looked as though it had not been made up in days. A dirty blanket hung over the small window. A bare light bulb hung from a cracked fixture in the ceiling above the table.

Standing beside the table, as though they had been interrupted in the middle of a meeting, were two other people. One was a tall, slim, attractive, redheaded woman in a short green dress and the other an angular, grey-haired man in a crumpled grey suit. They both stared at Kirsteen.

Gaston stood with his back against the door.

"You mentioned the Notre Dame Charities?" he said. "Who are you?"

"That's not what I'm supposed to hear," said Kirsteen matter-of-factly, though her heart was pounding and she could feel sweat breaking out under her armpits.

"I'm sorry." Gaston bobbed his head and then smiled his broad smile. "The Friends of Charity offer help to all in need," he said as though repeating a phrase he had learned parrot-fashion, which was probably what he had done, thought Kirsteen. She turned to the others in the room.

"And who are you?" she asked.

"Were you expecting her?" the redhead asked Gaston, ignoring Kirsteen.

"No! Not at all. But she has the words."

The grey-haired man bowed his head slightly to Kirsteen then looked her straight in the eyes. "You must excuse our caution," he said. "It is of necessity, I assure you." He brushed his moustache and stood up straight as though from habit. Ex-military, thought Kirsteen.

"I can imagine," she murmured. "So . . . I take it I'm in the right place?"

Gaston came back to the table and offered her a seat. They all sat.

"You are with friends," Gaston said. "You come from England?"

"That you don't need to know right now," Kirsteen replied. "It's enough that I'm here."

"No! It's not enough!" The redhead stared at Kirsteen, a frown on her face. "How do we know who you are? Just because you have the right words to say -- you could be working for the Gestapo."

"If the Gestapo knew you were here -- and who, or what, you are -- do you think they would send me?" Kirsteen asked. "No!   They'd be all over this place, and you. You'd be down at eleven rue des Saussaies before you knew what hit you!"

She had been well briefed and knew that all Parisians considered the rue des Saussaies address 'Gestapo Headquarters'. It was the old Sûreté Nationale building.

The older man nodded. "She's right," he said. "Allow me to introduce myself. I am Captain Antoine Lefaucheux. This is Paulette Cartier. Gaston you already know. And you are .. ?"

Kirsteen smiled at him. He had a certain old world charm which she liked. "My name is Marie Nègre. I've come north from the Free Zone. I was led to believe that you could help me."

The redhead snorted. "Marie Nègre! Obviously not your real name!"

"And Paulette Cartier is yours?" Kirsteen asked coolly. The redhead looked away.

"Come now!" Gaston spoke up. He spread his hands and smiled all around the table. "We are all on the same side, I'm sure. Let's not get off on the wrong foot. Marie, what can we do for you?"

"First of all, I need somewhere to stay."

"No problem."

She liked the warmth in his soft brown eyes. She could see why Madame Delestraint, the woman who had led her up the stairs, had mellowed when she had first mentioned Gaston's name.

"There are empty rooms here," Gaston continued. "In fact the one across the hall is empty, I believe."

"It is," Antoine affirmed. "I'll go and speak to Madame about it immediately. *Excusez-moi.*" He got up and left the room.

"Thank you," Kirsteen said. "Thank you very much. I knew I could count on you all."

The redhead sniffed and said nothing.

6: THE SEARCH BEGINS

Kirsteen unpacked her few belongings from the shopping bag and tucked them away in the top drawer of the battered chest standing beside the bed. Then she carefully weighed the Walther PPK in her hand and looked around for somewhere to hide it. There were no guarantees that someone might not get into her room at some time and search it. It wouldn't do to be caught with an illegal firearm. There was also her codebook to be secreted away somewhere; most damaging of evidence should it fall into the wrong hands.

As her eyes swept up to the ceiling they fell on the light fixture. Much like the one in Gaston's room, it was cracked and hung from crumbling plaster. She climbed up onto the table under the light and looked closely at it. Carefully she tugged at the base from which the short light cord extended. It came away from the ceiling altogether, powdering her hair with a fine cloud of plaster dust, and hung from the cloth bound wires that disappeared back into the darkness beyond the plaster. She peered up into the hole.

Within a couple of minutes Kirsteen had tucked her gun and codebook up into the ceiling and had wedged the light fixture back into place. It now leaned at a more grotesque angle, but certainly didn't look in the least suspicious. She just prayed that the plaster wasn't so weak that it wouldn't be able to support the 21oz weight of the Walther and the few ounces of the codebook.

The next morning Kirsteen left the rooming house and set off for a small restaurant that Gaston had told her about. There she would meet again with Gaston and Antoine -- Paulette claimed she had a previous engagement -- and they would introduce her to others in the Resistance. She glanced at the directions Gaston had scribbled down for her and turned off at rue Oudinot. When that street dead-ended she turned left onto rue Vaneau and quickly found the *Rescoe* she was looking for.

For those Parisians existing on a salary under three thousand francs a month there were community restaurants, known as "Rescoes", which offered a government-subsidized three course meal for a few francs. Kirsteen now found herself in such a place. She quickly spotted Gaston and Antoine and hurried over to their table. There was another man and a woman with them.

"This is Norbert Bastouette," said Gaston, in introduction. "He has been active here in Paris ever since the start of the occupation. And this is Colette Grenelle. She, too, is a long-time fighter for freedom. I've been telling them about you, Marie."

Kirsteen's eyes met the steel gray ones of the male Resistant. He seems awfully young, she thought. He had a shock of blond hair that fell forward over his right eye and which he would occasionally toss back with a jerk of his head. His face was handsome but still bore the pimples of adolescence. He had a cheery grin that he switched on and off like a light. When it wasn't turned on his brow was deeply furrowed. He nodded to her and seemed slightly ill at ease. Kirsteen liked the girl instantly. She was petite, with an elfin face and dark brown hair cropped short. She smiled shyly at Kirsteen.

"Norbert was asking what your mission might be," Antoine said. She noticed that the older man was constantly scanning the faces at the surrounding tables and keeping a weather eye on the door to check-out all newcomers. To an observer it looked as though he was simply looking out for a friend, but she knew he was acting as look-out for the little group. She was grateful for his vigilance.

"Of course," Kirsteen responded. She smiled at Norbert, hoping to set his mind at rest. His brow remained furrowed. "As I told Gaston and Antoine, I've come up from the Free Zone ..."

"Whereabouts in the Free Zone?" Norbert interrupted.

"Lyon. I'm a schoolmistress there."

"What is the situation in Lyon?" he asked. "Is it really free?"

She shook her head. She had been extensively briefed on her fictitious background. "Far from it. There are Gestapo all over the place; almost filling the main hotel. There is the S.S., the Vichy Police of course, and the Militia. No one feels the least bit free."

He nodded. The smile flicked on and off again. "And you are here for . . . ?"

Kirsteen pulled her chair closer. "I'm trying to make contact with a man known as Stonehenge." Her eyes had locked onto the young man's and she was rewarded by seeing them widen momentarily. He pushed back his chair and looked quickly around the restaurant. "You know the man?" she continued.

He nodded. "Very well," he said. "I'm one of his closest aides."

Kirsteen's heart skipped a beat. At last! Here was the sort of contact she'd been hoping to make. "You know where he is?" she asked. "You can arrange for me to see him?"

Norbert's furrowed brow was back in earnest. He gave a toss of his head to get the hair out of his eyes and looked around at the four of them. "Why do you want to see him?"

"That's my business," Kirsteen answered, smiling. "I've been instructed to speak to no one else."

"Instructed by whom?"

Now we're playing games, she thought. "You don't need to know," she said lightly. She didn't want to offend him, since he was her only contact. "Please, Norbert, trust me on this. I do need to see Stonehenge. Do you know where he is?"

"Norbert knows if anyone does," Gaston put in, his face beaming. "He's tops around here and especially in this arrondissement."

Norbert's smile passed across his face again. "That's true," he said, modestly.

"But hasn't Stonehenge disappeared?" Colette's brown eyes were big. "Didn't you tell me . . ."

Norbert cut her off. "Please, Colette!" He turned back to Kirsteen. "We must tread softly. Yes, as Colette says, Stonehenge has disappeared. We haven't had contact with him for almost five weeks now."

"Five weeks? *Sacré bleu!*" muttered Gaston. "I did not know this." He turned to Kirsteen. "Of course, I didn't work with him the way Norbert did. I suppose there's no reason I would have known." He turned back to the blond man. "But you hadn't mentioned it."

Norbert shook his head. "No. I've been trying to trace him."

"You think he's disappeared deliberately?" Antoine asked, momentarily stopping his visual sweep of the restaurant.

"I don't know. I hope that's what it is."

Kirsteen thought he sounded genuinely concerned.

"Exactly when and where did you last see him?" she asked.

"At the Ile de la Cité safehouse. We'd escorted a parcel out of the city -- he was to go down through the Free Zone to Tarbes and then, hopefully, over the Pyrenees into Spain. Everything had gone well and we took time to have a drink together and celebrate." He looked around the table at the attentive faces. "Stonehenge said he had to run up to Reims and would be in touch with me the following Monday. This was on a Friday. I never heard from him again."

Kirsteen knew that by "parcel" he meant a fugitive from the Germans, who had to be smuggled out of the country. "What did you do when he didn't show up for your next meeting?" she asked.

Norbert shrugged. "It happens. You wait for a while then you know -- or hope -- that he will contact you again soon. But he never did."

"And you still did nothing?" She couldn't help sounding slightly incredulous. Beside her Gaston made noises and Colette looked hard at Norbert.

"Of course I did something!" He sounded angry, Kirsteen thought. As though his loyalty was being questioned. "Stonehenge was -- is -- an important man. And he was my friend. I was really close to him."

"So what did you do?" persisted Antoine.

"I checked out all his old haunts. I talked with everyone I knew who had worked for him recently. I even went down through the Free Zone myself, through Lyon . . ." he looked hard at Kirsteen, ". . . and on down all the way to Toulouse, Tarbes and Pau. No sign of him and no one had seen him."

There was silence for several minutes. Finally Kirsteen cleared her throat. "I've got to find him," she said. "If anything's happened to him, then I have to know what it is. This is very important. Will all of you help me?" She looked around at them, moving slowly from one pair of eyes to the next.

"Of course!" They all nodded in support.

"Good. Now, where do we start?"

"As I said, I've checked all his old haunts," Norbert said.

"Then we have to assume he went somewhere new." Kirsteen realized she was taking command. She rather liked the feeling. "How can we check out the possibility of his having been taken by the Gestapo?"

Antoine scraped back his chair and stretched his long legs. "I can help there. I have certain contacts at rue des Saussaies and also at avenue Foch. I'll find out what I can."

"And I have contacts in the Gestapo offices in the Hôtel Majestic, off avenue Kléber," Norbert said. "I can check there."

Kirsteen nodded. "Do any of you know of a woman who goes by the name 'Canard'?" This was the name mentioned by Stonehenge in his last communication, Churchill had told her.

"Canard? Why, yes!" Gaston said. "That's a name Paulette uses."

Kirsteen's heart skipped a beat.

"Why do you ask?" Norbert said. "How do you happen to know this name?"

"I was told that Stonehenge had mentioned her," Kirsteen said smoothly. "I was also told that he'd last been heard of near somewhere called place Maubert."

"That's in the Latin Quarter," Colette said. "It's right near the river, not far from Notre Dame."

"Somewhere off boulevard St.-Germain, if I'm not mistaken," Antoine added. Colette nodded.

"Is there anything of any significance there?" Kirsteen asked. They all slowly shook their heads.

"Nothing we know of," Gaston replied. "But I'll check it out."

There was silence for a few moments. It was finally broken by Norbert.

"Marie, you said that you'd been told Stonehenge had mentioned 'Canard' . . . Paulette. Who told you? And in what way had he mentioned her?"

"I can't tell you who told me, but I can tell you that Stonehenge had said he was working on something 'special' with her and a friend." Kirsteen thought back to the redhead's very wary acceptance of her, back at the rooming house.

"We have to talk with her." Gaston made the statement.

"That's what I was thinking," Antoine agreed.

"Very well. We have work to do. We'll check up on these places, to see if the Gestapo has our friend, and I'll also look around place Maubert." Gaston got to his feet. His brown eyes met Kirsteen's. "Then, this evening, we'll all meet back in my room and I'll see that Paulette is there. She can fill us in on what she knows. Agreed?"

"Agreed." Antoine got to his feet.

"Good!" Colette said, also rising.

Norbert nodded, remaining seated, his brow once again deeply furrowed.

"And I will do a little investigating of my own," Kirsteen said. "Thank you all, very much. I appreciate what you're doing."

Norbert grunted.

Back at the rooming house Kirsteen opened the door to her room. The first thing she saw was a faint footprint in the light, white dust that had earlier fallen from the ceiling.

7: UNCOVERING CLUES

Earlier, after she had hidden her gun and codebook, Kirsteen had tried to clean up what plaster had fallen but some of the fine dust had managed to escape her attention. Now it was only noticeable because of the half-footprint on the edge of the worn carpet. Someone had obviously been into her room while she had been out. She dropped to her knees and examined the evidence.

It wasn't easy to tell whether it was a man's or a woman's footprint but Kirsteen suspected it was a woman's. It was only the left side of a sole but it seemed too small to be a man's.

Going to the chest of drawers Kirsteen noted that the hair she had pulled from her hairbrush that morning, and stuck across the crack of the top drawer, had gone. Whoever had been into the room had obviously gone through her things. She looked quickly up at the ceiling. The light fixture looked the same and there was no sign of any new plaster dust anywhere. She breathed a sigh of relief, knowing there was nothing incriminating in any of the drawers.

But who would have been here, she kept asking herself? Who was suspicious of her enough to want to check through her belongings?

Her first thought was that it might have been Paulette. Certainly the redhead had not been at all friendly; in fact had been downright suspicious. And she had excused herself from going to the restaurant with the rest of them. It was logical to assume that she was the one who had been into the room. Yet Kirsteen recalled Gaston saying something about old Madame Delestraint; that she could be very kindly but was also a notorious busybody. Perhaps the old boarding-house keeper was the one who had been in?

With nothing missing, and knowing there was nothing incriminating to be discovered, Kirsteen shrugged her shoulders and tried to put the incident out of her head. She had more important things to work on, she told herself.

She knew that Gaston was on his way to rue des Saussaies, with Antoine, and then from there they were going to the place Maubert on the boulevard St.-Germain. It would be some time before they came back to the rooming house. And on coming in she had passed Madame

Delestraint on the front steps, leaving the house with her shopping bag, so Kirsteen knew that at least the third floor was empty right now.

She eased open her door and stood still, listening. The only sound in the house came from the ground floor, where a toilet flushed and then someone broke into a few bars of the "Marseillaise", whistling it off-key. A door banged and then all was quiet. Carefully Kirsteen eased across the hallway to Gaston's door. Crouching down, she pulled a thin length of metal out of her belt buckle and used it to quickly pick the lock. In seconds she was inside the room with the door safely closed behind her. She stood still and listened. There was still no sound from the rest of the house. Breathing a little easier, Kirsteen looked about her.

The room was as she remembered it from the previous day. The blanket had been unhooked at one end and now hung down at the side of the window, allowing the weak sun to shine in through the grimy panes of glass.

Swiftly Kirsteen moved to the chest of drawers and ran her eyes over it. It didn't look as though the Frenchman had rigged any telltale signs to alert him to intruders, as she had done. She looked at the wooden-cased radio. It was at least ten years old and reminded her of the old

HMV radio in her father's room at the rest-home. She slid open the drawers, one at a time.

Of the five drawers, the top two held a few cans of food and a half-eaten packet of dry biscuits. The lower three held a variety of worn and threadbare underwear and shirts, a couple of sweaters and some gloves. Under the sweaters she found a few papers, including Gatson's birth certificate, his book of ration tickets and a creased and worn photograph of a naked woman, spread-eagled on a bed. The photographer had apparently been concentrating so much on what the woman had to offer that he had cut off her head. Scrawled across the back of the picture were the words: "To G. with love. It was good! Let's do it again sometime. S."

Kirsteen assumed that "G" was Gaston and couldn't help smiling at the thought of him having a sexual encounter. She wondered who "S" was.

Moving on to the wardrobe, Kirsteen found only worn clothing: a shabby suit, a top coat and a raincoat, hats, working coveralls and two or three well-worn pairs of pants. On the floor of the wardrobe lay a variety of shoes and boots. She was just about to close the door again when she had the presence of mind to check the footwear. As she reached down into a rubber gumboot her fingers encountered the unmistakable feel of a gun. She quickly upended the boot. Out slid a small "Woolworth" 0.45; one of the single-shot handguns that the allies dropped by parachute, by the tens of thousands, to the partisans in Axis-occupied Europe and Asia. If nothing else, she thought, this seemed to confirm that Gaston was a true member of the Resistance. She put the little gun back and closed the wardrobe door.

Running her hands along the bottom edge of the mattress on the bed she came across a small, thin parcel, wrapped in brown paper and tied tightly with string. Carefully she worked on the knots to undo them and, after what she felt was too long, unwrapped the package. Inside were the working papers and private identity cards and passes of someone named Jules Macé. The photograph showed a man who looked very much like Gaston and Kirsteen wondered if it was his brother. She recognized Category T ration tickets and Gestapo passes that would allow this Jules into the Forbidden Zone, listing him as a railway telegraph worker. She went through everything painstakingly, memorizing all that she could, then very carefully re-tied the package the way it had been and replaced it under the mattress. Feeling she had been in the room far too long, Kirsteen had a quick last look around and then slipped out and returned to her own room.

It was less than ten minutes later that she heard the soft tread of Madame Delestraint on the creaky stairs, accompanied by heavy breathing. Obviously the old woman had returned from shopping. With her ear pressed to the door of her room, Kirsteen heard the woman move to stand outside Gaston's room, obviously listening to see if anyone was in there, and then come across to stand listening on the other side of the door where Kirsteen stood. The old woman tried hard to suppress her gasping, wheezing breath but the climb up the stairs had been too much for her and Kirsteen smiled to herself at the obvious would-be eavesdropper. After what seemed a long time the old woman retraced her steps down the stairs.

Kirsteen left the rooming house and headed for Notre Dame Cathedral. She wanted to look around place Maubert herself. She took the *métro*, which was packed to bursting with all sorts of people. There were German officers dotted here and there but mainly businessmen, clutching their briefcases and with their noses buried in newspapers. There were no vacant seats so Kirsteen hung on to a strap and swayed with the movement of the car. At each stop more and more people piled in till they were packed so tightly she was no longer able to sway and she found she only had one foot on the floor, the other pushed and trapped between someone else's legs. She got a jab in the stomach from a woman's umbrella then had a large parcel stuck into the small of her back. The atmosphere was ripe with the smell of bad breath, reeking largely of stale cabbage. Next to her an old man clutched a poorly wrapped package of what was obviously very ripe Camembert.   Just when Kirsteen thought she could stand it no longer, the old man got off the train.   Several people around her smiled and nodded to her.

Kirsteen emerged from the *métro* and stood for a moment looking about her. It was mid-afternoon but there were many people moving along the streets. The sidewalk cafés were well patronized and she found it difficult to remember that this was an occupied city in the middle of a world war. But then the sudden appearance of a tall, thin-faced SS-Obersturmführer brought her rudely back to earth. Her eyes quickly took in the black uniform with the red, white and black swastika armband, the aiguillette across the right chest and the SS Service Dagger with its ornate "chains" hanging from the left side of the waist.

Kirsteen's mind flashed back to the lecture at the Wrexham manor house, with the London couturier detailing the uniforms of the occupying army.

"Out of my way!"

Kirsteen moved to one side as the German moved in the same direction. Quickly she moved back the other way, as he did. Angrily he grasped her arms and thrust her to one side.

"I-I'm sorry," she said.

He glared at her. "Your papers!" he demanded.

Out of the corner of her eye Kirsteen saw passersby looking down, so as not to be drawn in, and hurrying on their way. She fumbled with her bag and pulled out her identity papers. The Nazi studied them.

"Your name is . . . ?"

"Nègre. Marie Nègre. As it says there," she couldn't help adding.

He glanced up at her, scowling, then returned to scrutinizing her papers. "What are you doing in Paris?"

"I-I am on leave from my school in Lyon. I thought I'd come here to do some research."

"Research?"

"Prepare for classes. Prepare lessons for my students."

For a long moment he continued studying the papers and Kirsteen held her breath till she thought she would burst. Then he thrust them back at her.

"Keep out of my way!" he snarled. He turned on his heel and stalked away. Kirsteen let out her breath in a long gasp.

"They have no manners, these swine!" someone murmured as they passed her. She looked up, nodding.

"I know. I . . ." She gasped. The one who had spoken was a thin-faced man with prominent cheekbones and a sharp nose. He wore a beret pulled down on one side of his head and an old leather jacket with the collar turned up. For one brief moment his eyes met Kirsteen's and she recognized him -- it was her old classmate Greyhound! The next moment he was gone; swallowed up with the crush of people descending to the *métro*.

She had the presence of mind not to call after him, or try to follow him. Instead, she went into the nearest café and had a cup of *viandox*. She needed to pull herself together.

8: ENTER THE CANON

Kirsteen's first real view of Cathédrale Notre Dame came as she moved along the quai de la Tournelle. The huge edifice was silhouetted against the already dipping afternoon sun. Just beyond it she could see the great Hôtel Dieu, the oldest hospital in Paris and, possibly, in the world.

She couldn't resist a quick visit to the great cathedral. Later, she promised herself, she would come back with nothing else on her mind and retrace some of her steps from earlier, happier, freer days. But for now she moved along to pay her respects to Notre-Dame de Paris, the famous statue of the Virgin which had been venerated there for more than five centuries. She walked along the ambulatory and saw the choir stalls, decided to forego a visit up the 387-step climb to the north tower, and continued around to the east. There she had a good view of the apse and was able to gaze up at the spectacular flying buttresses.

Ten minutes later Kirsteen crossed the pont-au-Double and reached the quai de Montebello. A few feet south of the bridge, on her right, was a street called rue du Fouarre. Kirsteen found herself drawn down this, past its few houses, to the rue Galande with its quaint old buildings. Turning to her right, into rue Saint-Julien-le-Pauvre, she came to an old church by the same name.

She paused outside the church door and decided she was getting nowhere. She had ostensibly come to this section of Paris to find the last place from which Stonehenge had transmitted to London. But from exactly *where* -- in what building -- had he done this, Kirsteen asked herself? And would it help her to know anyway? It had been somewhere near place Maubert, she knew, and she was heading in that direction. She had better get on there.

"Bon jour!"

She looked up as the voice hailed her. An elderly cleric had come around the corner following the same route she had taken, it seemed, and now made to enter the little church. She realized she was blocking his way.

"Oh! Excuse me!" she said, and moved to one side. "I didn't mean to keep you from going inside."

The cleric smiled and inclined his head.

"I'm in no hurry," he said. "Please, don't let me distract you from your study." He looked up at the exterior. "This is a fine old building, isn't it? It's even a little older than the oldest part of Notre Dame, you know. And it was, for many years, the chapel of the Hôtel Dieu."

Kirsteen was impressed. "I didn't know that."

He smiled and nodded his head. "Few people do. I guess next to the Cathedral all else pales. But I think this church deserves a little more attention than it gets."

"Oh, I agree." Kirsteen found herself examining the exterior of old building with new interest.

"Won't you come inside?"

She didn't want to spend too long as a sightseer but couldn't resist following him into the dark interior. As her eyes adjusted she looked around in appreciation.

"The Gothic architecture is text book and the stained glass of the windows is without comparison," he enthused. "This present structure goes back to the Longpont monks who began work on it in 1170, though it was restored in 1651. The choir was the first to be patterned after that of Notre Dame. The nave originally possessed a triforium, though that was drastically altered in the seventh century. Beautiful, isn't it?"

Kirsteen nodded and stood looking about her.

"Oh! Now it's my turn to excuse myself." The cleric smiled and extended his hand. "I'm forgetting my manners. I am Canon Bizien. I'm actually *prêtre* of the little church of Saint-Denis, on rue Jean de Beauvais. But I love to sneak over here whenever I can. I just get such a tremendous charge of energy from Julien."

Kirsteen looked blank.

"Julien-le-Pauvre," Canon Bizien added. "This church."

"Oh! Oh, yes! Of course." She mentally kicked herself for being slow. But time was getting on and she had really allowed herself to be sidetracked. She must leave.

"You must come and see my humble church sometime," the loquacious canon continued. "Not a real pearl like Julien here, but a jewel none-the-less. It's not far from here; off boulevard St.-Germain, just a step across from place Maubert."

The name rang in Kirsteen's head like a peal of bells.

"Did you say place Maubert?" she asked.

"Why, yes. You know it?"

"As a matter of fact I was on my way there when I got sidetracked into Notre Dame," she said, smiling.

"Of course!" His head nodded up and down. "It's so easy to be seduced by Our Lady." His bright eyes twinkled. "And what was your business at place Maubert, if I may ask?"

"Oh! Er, just - just looking around." She knew it sounded lame as she said it.

For a short moment the canon's brow knitted. Then he was all smiles again. "Well, it does have its own charm. You know . . ." he glanced at his watch, ". . . I do have to get back there myself. Why don't we walk together?"

Canon Bizien turned out to be a wealth of tourist information. He had lived his whole life in the shadow of Notre Dame, he told Kirsteen, and loved every minute of it. She watched his animated face as he spoke of the beauties of the many buildings along this part of the Seine, and she couldn't help but get caught up in his enthusiasms. He was a little man, an inch or so shorter than Kirsteen, with fine white hair and a round, well-colored face that showed hardly a wrinkle. By his own admission he was nearly eighty years old but his slim figure and brisk walk gave the impression of his being two or three decades younger than that. Kirsteen found herself having to walk briskly to keep up with him.

"The occupation has made a big change to our lifestyle," said the canon. For the first time since their meeting his face took on a sombre look. "Not that I wish anyone ill, of course, but I do wish the Germans elsewhere!" The twinkle stayed away from his eyes.

"How has it affected you?"

"Oh, our fine church used to be one of the most popular in the arrondissement. We always had a full congregation, for every service. Now, of course, it's very much different."

"I always thought that people went to church more, in times of crisis," Kirsteen said.

"In crisis, yes." His white head nodded. "But we've got past the crisis stage now and are settled into the long term occupation. We have curfews. We have unemployment. We have rationing and permits and papers and need to justify our very existence!"

She glanced at him and saw how all the humor had gone out of his face. For the first time he looked close to his age.

"I wish I could do more for the people, but . . ." he spread his hands in exasperation. "The black market is more help to them than I am!"

They had turned the corner onto rue Jean de Beauvais and Kirsteen saw the church ahead of them.

"I'm sure they appreciate what you can do," she said.

"Oh, yes. Yes. Of course." He seemed to have sunk into self-examination and said no more till they entered the church. Then he perked up, as though remembering he had a guest, and was all smiles again.

"You never did tell me your name," he said. "Not, of course, that it matters. And many people these days don't want to share . . ."

"Oh, no! I'm sorry." Kirsteen quickly introduced herself and gave him a quick rundown on her teacher-from-Lyon background. He nodded his head, smiling, as though familiar with it all before.

"Of course," he said. "Welcome to Paris, Marie. And welcome to my humble church."

"Thank you."

They were approaching the nave, and Kirsteen was admiring the fine woodcarving of the pews, when she heard it. It was the unmistakable sound of a morse key. It was faint, coming from somewhere up above, but it was clear to anyone with her training. She stopped dead.

Canon Bizien turned to her. He had obviously heard it too, but tried to appear innocent. "What's the matter, my child?"

"Did you hear that?" she said.

"What?"

"Morse code! A telegraph key. Right here in the church. You must have heard it!"

The old priest's face lost its color and the smile disappeared. His right hand dropped to the folds of his cassock and suddenly came up again. Kirsteen found herself looking at the business end of a 9mm Beretta; the very gun she had almost chosen for her own use.

"I'm truly sorry, my dear," the canon said. "You are just at the wrong place at the wrong time. Normally the church is empty at this hour and I -- foolishly -- brought you here myself forgetting that we had to transmit right now. Normally we only do it very late at night," he added, more to himself than to Kirsteen. He waved the gun towards a small door leading off from beside the altar rail. "If you please!"

In a daze at the sudden turn of events, Kirsteen walked across to the door, opened it and passed through. She found herself in a small robing room. The canon indicated a chair and she sat down.

"I truly hate to have to do this," said Canon Bizien, going to a small closet and taking out a length of thin rope. "But you do understand? These days we just don't know who can be trusted and who cannot. We've got to take every precaution."

Kirsteen took a deep breath. "You're right," she said. "You have to take every precaution. Just as I do. Canon Bizien, I told you I had come up from Lyon. I didn't tell you why I had come. Perhaps we are on the same side?"

Quickly she told him the story of having come from the Free Zone to look for a missing Resistance worker -- she didn't give Stonehenge's name. She told him that the reason she had been coming to the place Maubert was to follow up on a clue she had about his last whereabouts. As she spoke, the old cleric's hand wavered and, finally, dropped down to his side. He slipped the Beretta away again. She noticed that his face had regained some of its color.

"My dear! What a coincidence that you should meet me and come here at just this time." His eyes lifted skywards. "I do believe it is His intervention."

They were interrupted by a light tapping noise from the ceiling. Looking up, Kirsteen saw a trapdoor.

"Don't worry. It is Michel, my radio man." He smiled broadly. "We must let him down."

He went across and tugged on a thin bell cord that ran up through the ceiling. Immediately the trapdoor opened and a ladder was pushed through. No sooner did its end hit the floor than a skinny, pale-faced man, with a small mustache and a day or two's growth of beard, clambered down and turned to the canon. When his eyes fell on Kirsteen his mouth dropped open and his eyes went wide.

"Relax, Michel," Canon Bizien said. "The young lady is a friend. Now! How did it go?"

Not taking his eyes off Kirsteen, Michel jerked his head up in the general direction of the loft. "It's no good. We're not getting through or something. There's no response at all."

"Oh, dear!" The cleric's eyes found Kirsteen's. "It was very important that we send a message at this time but we seem to be having trouble with our equipment." He sighed. "It was a patch-up at best and, though Michel here is the best radioman in Paris -- or so he tells me . . ." his eyes twinkled, ". . . you can only do so much with the equipment you have."

"Perhaps I can help. Might I have a look at the set?"

Both men looked at her in amazement.

"Really!" Kirsteen smiled and nodded her head at them. "I do know something about this sort of thing, as it happens. I've had some training."

She was halfway up the ladder, behind Michel, when they heard the church's outer door bang open. Jackboots pounded on the flagstone floor of the old church.

"Quickly! Up and out of sight. Don't even breathe!"

The old cleric sprang to the door and went out into the main church, pulling the door closed behind him. As Kirsteen hurriedly helped Michel pull up the ladder and close the trapdoor, she heard the Canon saying:

"Ah! Welcome to my humble church, Oberstleutnant. To what do I owe the pleasure of this visit?"

9: THE BELFRY

There was a rough, steep, wooden stairway that led up into the bell-tower. Though ancient it looked solid and Kirsteen followed Michel as he climbed carefully upward, away from the trapdoor through which they had come. At three different spots the Frenchman stopped and, with a finger to his lips, indicated to Kirsteen that she was to avoid stepping on a certain stair. She assumed it was because it would creak.

When they arrived at the top Michel collapsed in a corner and Kirsteen could see that he was sweating profusely. She guessed it was from the visit of the Gestapo rather than from the exertion of the climb. She regained her own breath and said nothing. Looking around, she saw a Type A, Mk. II, English-made radio receiver-transmitter of the type specially designed for the Resistance. It sat on the edge of the wooden platform around the church bell.

Finally Michel pulled a soiled handkerchief from his pocket, mopped his brow, and smiled at her. She saw that three of his front teeth were missing.

"We're safe for the moment," he whispered. "They won't be able to hear us up here."

Kirsteen wasn't so sure, remembering how she had distinctly heard the tap of the Morse key.

"Do the Gestapo often come here?" she asked softly.

He shook his head. He crawled to the edge of the
tower and pulled himself up to look out over the open side. She heard his sharp intake of breath.

"What is it?" she asked, crawling over beside him.

He nodded down to the street, far below. There was a black, unmarked van parked at the near corner. With sinking heart, Kirsteen realized it was a German radio detection van. She had been warned that there were many of them cruising the streets of Paris, and other cities, using their finely-tuned antennas to pinpoint buildings from which radio transmissions were being emitted. Obviously they had managed to pick up Michel's earlier transmission attempt.

"What can we do?" she asked. "They'll come up here, won't they?"

Michel, eyes starting out of his head, nodded vigorously. "Don't worry," he said. "We've prepared for something like this."

He moved across to one side of the belfry and started tugging at one of the wooden planks of the wall. Suddenly a section of the wall swung up on hinges. Someone had made a hiding place behind the wooden facing of the belfry. Kirsteen moved across and looked in.

It was long and narrow; small, dark and dirty. Michel scooped up the two halves of the radio, pulled down the antenna wire and wrapped it around the set, and stuck them inside the opening. Then he pushed Kirsteen to get in.

"You're joking!" she said. "We'll never both fit!"

"It was made only for me," he said, "but we've both got to get in."

He gave her another push, harder this time. At that moment they both heard the trapdoor, far below, slam back on its hinges. Kirsteen needed no more urging to get down on her knees and crawl into the murky opening. She had no sooner lowered herself flat on the floor, face down with the radio pressed against her cheek, than the skinny Frenchman dropped down on top of her, his body pressed hard against hers. She was about to object when he lowered the flap of the door and she realized that the enforced intimacy was not a matter of choice; they had to press together as tightly as possible to ensure the door stayed closed.

Kirsteen tried to hold her breath to keep from sneezing at the dust. Through a small crack between laths she was able to make out the space to one side of the bell opening. After what seemed like an age two figures emerged from below and stood glowering around the belfry. They were a German SS-Scharführer and an SS-Unterscharführer. The Sergeant moved across to the outer edge and waved to the men by the van, on the street below. The Corporal prowled around the belfry, occasionally tapping at the walls, and peering up into the underside of the roof.

Kirsteen's recently reviewed knowledge of German told her that they were disappointed and annoyed, as they cursed the French Resistance and stomped around the cramped belfry. Finally they started down the steps again, shouting down to their officer.

"Nichts! Es ist ausleere!"

As soon as the trapdoor flap banged shut again Kirsteen jerked her head up.

"Get off me!" she said.

It had become obvious to her that the little Frenchman wasn't exactly suffering in the enforced closeness; his foul-smelling breath was wheezing in her ear as he started to press himself rhythmically against her taught buttocks. She reached back, grasped his hair and gave it a solid tug. With a howl, Michel flung open the cover and rolled off her, rubbing his smarting head.

"Don't you ever try to take advantage of me, or any other woman, again!" Kirsteen advanced on him and snapped out a hand to slap the little Frenchman soundly on the side of the face. "So help me, I'll have you in the hands of the Gestapo in no time flat, and then see what they do with your manhood!"

Michel winced and darted away. He moved rapidly down the wooden steps, though still having the presence of mind to step warily in case the Gestapo were still in the church.

"Do you think they'll be back?" Kirsteen asked.

Canon Bizien nodded his head. "Yes, I'm afraid so. Now that they've been alerted they'll keep checking here, at all hours of the day and night. Just because they didn't find anything this time doesn't mean they think we're innocent." He sighed. "Ah, well! We'll just have to move around to another church.' He smiled at her. "Church towers and steeples are really excellent places for transmitting, you know."

"I bet they are." Kirsteen's eyes were fixed on Michel, who stood by the church door, peering out. He gave her a quick, surly look then disappeared outside. "How long have you known Michel?" she asked.

"What? Michel? Oh, I've known his family for years."

"His family . . . including Michel?" she persisted. She had not told the priest of the Frenchman's attempted violation.

"Well, actually no. I haven't known Michel himself as long as the others. He lost his wife and daughter at the beginning of the war and came to live with his uncle and aunt here just a year ago. He seems a conscientious fellow. He volunteered to work the radio for us. Unfortunately we haven't had a lot of luck with it, though. I think the set must be faulty."

"I rather doubt that," Kirsteen muttered. "I'll have a look at it for you later, canon, when the pressure is off. For now, I'd better get back. I have to meet with some other people."

"Of course. Of course." The cleric walked with her to the church door and they both peered out, carefully looking up and down the now deserted street.

"You keep speaking of 'we'," Kirsteen said. "I take it there are several in your group, Canon?"

"Just five of us. But we are all dedicated." He thought for a moment. "I think I would like you to meet them, Kirsteen. I think we may be able to help you trace that man you are looking for. By the way, you never did tell me his name."

Kirsteen smiled at him. So he hadn't missed that fact, she thought. "It was Stonehenge. At least, that was the name he was known by."

"Stonehenge!" Canon Bizien's face was pale. "It's Stonehenge you seek?"

Kirsteen was nervous as she prepared to cross the hallway to the meeting in Gaston's room. She had bad feelings about Paulette. She was half certain that it was the redhead who had been through her room, though she had no proof of that. Certainly the woman had made no attempt to hide her animosity and this was a situation where animosity could be dangerous.

"Ah, Marie! Come in, come in!" Gaston beamed his usual smile at Kirsteen and shepherded her to a seat at the table. Norbert was already seated there, as was Paulette. Colette was perched on the edge of the bed. As Kirsteen sat, between Gaston and Norbert, the door opened and Antoine hurried in.

"I hope I'm not late," he said. "I was doing some last minute checking with a friend at the *Soldatenheim* next door."

"You have a German friend?" Kirsteen asked, surprised.

"'Friend' is, perhaps, a misnomer," Antoine smiled. "It's a contact I've developed. He's a young man with a healthy appetite for French women and I've made myself useful to him in arranging contacts."

"All whores!" Gaston chuckled. "But the German thinks he's getting young virgins." They all laughed.

"It serves a purpose," Antoine continued. "In return he has been able to give me important information from time to time. Not that he realizes how important it is, of course." He sat on the bed beside Colette.

"Well, before we get down to business," Gaston said, "we must check the BBC. It's just coming up to nine o'clock."

He switched on the radio, which took an inordinately long time to warm up. Finally it gave out with a loud hum. Gaston hit the top of the set with the flat of his hand and the humming stopped. It was replaced by the voice of Alvar Lydell, the BBC news reader with the French-Language Service. At the end of the news round-up the announcer started reading the coded messages aimed at the various Resistance groups and individuals in the occupied land.

"Michelle needs a new hat ... Lyons must see the return of Napoleon ... Winter mittens are in demand ... Crocodiles make poor pets ..."

Each message was said twice; slowly and clearly. The group in Gaston's room listened intently until the end then the Frenchman turned off the radio.

"Is there ever a message for you?" Kirsteen asked.

Gaston shrugged. "Not so far." He smiled. "I doubt there ever will be, but we like to listen; to know that there are others out there, like us, who fight the Bosch!"

He glanced around the room at the other five. "Now then, as you all know Marie, here, is anxious to make contact with Stonehenge. But it seems Stonehenge has disappeared."

"What! What do you mean, he's disappeared?" Paulette came to her feet. "When did this happen?"

Kirsteen eyed her carefully. Paulette didn't seem to be acting. Her reaction looked decidedly genuine; she really seemed shocked to hear that Stonehenge was missing.

"You didn't know?" Gaston asked.

"Know? Of course I didn't know! Did you?"

"Well, no," Gaston admitted. "Until this afternoon, no I didn't."

"How long has he been gone?" Paulette demanded.

"About five weeks."

"What!"

"But weren't you supposed to be his girlfriend?" Antoine asked.

"*Supposed* to be?" Paulette spluttered. "I *was* -- I *am* his girlfriend! We have a very special relationship."

"Yet you didn't know he'd disappeared?" Kirsteen asked, her eyes fixed on the redhead.

"You all keep saying that," Paulette said, looking around at them in disbelief. "But I've been in touch with him all the time. I've spoken to him regularly; recently. He's not missing."

There was a stunned silence.

"You're saying you've been seeing him?" Kirsteen finally asked.

"Yes. Well, no -- not exactly. I haven't actually been seeing him. But I have been speaking to him . . . on the telephone." The redhead sat down again and looked from one to the other of them with a quizzical look on her face. "What's going on?"

"A good question," Norbert said.

"All right. Let's talk this through." Gaston spread his hands on the table. "Marie, here, turns up and says she's looking for Stonehenge. Norbert admits he hasn't seen him in weeks and did a thorough job of looking for him. He's now checked his contact with the Gestapo at the Hôtel Majestic and . . . ?" he looked expectantly at Norbert.

"Nothing. The Gestapo have no knowledge of him, so far as my man can tell."

"And my lady at the Gestapo offices in rue des Saussaies says the same thing," added Antoine. "He's not in custody and has not passed through their hands."

Gaston nodded. "Right. But now Paulette, here, says that he's not missing at all; that she's been in constant touch with him."

"I'm not just saying it. I have been!" insisted the redhead.

"Of course. Of course,' Gaston's head kept nodding up and down. "Yet," he spread his hands, "how can that be?"

Kirsteen looked into Paulette's green eyes. She noticed that they were beginning to water. She spoke gently. "Tell me, Paulette, when did you last actually *see* Stonehenge? In the flesh?"

"I guess it was some time ago. He'd been down to Tarbes, or somewhere, escorting a parcel. You went with him, didn't you Norbert?"

The blond young man grunted. "Yes. I've already been over that."

"And you saw him after that?" Kirsteen persisted.

"As soon as he got back. A Saturday, I think it was. He was going to Reims. He said he'd call me but I didn't hear from him for a while."

"How long a while?"

"I - I guess it was over a week, now that I think about it. But then I got a phone call," she added quickly. "And he's called me a couple of times since."

"Why hasn't he seen you?" asked Colette, from the bed.

"I don't know. Various reasons I guess."

"In these phone calls," Norbert said, his brow deeply furrowed. "Did he say where he was calling from?"

"And did he sound normal?" added Colette.

The redhead wrinkled her brow. "I guess he didn't sound normal, though it was hard to tell."

"What do you mean?" Kirsteen asked.

"Well, each time he said he was calling from out of town and it was dangerous to talk for long. His voice sounded sort of strained. It was always a bad connection, it seemed."

"And what did he call for? What were your conversations about?"

"He asked me to get him some things and send them to him."

"What?"   Kirsteen and Norbert spoke together.

"His special papers to get into the Forbidden Zone. I knew where he had them hidden. And his code book."

There was silence for a moment.

"How did you get them to him?" Kirsteen finally asked.

"It was a dead drop," Paulette said. "I wrapped them in an old piece of newspaper and left them under a pew at Notre Dame."

"You didn't watch to see if he came to pick them up?" Colette asked. "I would have done!"

"He told me not to." Paulette's voice sounded uncertain and, to Kirsteen, innocent.

"You say that the phone calls were bad connections," Kirsteen said, pondering. "Is it possible, do you think, that it wasn't Stonehenge at all on the phone, but someone else, pretending to be him?"

"No! No, of course not . . . I - I don't think so anyway." Paulette's voice tailed off as she began to think about the suggestion. "I - I guess it's possible," she finally admitted, speaking quietly with her eyes cast down.

Kirsteen looked at her and revised her earlier suspicions of the other woman. Perhaps Paulette was telling the truth.

10: CLOSE CALL

It was near noon and Kirsteen hurried along the boulevard St.-Germain. She didn't want to be late meeting Canon Bizien since the old cleric had promised to introduce her to his group of Resistants. She turned the corner from rue Jean de Beauvais onto rue Michel-Ange and slowed down.

In front of the church, a block ahead of her, a German staff car and two *Küblerwagens* were pulled into the curb. As she watched, an SS-Sturmbannführer came out of the church followed by a squad of Waffen S.S. In the middle of the soldiers Kirsteen immediately spotted the white head of Canon Bizien.

Knowing it would look suspicious to turn around and walk away, Kirsteen continued on towards the church, though she crossed to the far side of the road. As she passed the group the cleric happened to look up and caught Kirsteen's eye. He made no sign of recognition and she saw him being bundled into the staff car. As she continued her walk the small group of vehicles drove off.

At the far end of the block, just before turning the corner, Kirsteen looked back to the church. She was surprised to see Michel come out of the old building and hurry off in the opposite direction.

"So you've been in touch with other *Réseau*?" Gaston said. "There are a lot of us at work, you know. We're not taking this occupation lying down."

"I know," Kirsteen said. "You're all doing excellent work. Tell me, Gaston, did you know of the Canon?"

"No. There are so many small groups of Resistants and most of them are independent. We usually know of a few others but no one knows them all."

"Where do you think they took him? And what will happen to him?"

"Your *prêtre*?" Gaston shrugged his shoulders. "He'll be taken down to rue des Saussaies for questioning. He'll perhaps be kept for a few hours; maybe overnight. But they'll almost certainly let him go. If they have no evidence they'll just try to scare him."

Kirsteen wasn't greatly comforted. She didn't know whether or not the Gestapo had found the radio, though there was no evidence of it from what she could see in walking by. But she wasn't happy at the sight of Michel leaving the church after everyone had gone. Why hadn't he been taken, along with the canon, she wondered?

"Can you contact Antoine's inside lady, at rue des Saussaies, and find out what's happening?" she asked.

Gaston scratched his head. "We don't want to use her more than we have to. Why don't we wait twenty-four hours and see what develops? If Canon Bizien isn't out by then, yes, I'll do some questioning."

Kirsteen would have liked to have found out right away but realized that what Gaston said was right. If they had an informant inside the Gestapo offices it made sense to use her as sparingly as possible, so there would be less chance of her being discovered.

"I'll be guided by your judgement, Gaston," she said with a smile. "You know this area better than I do."

They were seated together on a bench beside the river, at pont des Invalides. A tugboat moved slowly past them, pulling a string of barges.

"Have you asked this Canon Bizien about Stonehenge?"

Kirsteen nodded. "Yes. And he knows him. Like you, he hasn't seen Stonehenge in weeks but he did see him more recently than Norbert or Paulette did, it seems. About a week after Norbert last saw him, Stonehenge was at the church using the radio up in the belfry. Canon Bizien says that he was a frequent visitor. He used the radio that night, just before midnight, came back at dawn and used it again very briefly, and then disappeared."

"Did he say where he was going?"

She shook her head. "He indicated he'd be back within a couple of days but, of course, he wasn't."

"Hmm. So another trail goes blank."

They fell silent as two men on bicycles rode past them. It had started to rain and Kirsteen pulled a headscarf from her pocket and slipped it over her head.

"Where do we go from here?" she asked.

Gaston turned up the collar of his jacket and they both got to their feet.

"Paulette didn't believe he'd disappeared. She said Stonehenge had been telephoning her. Perhaps he'll call again?" the little Frenchman said hopefully.

They started to walk back towards the boarding house. The rain got heavier and they walked faster.

"You know, you may have something there," Kirsteen said. "There's no reason he shouldn't continue to call -- Stonehenge or whomever it is that's actually talking to her."

The next day Canon Bizien was back at the church. Kirsteen sat with him in a pew and listened to his story.

"The Gestapo suddenly turned up, did another quick search, then took me away with them, as you saw," he said. "Again they had found nothing so I wasn't too worried about the arrest."

"They took you to rue des Saussaie?" Kirsteen asked.

He nodded. "And there they asked me question after question. Did I know that a radio was being operated in my church? Was I suspicious of any of my parishioners? Who had a key to the church? Who would be there late at night, and so on. They asked each question at least twenty times and I answered everything at least twenty times." He sighed. "I don't know if they suspect me or not. I rather feel they do, though they said I was free to go."

"You'd better lay low on the Resistance activities for a while," Kirsteen said.

The old cleric smiled at her. "Have no fear, my child. I'll be careful."

They rose and walked slowly and silently to the door of the church.

"Where was Michel while all this was going on?" Kirsteen asked suddenly.

"Michel? I don't know. He wasn't at the church when I was picked up, and I haven't seen him since I've been back."

It was on the tip of Kirsteen's tongue to say that Michel *had* been at the church when the canon had been arrested, but she kept quiet.

"I still want you to meet the other Resistants," Canon Bizien continued. "Go to Notre Dame tomorrow at noon. I will be at the foot of the North Tower. I'll be giving a group of students a tour of the cathedral. Perhaps you'd like to join us?" His eyes twinkled.

Kirsteen smiled at him and nodded her head. "Yes. I'd like that very much."

All the way back to the rooming house Kirsteen went over and over her feelings about Michel. The canon said he had not known the man a great time but had known his family. Michel operated the radio for the Resistants, the cleric said, but had encountered a number of problems doing it, despite claiming to be something of an expert. As she thought about it, with a calmer mind, she felt she could excuse the Frenchman his tentative sexual advance. It was probably just due to the closeness -- the tightness -- of the hiding hole. Being pressed up hard against a woman's *derrière* like that would probably have turned-on any red-blooded male. She smiled to herself, thinking about it. Too bad it hadn't been a handsome young man in there with her!

She mentally shook herself. Whatever the circumstances in the hiding place, there was an explanation needed for Michel being at the church when the canon was taken by the Gestapo. What was he doing there? How long had he been there? Was there any connection between him and the Gestapo's visit?

Kirsteen sighed. Winston Churchill had certainly dropped her in on an adventure. Find Stonehenge, he'd said. Just like that.

She went into the old house and climbed to the third floor.

"Kirsteen! Quickly! Come with me!"

Paulette literally jumped out of the doorway to Gaston's room and grabbed Kirsteen's arm.

"W-what? Why, . . . ?"

"Gestapo!" The redhead spoke through clenched teeth. "They're on their way up here."

Kirsteen heard voices down below and the sound of heavy boots on the stairs.

"No time! Let's move!" Paulette ran towards the bathroom at the end of the corridor, dragging Kirsteen after her. They went in and closed the door, Paulette locking it behind them. The tall Frenchwoman climbed up on the toilet seat and tugged at a short knotted cord hanging from a wooden trapdoor set into the ceiling. The flap came down and Paulette unfolded a frail-looking ladder.

"Quickly!" she said. The two women climbed up the ladder into the unlit roof crawl-space and then pulled up the steps after them and secured the trapdoor.

"Keep tight behind me," Paulette said.

Kirsteen reached out a hand and grabbed the other woman's belt. Slowly they inched across the dark attic floor, occasionally bumping into boxes and trunks.

"It's somewhere here . . . ah! Here it is," Paulette said. With a loud creak, from un-oiled hinges, another flap opened, this time in the attic's sloping ceiling. Daylight streamed in. "It's the way out to the roof. Come on!"

Kirsteen followed, climbing up onto an old wooden box and stepping over the low sill onto a flat area of roof. Paulette closed the flap behind them.

"Okay," Kirsteen said, getting her breath. "Now what on earth is going on, Paulette?"

"I told you -- Gestapo!"

"But - but here? I mean, why? How did they know about us; about me?"

The Frenchwoman shrugged. "Who knows? They have their spies everywhere. I wouldn't be surprised if old Madame Delestraint tipped them off. She never did like me, that old bat!"

"But she adores Gaston," Kirsteen said. "Why would she . . . ?"

"Oh, I don't know!" The redhead irritably turned away and moved along the flat section of roof towards the brick parapet. It didn't look at all secure to Kirsteen but she followed.

"We can jump down onto the roof next door," Paulette said, pointing the way. "And from there we can get into their attic and down the way we came up this one."

"It sounds as though you've done this before," Kirsteen observed.

"Come on!" Before Kirsteen could get a response the redhead swung a leg over the parapet and jumped off.

The whole row of houses were attached to one another, each stepping down slightly from the previous one due to the slight incline of the street below. Kirsteen noted that it would be possible to hop from housetop to housetop for about eight houses before coming to the end of the row. She wondered why Paulette didn't choose one of the further houses for re-emergence. But she followed the redhead anyway.

"I don't understand it," Gaston said, some two hours later as they sat around a table at the *Rescoe* where Kirsteen had originally been introduced to Norbert and Colette.

"Nor do I." Antoine was in his usual position, keeping an eye on the door and on the other customers. "Who knows how the Gestapo would find out about us?"

"Will it be safe to go back?" Kirsteen asked. She was thinking of her gun and codebook, safely tucked away in the ceiling of her room.

"You have stuff there you need?" Paulette's eyebrows rose in question.

"I have very little in the way of clothing," Kirsteen said, "but what I do have I don't want to lose. You can't buy anything worthwhile these days, except on the black market of course."

"Well *I* need to go back," Gaston said. Kirsteen thought of the gun in his wardrobe and the work papers under his mattress. "I'm not going to be frightened away so easily."

"Paulette thinks it was Madame Delestraint who tipped them off," Kirsteen said.

Antoine snorted. "Nonsense! That old biddy loves young Gaston here. She'd never turn him over to the Germans."

"I just offered that as a suggestion," Paulette said, sniffing. "It could have been anyone."

"We must be extra careful from now on," Gaston said. "And we'd better have someone on watch anytime we're having a meeting there."

They all nodded agreement.

"I do have to thank you, Paulette," Kirsteen said, turning to the redhead. "You got me out of there pretty quickly. I'm grateful." The other woman nodded and smiled, though she didn't look up. I guess that does prove her loyalty, Kirsteen thought to herself.

11: THE SAFE HOUSE

She could hear Canon Bizien's voice before she saw him. He was describing the construction of the cathedral, started eight centuries ago, and enthusing over the standard of workmanship in those early times. Kirsteen smiled to herself as she listened knowing, even from her short acquaintance with the man, how inspired the cleric became when emersed in the ambiance of Notre Dame and its surrounding ancient churches.

She rounded a corner and saw the white-haired figure standing with a small group of men and women.

"The building was started in 1163 on the site of an old Roman temple. The chancel and altar were consecrated in 1182. It was another sixty years before the wonderful sculptures around the main doors were put in and the north tower wasn't added till 1250. Later we'll visit the Treasury, where the reliquaries of the Crown of Thorns and the Nail of the True Cross are kept, together with Thomas à Becket's cross, gold and silver plate, and other relics. There, too, you'll see Napolean's coronation mantle -- in May of 1804 he crowned himself emperor here."

He looked up and saw Kirsteen.

"Ah! Here's our other student. Won't you join us, Marie?"

She moved forward, smiling.

"This is Marie Nègre, fresh from Lyon." The canon introduced her. "And these, Marie, are my students: Albert, Claude, Elise, Lucie and Hélène."

Kirsteen smiled around at everyone until her eyes met those of the man introduced as Claude. She felt a shock of recognition when she looked at the thin-faced, bright-eyed man wearing a black beret and black leather jacket . . . it was none other than Greyhound, her Gypsy co-trainee at the Wrexham school!

Greyhound was quick to cover any reaction she might have at seeing him.

"Bon jour, Mademoiselle," he said. She was surprised that his French was so excellent, with just a trace of a Belgium accent. "I am the new one here; like yourself I've just arrived in Paris, from my native Brussels."

"But Claude is a not infrequent visitor," added the canon. "We're always glad to have him here."

Greyhound inclined his head in acknowledgement of the compliment. "Thank you, canon," he murmured. "You're too kind."

The canon led the group around the cathedral for about twenty minutes, so that anyone who might be watching would have been assured that he was lecturing a group of students. Eventually he led the way out to the Square Jean XXIII, located between the river and the building. From it there was a breathtaking view of the east end of the cathedral, ringed by flying buttresses and surmounted by the spire. The square was deserted except for their little group.

"I've had enough history for today, thanks very much," muttered Albert, a short, fat, ruddy-faced man who made Kirsteen think of a butcher. "Do we have to keep up this pretense any longer, Pierre?"

"Pierre?" said Kirsteen.

The canon smiled. "My name in the *Réseaux*. No, Albert, we can relax now. But it was necessary to establish ourselves. You just never know who may be watching."

"I enjoyed it," Elise said. She was a skinny brunette who wore a large beret pulled down around half her face. Her bright brown eyes caught Kirsteen's. "I'm fascinated by history, aren't you, Marie?"

Kirsteen nodded and smiled.

"Marie!" Canon Bizien spoke in a low voice. "These are my compatriots; my fellow Resistants. Friends, Marie is searching for Stonehenge. You all remember Stonehenge, of course?" There was a general murmur of assent. "Have any of you seen him lately, by any chance?"

They all looked at one another, but no one offered any information.

"I haven't seen him for weeks," Lucie said. She was a pretty blonde girl who looked young enough that she should have been in school, Kirsteen thought. "He'd said he was going to take me to the Louvre but he never did."

"You didn't miss much," grumbled Albert. "There's no true art there today. All the famous paintings are either hidden away or hanging in some high-ranking German's home somewhere."

Kirsteen looked around. "Where's Michel? I would have thought he'd be here with you."

Hélène gave a snort. "Michel come to a lecture? Even a pretend one? I don't think so!" She was a gray-haired, middle-aged matron who peered over the tops of steel-rimmed spectacles. Kirsteen picked up on the fact that she kept giving Albert long, searching looks, with little smiles. For his part the rotund butcher -- as Kirsteen was sure he was -- ignored her.

"As a matter of fact I did ask Michel to try to be here," the canon said. "I don't know why he's not. I really thought this was a good way of having a meeting without attracting attention. He should have been here."

"I don't care for Michel!"

Kirsteen was surprised at the bitterness in Lucie's voice. The girl turned her back on the group and stood gazing out at the Seine. Canon Bizien tut-tutted and shook his head at Kirsteen as though to assure her that she should not take Lucie seriously. But Kirsteen made up her mind to speak further to the young girl later.

"Why do you want to see Stonehenge?" Elise asked.

"That's not what's important," Kirsteen said. "The fact is that he's missing and we need to find him."

"*You* need to find him! We don't have to."

"Now, Albert," the canon admonished.

"Don't worry. We'll help." Lucie turned back to the group. "Albert too. He just likes to be difficult."

The others laughed and the tension that had been building disappeared.

"I will certainly help all I can." Greyhound's eyes met Kirsteen's and she felt comforted. "I - we do have our own particular tasks but I understand Stonehenge is important.

And, of course, we'll always help a fellow Resistant like yourself, Marie."

She returned his smile. "Thank you, Claude," she said.

"What about the Leycuras safe house?" Hélène spoke up. She pushed her glasses up on her nose. "Pierre! Didn't you mention, once, that Stonehenge had used that?"

"Of course!" The cleric nodded. "I had forgotten. Thank you, Hélène." He turned to Kirsteen. "Stonehenge did occasionally bring parcels to this particular safe house. And it wasn't unknown for him to stay there himself once in a while. That would be a good place for you to start enquiring, Marie.'

"I'd be happy to take her there," Greyhound offered.

"And I'll go too -- if I may?" Lucie looked to the canon, for permission. He smiled.

"Of course, my child."

The three of them hurried across the pont au Double, on to quai de Montebello, and headed down rue Dante, towards rue Bièvre.

"So what brings you to Paris, Claude?" Kirsteen tried to sound casual, conscious of Lucie walking between the two of them.

The brown-faced Gypsy grinned. "Oh, nothing special, Marie. I get away from Brussels whenever I can, knowing I can do more good for the Resistance here in Paris than I can in Belgium. And what about yourself? This fellow Stonehenge must be important."

"We're all important," Kirsteen said, sidestepping the question.

"That's true," Lucie put in. "Marie, you'll have to remember that when we get to the Leycuras safe house. Godefrois and Victoire Leycuras are a strange couple."

"Oh? What do they do?"

"They deal in antiques. Have done for years. They also deal with the Germans."

Kirsteen was surprised. "They deal with the Germans? Yet they run a safe house and hide people from the Germans?"

"Uhuh!" Lucie was pleased to be able to explain.   "Apparently they dealt with many Germans before the war, in their antique business. So they've just kept up the connections, hoping they would turn out to be useful to us all."

"And have they?"

"Oh, yes." The young girl laughed. "It seems that several times they've got important information out of some unsuspecting Wehrmacht General or Colonel who was decorating his new Paris apartment. They even managed to pass the word about some French works of art being transported off to Germany. The *Réseau* was able to intercept them and save France's treasures. Ah, here we are."

They had arrived at a small row of stores on rue Bièvre. Kirsteen immediately spotted the antique shop. They opened the door and went in.

"Lucie! What a delight."

A stout, elderly gentleman dressed in a charcoal-grey, three-piece suit, and sporting a red carnation in his buttonhole, bore down upon them from the back of the store. He wore a dark green, silk, polka-dot bow tie and Kirsteen couldn't help but notice the heavy gold watch-chain that stretched across his vest. His hair was black, with generous borders of silver-gray on the sides, and was overly oiled and swept back in an exaggerated wave. He had a large walrus mustache which didn't hide the glint of gold in his teeth when he smiled, which he now did as he thoroughly looked over Lucie's two companions.

"And who do we have here . . . ?"

"These are two 'friends', Godefrois," Lucie said, introducing them. "Claude is from Belgium and has been here to help us before. Marie is new in town. She's from Lyon."

Godefrois Leycuras extended his hand and greeted Kirsteen. "Delighted, my dear. Any friend of Lucie's is welcome here." He turned to Greyhound. "And any friend of France is a friend of mine. Come! Into the back room."

He turned and strode off, the three of them hurrying after him.

"Where's Victoire?" Lucie asked, when they were settled in the small sitting room behind the shop.

Godefrois waved his hands in the air. "Out and about! I can't keep up with her half the time! She'll be back soon enough. Now -- what can we do for you?" He looked first at Greyhound.

The Gypsy deferred to Kirsteen.

"It's extremely important that I contact a man who goes by the name Stonehenge," she said. "I understand you know him; you've had dealings with him?"

"Indeed we have. An excellent chess player, as it happens -- though I don't suppose that's why you're looking for him." Godefrois's eyes were locked on Kirsteen's and she sensed he was feeling her out.

"I'm afraid I can't say why I need to see him; I just do," she said.

He nodded. "I understand." He walked across to peer out the door into the shop, as though to be certain it was empty. He came back to where they were sitting and lowered himself into an ornate but delicate-looking Louis XVI chair. He was a large man and Kirsteen wondered if it would support him.

"Stonehenge seems to have disappeared," Greyhound said. "Apparently all his associates have been looking for him but no one can find him."

"We thought perhaps you could help," Lucie added. "Have you seen him recently?"

Godefrois looked up at the ceiling and tugged at one ear, as though deeply searching his memory. Finally he said, "No. No, we haven't seen Stonehenge in about a month. It's funny you should come asking about him. He brought two Englishmen here -- downed RAF pilots -- late one night and said he'd pick them up again in two days. He'd often used our, er, 'facilities' and we're always glad to help. Anyway, he didn't show up. We waited five days before making our own arrangements to pass on the parcels to someone else. We haven't heard a word from him since."

They sat in silence for a while. Finally Kirsteen broke it. "Did you try to find out what had happened to him?"

"No."

Kirsteen was surprised.

As though reading her mind, Godefrois continued. "This is an extremely dangerous game we're in. People come and go; one day they're here, the next they've disappeared. We take a big risk using our home as a safe house, as I'm sure you're aware. It wouldn't do for it to become known -- in certain circles -- that we were inquiring as to the whereabouts of anyone. Anyone!"

"But surely . . ."

"We're not like so many in the Resistance. If it gets hot, they can just pick up and move elsewhere; go into hiding for a while. But what Victoire and I have here is a long-established business set-up that can effectively act as a go-between for France with the occupying forces. These days we just don't know whom we can trust. Times are hard and getting harder, as you well know. When pressed to put food on the table people will do terrible things. There's no way we can risk this safe house by asking one single question that might be out of line. You understand?"

Kirsteen nodded. "Yes," she said. "Yes, I think I do." She stood up. "Thank you. Thank you, Godefrois, for all that you have done and are doing."

12: QUESTIONS

"Gestapo? What Gestapo? There's been no Gestapo here!"

Kirsteen looked at the old woman in amazement. Madame Delestraint returned her stare, her mouth set in a straight line.

"You're sure about that? It was yesterday morning, just before noon."

"I know. I saw you come in, not long after that redheaded Paulette. I don't know about that one, you know? And that isn't her natural color hair either!"

"But I heard them -- heard their boots on the stairs," Kirsteen protested.

The old crone laughed a cackling, humorless laugh. "Oh, you heard Vincent and Guillaume, the Cognacq brothers in 2B. They're always heavy on their feet. Work at the railway they do."

"I see. Thank you. Thank you very much, Madame."

Kirsteen turned away and climbed the stairs to her room. What was going on, she wondered? Had Paulette been mistaken also, when she led them out over the rooftops? Had she truly believed it was the Gestapo coming, or was she playing some kind of game with Kirsteen?

"Hello Marie!" It was Gaston, standing at his door.

"Oh! Hello, Gaston. Say, do you have a minute? Could I speak to you?"

"Of course. Come on in."

He led the way into the room, then closed the door after her. They sat down at the table and Kirsteen told the little Frenchman what she had learned about the false alarm with the Gestapo.

"What do you think, Gaston? Did Paulette know it wasn't really the Gestapo? Or do you think she really believed it was?"

Gaston shrugged his shoulders. "Who can say? I know she'll never tell. If she was mistaken she would never admit it." He laughed. "She's a proud one, our Paulette."

"I wasn't thinking so much about her being mistaken," Kirsteen said. "I was wondering if there could be any reason for her deliberately misleading me?"

Again he shrugged. "Perhaps she wanted you to feel indebted to her, for saving you! Who knows? I don't."

Kirsteen thought for a moment. Yes, perhaps that was it; perhaps the redhead did want Kirsteen to feel indebted to her. Or perhaps she used this to 'prove' that she was a true partisan and above suspicion. But did it prove that   . . . or did it raise more questions than it answered? Kirsteen couldn't make up her mind.

"Well one thing is good," Gaston said, flashing his cheery smile. "We'll no longer have to worry about moving out. We can stay in these rooms and relax."

"That's true," Kirsteen agreed, smiling herself.

"Now, tell me about your canon and his people. How many does he have?" Gaston asked.

Kirsteen told him of the meeting held at Notre Dame, though without mentioning that she had known Greyhound previously. She also told of the visit to the antique shop.

"Do you know of the Leycurases?" she asked.

He nodded. "They are highly respected in the *Réseaux*   -- the Resistance network. They've had many, many people pass through their house. They'll hide them and feed them and then pass them on to others in the line to freedom."

"Have you ever met them?"

"No. But I'd like to, one day."

They sat and talked for half an hour then Kirsteen left and went to her room. There she sat quietly and, in her mind, went over everything that had happened since she had landed in France. She felt depressed. She decided she hadn't really accomplished anything. She was no nearer finding Stonehenge than she had been when she arrived. She had made contact with Gaston's group through information she had been given on leaving England. She had made contact with Canon Bizien's group on her own initiative. But neither had been able to help. What should she do now, she wondered? There was a knock at the door.

It was Gaston. "Marie! It's Paulette. Madame Delestraint says she telephoned to say we should both meet her at the *Rescoe*. She's had another phone call from Stonehenge!"

"This time I listened very carefully," the redhead said. "I'd swear it was his voice, though again it was a bad line. He said he was calling from Falaise, up near Caen."

"That's in Normandy; in the Forbidden Zone," Kirsteen said.

"What did he want?" Gaston asked.

"He said he wanted me to join him there." Paulette sounded excited. Kirsteen noticed how her green eyes sparkled and how she held her head high and seemed far more animated than she had in a while. If this was all an act, Kirsteen thought, Paulette should have been a professional.

"You'll need travel papers," Antoine said. He had joined them at the restaurant. "We should be able to arrange that."

Gaston nodded. "Yes, Abbé Carpentier can take care of that all right, though it'll take a day or two. He has a small printing press in his cellar, Marie. He can produce identity papers on demand; passes into the Forbidden Zone, demarcation line cards, and any other documents we might ever need. How soon do you have to go, Paulette?"

"He asked me to be at Falaise within a week. I'm to take a room at the small hotel there and he'll contact me."

"But wait a minute!" Kirsteen wanted to know more. "Didn't he say why he wanted you there? Did he say what he was doing?"

Paulette shook her golden curls. "No. Just that he needed me there with him."

"Did you ask him about his disappearance?"

"Well, er, no." The French woman hesitated. "Since he was right there, on the phone, it seemed silly to say that he'd disappeared. I mean . . ."

"No matter," Gaston said. "If it really is him then you're right -- he did <u>not</u> disappear, not in the strict sense of the word."

"But you're certain it was his voice?" Kirsteen persisted.

"Yes! I told you, it was a bad line. It always is, these days, it seems. Why even right here in Paris you can be calling . . ."

"Paulette!" Kirsteen interrupted her. "I want to go with you."

"What?"

"I want to go with you, to see Stonehenge."

The redhead looked around at each of them, uncertainly. "I - I don't know," she said. "I mean, Stonehenge did say that this was top secret. In fact I shouldn't even have told you he called, except that I knew you needed to know."

Kirsteen turned to Gaston. "Can you arrange papers for me, too? I may also need a Gestapo pass -- 'love bird' papers? Can you do that?"

In order to cross into the Forbidden Zone it was necessary to have a special pass from the Gestapo. This pass had a rubber stamp on it showing two birds facing each other, in a circle.

The stamp was generally referred to as 'the love birds'.

"We can get you papers all right, Marie," Gaston said, nodding his head. "But Paulette may be right. Do you think it wise to go with her?"

Kirsteen looked him in the eyes. "I can't say why I have to find Stonehenge. I've already told you that. But you must trust me, I do need to see him. It is *very* important."

His brown eyes looked hard at her for a long moment. Then he shrugged. "So be it! I'll see that you have the papers."

"Thank you, Gaston. Thank you."

Paulette said nothing.

That evening Kirsteen paid another visit to Canon Bizien. She found him in the robing room of the church, packing some vestments into an old cardboard box. Michel was with him.

"Marie, my dear! What a pleasant surprise," the old priest greeted her. "To what do I owe the pleasure of this visit?"

"I need to use your radio, canon? May I?"

The cleric and Michel exchanged glances.

"You can't," said the sullen Frenchman. "It's not working."

"And apart from that, we're just in the process of moving it," added the canon. "We're taking it over to our neigbouring Sainte-Eleanore church. They have a shorter bell tower than ours, but they are on higher ground, so we should get better reception."

"But it's still not working," repeated Michel.

"You mean, you've got the radio there, in that box?" Kirsteen asked.

The old man nodded. "Just an old box of church vestments I'm taking across to my good friend Canon Cruse," he said, with a twinkle in his eye.

"Would you mind if I come with you?" Kirsteen asked, ignoring the dark looks of Michel.

They reached the neighboring church with no problems. Canon Bizien led the way down the aisle and into the robing room, the church layout being almost identical to that of Saint-Denis.

"Canon Cruse told me to make myself at home," said the cleric, indicating a small table to Michel. The Frenchman thankfully put the box containing the thirty pound radio covered by the vestments on the table. "He said I was welcome to come here to do whatever I needed to do, just so long as I didn't tell him what that might be!"

Ten minutes later the three of them were up in the bell tower, Michel laying out the wire for the antenna. He still protested that the radio was inoperative.

"Now, let me have a try with the set," Kirsteen said, putting on the headphones and settling herself in front of the twin boxes. "You know, they've now got out the Model A Mark Three, which is a whole lot lighter than this and can transmit over six hundred miles." She busied herself with adjusting the knobs on the transceiver and listened intently for any sound in the headphones. She flipped the toggle-switch back and forth, a frown creasing her brow.

"See?" grunted Michel. "I told you."

"Wait a minute." She unscrewed the black bakelite knob on the lower right side of the set and examined inside. "As I suspected. It's a fuse!" Kirsteen waved the small holder in Michel's direction then bent to the task of fastening a fresh strand of fuse wire, taken from the small receptacle marked *SPARES*. In less than a minute she had the fuse-holder back in place and a smile spread across her face.

"Is it working?" the canon asked.

Kirsteen nodded. "Oh, yes," she said. "It's fine."

Michel grunted and moved off to look around the bell tower.

Kirsteen took out her code book, removed from the apartment ceiling for the occasion, and set it on the ground beside her.

"I have to be out of town for a few days and need to send out a report before I go."

"You're going back to Lyon?" the cleric asked.

"No. Just a quick trip up to Falaise."

In no time she was tapping away at the telegraph key, sending groups of five-letter ciphers over the transmitter to London.

Across the English Channel the message was relayed from a station in Kent to the Bletchley Code and Cipher School fifty miles north of London. There it was received and acknowledged. From its opening identifier it was recognized as a message for the Prime Minister's eyes only and again relayed to a basement in Whitehall. There, during a brief lull between air raids, it was sent by special messenger across to the basement War Office where Winston Churchill was finishing up a meeting with the War Cabinet.

"Gentlemen," he said, looking at the yellow sheet of paper covered in neat rows of numbers, each of five digits, "You must amuse yourselves for a few minutes, I'm afraid, while I see what this epistle has to say. I will rejoin you shortly."

He pulled himself up out of the chair and shuffled off to the small back room that served as his sleeping quarters on many nights. When he returned his face bore the slightest of smiles.

"I am happy to report, gentlemen, that events are finally showing signs of moving, amongst our French cousins over the water."

"With regards to what, Prime Minister?" asked Clement Attlee, the Deputy Prime Minister.

"Ah! That I'm not at liberty to say!" smirked Churchill.

Kirsteen was in her room, packing her few things for the trip north, when there came a tap on the door. Cautiously she opened it. A thin, slight figure quickly eased around her into the room. It was Greyhound.

"Close the door!"

She did. "Greyhound! What are you doing here?"

"'Claude', please. We'll leave Greyhound and Casey for other meetings." His eyes swept rapidly around the room, then he moved over to the window and, lifting the edge of the heavy blackout curtain, peered out.

"Are you on the run?"

"No." He turned back to face her and smiled, his body visibly relaxing. "Just thought I'd drop in on you and see how you are." He pulled out a chair from the table and sat down. "I see you're packing. Going on a trip?"

Sitting opposite him, Kirsteen quickly told him of Paulette's call from Stonehenge and the fact that she was going with the redhead, to meet the elusive agent.

Greyhound studied her face intently. "Was she sure it was Stonehenge?" he asked.

"That's what I asked. She said she couldn't swear to it but it sure sounded like him."

The Gypsy was silent for a moment, then he leaned forward. "I must go to Falaise as well."

Kirsteen sat back. "Wait a minute. I'm the one who's looking for Stonehenge. Why do you have to go?"

Greyhound chuckled. "I don't know what your mission is, 'Marie', nor what department you're working for -- and I'm not going to ask. But I do know that part of *my* mission also happens to be to make contact with Stonehenge."

"It does?" She was momentarily nonplussed. Then she had an idea. "You're with MI6, right?" She said it as though she already knew, hoping that the dark-skinned little man would simply agree. But Greyhound was too canny for that. He grinned broadly.

"Like I said, Marie, I'm not going to ask who you're working for . . . and I don't expect you to ask me. I just know we're on the same side and we both have our orders. Okay?"

She smiled. "Okay, 'Claude'."

"I'll be going under my own steam so you won't have to explain me to this redhead."

There came a tap at the door.

"Marie!" It was Gaston's voice.

"One moment, Gaston," she called. Then, to Greyhound, she whispered: "If you need to, you can get out over the rooftops. Just go to the bathroom at the end of the hallway and there's a trapdoor up to the attic."

Greyhound nodded and moved swiftly to stand behind the door as she opened it.

"Gaston. What is it?"

The short Frenchman smiled his usual smile. "We need a photograph of you for the identity papers, Marie. Come on over to my room. I have a friend there who will take it for you."

With the briefest of glances at the man in hiding, Kirsteen went out into the hallway and closed the door.

13: NORTH TO NORMANDY

The train was forty-five minutes late pulling out of the station. Kirsteen and Paulette had shown their papers at least a half dozen times to different officials before they were finally able to relax in the crowded corridor of the ancient wooden carriage. There had been no question of getting a seat in any of the compartments, which were full to overflowing more than an hour before the old locomotive got up steam enough to drag its load out of the Gare d'Austerlitz. It was a short train, with only two passenger cars together with three freight cars carrying army supplies.

Kirsteen wedged herself against a pile of suitcases belonging to a family of five, filling the corridor to their left. She had no sooner made herself comfortable, perched on half of Paulette's battered suitcase, than she was thrown forward as the train suddenly and sharply decelerated and ground to a stop. There were shouts up and down the train and Paulette managed to stick her head out of the nearby window to see what was going on.

Kirsteen strained to peep out also, but her view was partially blocked by the redhead and other passengers equally anxious to see what was going on. She finally managed to make out a small group of people, down on the track, walking back in the direction of the station. As they came abreast of the window Kirsteen saw that it was a man and a woman with two young children, being driven along by a Waffen-SS-Hauptsturmführer   and   two   burly   SS-Scharführers. The family was each wearing a yellow, six-pointed star.

"Jews!" hissed Paulette.

As Kirsteen watched the family being prodded along by the rifle-butts of the Gestapo men, the train started up again and slowly began to gather speed once more till the escorted family disappeared from sight.

"What will happen to them?" Kirsteen asked.

Paulette looked at her briefly then stared down at her toes. "They've been shipping foreign Jews out of Paris for over a year now. The Propaganda-Staffel started with a lot of propaganda against Jews, to build up resentment among Parisians. They smashed windows of Jewish stores and residences. They provoked the

Jews into a huge demonstration, last June; they were all over the main boulevards, between the Place de la République and the Opéra. Then the Germans swooped and got rid of five thousand of them. With less than an hour's notice they shipped them out in buses, trucks and trains. There are still about a hundred thousand French-born Jews here but they seem to have become a target for the Germans and, in particular, the Gestapo."

"Why do they wear those yellow stars?" Kirsteen asked.

"They have to. It's something the *Militärbefehlshaber* is trying out. They say that by the beginning of June all Jews over the age of six will have to wear a yellow star so they can be easily identified." Paulette kept glancing around, as though afraid to speak on the subject. "I also hear that General Oberg is about to issue a decree banning them from just about everywhere: the cafés and restaurants, theaters, concert halls, cinemas, beaches, even libraries and museums."

"But - but, why?" Kirsteen was bewildered. "What have the Jews done?"

"*Le Petit Parisien* newspaper, which is now run by the Germans of course, said that it was the Jews who wanted the war. They said that they were an evil-minded race that plunged the world into this terrible conflict." She paused for a moment, as though deep in thought, then continued. "I think they plan to get rid of all the Jews. We -- our little Resistance group -- have heard that within the next two or three months there will be tens of thousands of Jews taken from their homes and sent off to some sort of camps in Germany."

They continued the journey in silence.

Normandy was a beautiful part of France, with many small lakes and rivers, woodlands, and rich farmland producing dairy products and fruit crops. Many were the herds of cows Kirsteen saw as the train traversed the fields of Normandy and, as the engine steamed into the station at Falaise, she saw hundreds of anemones and camellias plus many fine magnolias. Every little cottage seemed to have its own small orchard.

There was one hôtel close to the station, though "inn" would have been a more apt description, Kirsteen thought. It was at least three hundred years old; all oak beams with walls and doors out of alignment. Despite its age it was clean and welcoming. They had no trouble getting a room. In fact the landlord seemed surprised that anyone was still traveling away from home. But they had their story ready.

"We were in Evreux all through the bombing," Kirsteen said, conversationally. "We had hoped to stay out the war there but my sister ..." she indicated Paulette, "... is a nervous wreck. We are going to Paris to stay with our brother but thought it would be nice to stop a few days here, in Falaise, first. It's just nice to see the fields and trees and get away from bombed-out buildings."

The landlord, an old man with a heavily-wrinkled face and a head covered with close-cropped grey hair, nodded glumly. "Yes. I heard Evreux was badly hit. They even destroyed the cathedral, didn't they?"

Kirsteen and Paulette nodded in unison, their faces blank.

"Ah! War is hard! I made it through the first one, myself. They said as how that was the war to end all wars but, well, here we are again it seems." He shook his head somberly and passed them an old iron key. "Here you go, ladies. Room number nine. My best. It's got a nice view to the north."

They thanked him, went up the well-worn stairs and along the narrow passageway to a heavy oak door at the end, bearing the number nine. Inside they sank down on the big four-poster bed and let out long sighs.

"I've never had a sister," Paulette said, after a few moments of silence. "I think I might like it."

"I've never had one either," Kirsteen said. "This will be an experience for both of us."

That evening they went down to the small hôtel dining-room and ordered the chicken and duck pie; specialty of the region and of the hotel. The portions served were large and well adorned with early fresh garden peas and potatoes. The meal was washed down with hot apple cider.

"What a change from Paris's rationing," Paulette said. "Even on the black market you can't get a meal like this."

Back in their room the Frenchwoman poured some hot water from an antique china pitcher into a matching washbowl and started to wash her face.

"I wonder when Stonehenge'll get in touch with me," she said. "I wonder if he knows I'm here yet?"

"Oh, I'm sure he does," Kirsteen responded. She put away her few belongings in the top drawer of the large chest of drawers alongside the window. "I doubt that there are many people get off the Paris train at Falaise. Most of them must go on to Caen. I'm sure he's been watching the station and knows we're here."

"What should we do? How will we get in touch with him?"

"You said that he told you he'd get in touch with you. We just have to be patient and wait. We could be here for several days. We might as well enjoy it."

"I suppose you're right."

Kirsteen watched the redhead slip into a flannel nightgown and climb up into the big old bed. There was plenty of room for the two of them on the feather mattress, under the multi-colored eiderdown that promised plenty of warmth despite the small fire that was already dying down in the fireplace.

Tomorrow is another day, she thought, and climbed into the bed also.

Kirsteen wasn't sure where she was when she first awoke. It took a moment to realize that she was in the old inn and a moment longer to notice that Paulette was gone. The sun streamed in at the window and, reaching over to the nightstand for her watch, Kirsteen saw that it was already eight o'clock.

She's probably gone out for an early morning walk, Kirsteen thought, though the redhead had never struck her as the athletic type. Or perhaps she's gone down for an early breakfast. Then she heard footsteps in the corridor outside.

"Paulette!" Kirsteen called. "Why didn't you wake me ..." Her voice trailed away as the door was flung open and a tall, grey-faced Gestapo officer stepped into the room.

Kirsteen instinctively clutched the bedclothes about her. "W-What are you doing here?" she asked.

The German, an SS-Sturmbannführer, stood looking around the room. He was dressed in the usual black tunic and breeches over which he wore a heavy field-grey greatcoat, open at the front. Highly polished black boots gleamed beneath the coat. Despite her surprise, and near panic, Kirsteen's mind was able to run through the lesson on German and Nazi dress, learned back at Wrexham.

"You will come with me," the German said. He spoke very poor French.

"What? B-but -- I mean, why ... ?"

"You will come with me. Now!" There was no room for discussion.

"May I get dressed?"

He took a silver cigarette-case from his overcoat pocket and selected a cigarette. He nodded briefly before he lit it.

"W-would you mind waiting outside?" Kirsteen hardly dare ask.

The Gestapo officer looked hard at her then glanced at the window.

"Oh, don't worry," Kirsteen quickly added. "I won't try to jump out of the window. We're on the second floor."

He strode casually across and stood for a moment looking out of the window, as though to assure himself that it did not represent a means of escape. Then he turned and walked to the door.

"You have three minutes," he said as he went out. He left the door ajar.

The hôtel seemed to be deserted as they passed through it. There was no sign of the landlord or any of the few staff, and no sign at all of Paulette. Kirsteen had a quick look around outside before she was bundled into the back of a large German staff car. Again, there was no sign of anyone. The place was deserted.

"Now can you tell me why and where you are taking me?" Kirsteen asked, as the big black Citroën turned from a secondary road onto a main highway and picked up speed.

"Be silent!"

Kirsteen sat back and said no more, as the reticent officer stared out of the window and puffed his way through a succession of cigarettes.

Thoughts came and went in Kirsteen's head. What had happened? Had Paulette betrayed her or had she just happened to get out before the Gestapo officer arrived? Was it the landlord of the hotel who had turned them in? And what was the charge? So far as she knew her papers -- forged as they were -- were in order. She was listed as a schoolteacher on break from her school in Lyon. She knew that there was even documentation in Lyon -- courtesy of Winston Churchill -- to back up this story. No one, so far as she knew, had any idea why she and Paulette were going to Falaise. Certainly no one knew they were going there to meet Stonehenge.

But wait! She almost gasped out loud, and then glanced in the direction of her silent companion to make sure she hadn't alerted him. Suppose it wasn't really Stonehenge who had called Paulette and arranged the rendez-vous? Certainly that had always been a question in her own mind. But that would have been an unnecessarily elaborate way to set them up for arrest. They could just as easily have been arrested in Paris.

As she thought this through she realized that they were coming into the outskirts of Paris.

So, she was being taken back there, probably to Gestapo Headquarters.

The car moved along the Champs-Elysées and turned into the avenue Kléber, eventually stopping at a barricade across one of the side streets. When the barricade was raised the car proceeded along to a building that looked like a hôtel. The Gestapo officer got out of the car unhurriedly and motioned for Kirsteen to get out also. Then he led her into the building.

There were many Germans there, most in uniform but some in civilian dress. Kirsteen guessed that this was the famous Hôtel Majestic; now Gestapo Headquarters. The officer took Kirsteen up to the one-time reception desk where a Gestapo sergeant presented a clipboard which the officer signed. They then proceeded up the wide stairway to the second floor and along a corridor to one of the rooms.

"Wait here," snapped the German. He turned and went out again, closing the door behind him. She heard a key turn in the lock.

Looking about her Kirsteen saw that she was in a small room, probably once used as an office. It was completely bare of furniture. There was an inner door, possibly leading to a larger room. Kirsteen tried it and found, as she expected, that it was locked. She moved to the one window and looked out. It looked onto an inner courtyard surrounded on all sides by walls. There were other windows, reaching up the seven floors of the building, but she could make out nothing in any of them.

It was almost an hour later that she heard the key turn in the lock and the door opened again. The same officer who had brought her from Falaise -- though now he had shed his greatcoat -- beckoned her to follow him. They walked down the corridor and turned into another, much larger, room. There were desks scattered about at which men and women worked, most in uniform but not all. Kirsteen was taken up to a large desk at the far end of the room, near the windows which, she noticed, looked out toward avenue Kléber.

Seated at the desk was an SS-Standartenführer, who had a pile of blue folders beside him. As she approached he pulled one of the folders off the top of the pile and opened it.

"You are Marie Nègre?" he asked. He spoke German. Kirsteen understood him well enough but remained silent. He repeated the question in French.

"I am. May I ask ... ?"

"No! Where is your residence?"

"I am from Lyon," Kirsteen said, trying to keep her voice from shaking. "But while I'm staying in Paris I'm at number seventeen, avenue de Villars."

He nodded, as though she had just confirmed what he already knew.

"You share a room with a Gaston Dissart." It was a statement rather than a question.

"No! I do not share a room with Gaston, or with anyone. I have my own room."

"Silence! You do know Gaston Dissart?"

"Yes. Yes, of course I do. He has a room on the same floor. The third floor," she added. So that was it, she thought. They had discovered the group of Resistants and linked her with them.

"Where is he now?" asked the officer.

So, they hadn't caught Gaston. Good! "I don't know," she said.

Her interrogator looked up from the folder and stared her in the eyes for a moment. Then he looked down again. "Take off your clothes," he said.

"W-what?"

"Take off your clothes! Or do you need some help with that, Mademoiselle?"

There was loud laughter and Kirsteen looked around to see that most of the people sitting at the surrounding desks -- men and women -- were staring at her. Slowly she put up her hands and started to unbutton her blouse.

14: INTERROGATION

"But why do I have to take off my clothes?" Kirsteen realized it would probably be in vain but couldn't help fighting against the order.

"Do as you are told!" The officer slammed his fist down on the desktop, causing some of the folders to fall to the floor. He ignored them and a man out of uniform, sitting at a nearby desk, moved across and picked them up for him.

Kirsteen saw that she was only attracting more attention. In fact she now had quite a little circle of Gestapo officers standing studying her. Reluctantly she took off her blouse and stepped out of her skirt. She removed her shoes and unfastened the suspenders from the tops of her stockings. She was thankful that her preparation for the trip had included underwear suitable for a schoolteacher in occupied France. Her stockings were cotton, rather than silk, and there was little lace on her bra and panties. She removed her stockings then, with a sigh, reached back to unclasp her bra.

"What the hell's going on here?"

She swung around and saw an immaculately attired SS-Brigadeführer standing in an open doorway behind her. She almost laughed at the way the assembled men and women almost fell over themselves, bumping into one another in their haste to move off and look as though they were going about their business. Those at the desks immediately looked down and busied themselves with their work.

The officer at the desk, who had ordered her to disrobe, sprang to attention.

"Herr Brigadeführer!" he cried.

"I said, what the hell's going on here?" repeated the senior officer, coming into the room and glaring at everyone. He briefly looked at Kirsteen. "Get your clothes on," he said in French.

"Yes, sir. Thank you," she murmured, and lost no time in dressing.

"Well?" he snapped at his red-faced subordinate. "Answer my question."

"Yes, sir. I'm sorry, sir. We -- that is to say, I -- was interrogating this prisoner."

"And you found it necessary to have her naked, in order to answer your questions?"

"Yes, sir. I mean, no sir."

"Did you not read the memorandum from the Kommandant von Gross-Paris, Herr General von Schaumburg, and the one from Militärbefehlshaber Herr General von Stülpnagel, commanding all personnel to treat Parisians with courtesy and respect?"

"Yes, Herr Brigadeführer."

"This is a delicate situation we have here. Is this woman a spy?"

"No, Herr Brigadeführer."

"Is she accused of sabotage? Or of conspiring against the Reich in any way?"

"No, Herr Brigadeführer."

"Hmm. I see." He stroked his chin and then, with hands clasped behind his back, walked up and down the rows between the desks.

Kirsteen dared not look the officer in the face but, under lowered eyes, she studied him. He was young for his rank; probably in his mid-thirties. He was tall and thin, with the blond hair and blue eyes of the true Aryan. His face was sharp-featured yet pleasant. His uniform was obviously tailor-made; the silver aiguillette on his right shoulder complemented by two rows of medals above his left breast pocket. He wore the SS Service Dagger, with its ornate chains, hanging from the left pocket of his tunic. His black jackboots gleamed like obsidian.

He finally turned and came back to the desk, where he scooped up the open file from in front of the still-at-attention would-be interrogator.

"I will take over this case," he said. Then, to Kirsteen, "Come!"

She followed him into the office and he closed the door firmly behind them.

"Sit, please," he said. He indicated a comfortable-looking chair in front of the desk, behind which he ensconced himself. "I apologize for my officer. He is over-zealous and tends to forget that we are here as temporary guardians of your fine city."

His French accent was excellent, Kirsteen thought. She murmured something noncommital and looked about her. It was a medium-sized office dominated by an enlarged colored photograph of the Führer. Kirsteen felt as though his eyes were looking straight at her. She shivered. On the wall there were large-scale maps of Western Europe and of the environs of Paris, with the arrondissements highlighted in contrasting colors. Filing cabinets lined two of the walls. A large window looked out toward avenue Kléber.

"Pardon me, I have not introduced myself," said the blond young man. "I am SS-Brigadeführer Artur Ebernach. And you are ... ?"

"As it says in the file," Kirsteen nodded at the folder open on his desk, "I am Marie Nègre."

Ebernach smiled. "Ah, yes. Of course." He studied the file for a moment. "You seem to have been keeping some very bad company, Mademoiselle, if I may say so?"

"Sir?" Kirsteen decided to continue playing total innocence.

"You have been seen in frequent company with Gaston Dissart, Antoine Lefaucheux, Norbert Bastouette, François Muller and Colette Grenelle." He ticked them off with his finger as he read off the names.

Kirsteen did not recognize the next to the last name and seized on it to protest her innocence.

"I know Gaston, of course. He lives in the same rooming house that I do. And most of the others I think I have met, for they are friends of Gaston's. But this Muller man I am not familiar with."

"Hmm." He pondered the list, then suddenly looked up and threw a question at her. "What were you doing in Falaise?"

Kirsteen knew the questioning would eventually get around to this and was not thrown off guard.

"I went there with a good friend of mine, Paulette Cartier, to get away from the city for a few days." It suddenly struck her that there had been no mention of Paulette by the Germans, even though they must have known that she was with Kirsteen in Falaise and that she was a close friend of Gaston's.

"Falaise is just down the road, as it were, from Caen," Ebernach said, ignoring the reference to the redhead. "That, as I'm sure you are aware, is in the Forbidden Zone."

Kirsteen said nothing.

"The papers which were found on you show that you have a pass to enter the Forbidden Zone. Why is that?"

"I am a teacher with a thirst for knowledge. Caen is of historical significance. I wanted to visit it to prepare my future lessons."

He nodded, though Kirsteen didn't know whether that meant he accepted what she said or not. "And where did you get this pass?"

She swallowed. "At the Kommandantur, on the Place de l'Opéra," she said, naming the offices of the Kommandant von Gross-Paris where everyone had to go to get every conceivable kind of permit. She prayed that he would not check-up on her.

"Hmm." He was silent again, pulling at his lower lip as he studied her folder. Suddenly he stood up. "All right," he said. "You may go. Here are your papers, though I will retain the pass into the Forbidden Zone . . . for your own protection you understand, mademoiselle?"

She wasn't sure what he meant by this last but was thankful to be off the hook. She took the papers he had taken from the folder and tucked them into her handbag. She turned and went to the door.

"Again, my apologies for the inconvenience." Ebernach smiled at her, clicked his heels, and inclined his head in a little bow. In other circumstances Kirsteen would have accepted it as a very friendly smile. She couldn't help but smile back.

"You've been very kind," she said, and went out.

Kirsteen had now been in occupied France for a week yet she seemed no closer to finding Stonehenge than she had been when she first arrived. Not only that, but she was now under suspicion by the Gestapo. She felt she was letting down Winston Churchill.

She returned to her apartment and seriously considered moving out and finding another place to live. Yet to do so would surely indicate to the Germans that they were right to suspect her, she reasoned. No, she would stay on at Madame Delestraint's. But she needed to tell Gaston that he and the others were apparently well known to the Gestapo. There was no sign of the likable Frenchman so she set off instead to find and talk to Canon Bizien.

As she left the house she checked to see if she was being followed. It wasn't difficult to spot an overweight German, in civilian clothes, leaning against a lamp-post across the street, pretending to read a newspaper but watching the house. As Kirsteen emerged and descended the front steps, he folded up the newspaper and tucked it under the arm of his black leather coat.

Kirsteen moved off down the avenue. She paused at the corner of the street to look into a shop window verifying, by checking his reflection, that the German was indeed following her. She made for the *métro* and stood patiently on the platform waiting for the train. The black-coated German stood behind her and a little to one side. When the train pulled into the station Kirsteen moved off slightly to the right to enter the opening door there. The German moved to his left and entered that door. Just as the doors closed, Kirsteen slipped out again. She smiled at the angry and bewildered look on the German's face as the train moved off with him looking helplessly out at her.

To be on the safe side Kirsteen took a number of different trains to get to her destination. When she finally emerged from the *métro* station on boulevard St.-Germain, near

Notre Dame, she was certain she was no longer being followed. She lost no time in walking over to rue Jean de Beauvais and to the little church of Saint-Denis.

She found the canon standing at the rear of the church, studying a small chestnut tree. He spoke to her as though he had seen her only an hour or so before.

"Poor little tree. I put it in here only about two weeks ago. It may have been a trifle early to try to plant it but I think it will survive, if the weather warms up just a bit.'

"Canon, I have much to tell you."

"Of course, my child. How silly of me to prattle on about the tree. Come! Come into the church."

He led the way. They went halfway down the aisle and sat in the pews of the empty building.

"Michel is not here, is he?" Kirsteen asked, glancing around.

"No. I haven't seen him all day."

Quickly Kirsteen went over the events from the time she left for Falaise, with Paulette, to her release from Gestapo Headquarters two hours earlier. The Canon listened silently, occasionally nodding his head in understanding. When she was finished he reached out and patted her arm.

"I know exactly what you've been through," he said. "Mine was a similar experience, when they took me the other day. Though . . ." he chuckled, ". . . they didn't ask me to disrobe!"

Kirsteen couldn't help laughing. She felt comforted by the old cleric.

"They didn't ask you about me, then, or intimate that they knew we had met?" he asked.

"No." Kirsteen had been relieved at that, and had consequently been at such pains to ensure she was not followed to the *prêtre*'s church. "Tell me, canon, do you know who this Gestapo officer is, this Artur Ebernach?"

"No." The old man shook his head. "I did not encounter him when I was there. I had a much harsher interrogator; an SS Sergeant who obviously would have relished an excuse to torture me." For a moment his voice was bitter, and then it softened again. "You were very fortunate, my dear. For which I thank the good Lord."

"So do I, canon . . . what is it?"

She saw that he was looking at his watch. It was the second time he had done so since they had sat down in the church so she knew there was a reason.

"Forgive me, Marie. I don't mean to be impolite. It's just that it is coming up time for the

BBC French-language broadcast. Would you like to come and listen?"

Together they went back to the robing room, which Kirsteen felt was becoming really familiar to her. As she sat on one of the two chairs there, the Canon moved aside a pile of prayer books and hymnals to reveal an old wireless set. He turned it on and, as it warmed up, fine-tuned the dial. Soon they heard the voice of the BBC announcer. He dealt with the latest news and then went on to the messages for the occupied country.

Kirsteen listened carefully. She wondered who dreamed up some of the messages and how they could possibly relate to the instructions they were actually giving.

". . . The donkey is braying; the donkey is braying . . . Wheat fields gleam in the brightness of the sun; wheat fields gleam in the brightness of the sun . . . The wind blows the rain in from the west; the wind blows the rain in from the west . . . Mary had a little lamb but Bo-Peep's sheep come home; Mary had a little lamb but Bo-Peep's sheep come home . . ."

Kirsteen suddenly sat forward. That was for her! The message being broadcast was for her. She could hardly believe it. Churchill had arranged that if he needed her to return to

London the message about Bo-Peep's sheep would be broadcast.

Canon Bizien had noticed her reaction. He was a sharp old man, Kirsteen thought.

"Something in there for you?" he asked, quietly.

She nodded. He asked no more.

"In a couple of days I have to, er, to return home for awhile."

"Back to Lyon?"

She nodded. She wasn't willing to confide in anyone, not even the old priest, the fact that she had actually come to Paris from London. "I won't be gone long, I don't think."

He took her hands in his and looked intently into her eyes. "You be very careful, Marie Nègre," he said softly.

She nodded.

That evening Kirsteen visited Gaston in his room and brought him up to date on what had happened to her.

"Have you heard anything from Paulette?" she asked.

He shook his head. "No. Not a word. I thought you were both still up in Normandy. What a surprise to see you back again so soon."

"Don't you think it surprising that she disappeared like that, just before the Gestapo arrived? And then the fact that they never mentioned her at all, though they knew about you and all the others?"

The Fenchman shrugged his shoulders in his characteristic way. "I don't know. There could be several reasons for Paulette's disappearance. She might have got up early and then seen the Gestapo car arrive but not had time to run back into the room and warn you. Or she might have been outside somewhere and not even known what happened; she might even be wondering where you have disappeared to!"

Kirsteen had to admit that what he said was true, though she felt sure that someone -- possibly the landlord? -- had known what was going on and could therefore tell Paulette what had happened.

"But you say the Gestapo know all about us; about our *Réseau*?" Gaston was nervous.

Kirsteen nodded. "They know all your names, that's for sure. Though just what else they know I have no idea."

"I'll have to get in touch with everyone; tell them we must lie low for a while." His brows knitted as he thought it through. "Perhaps we should not meet for a time?"

"Actually I have to go home for a day or two."

"You do?" He was surprised. "Because of this run-in with the Gestapo? Don't let them frighten you, Marie."

"No!" She smiled at him. "It's not that. They didn't really frighten me -- I don't think! No, I have to go home anyway. I just got a message that I'm needed at home for a short while. At least I hope it will just be a short while."

He didn't ask how she got the message. "Will you give up your room here?"

"No. I'd like to keep it on, if that's all right with Madame Delestraint. I'll pay her rent in advance and somehow let her know if, for any reason, I won't be coming back to it."

Gaston nodded. "I will keep an eye on it for you, Marie. When will you be leaving?"

"Tomorrow night."

15: HOME AGAIN

As Kirsteen stepped down from the front steps onto the sidewalk, and started walking away from the apartment house, a soft-treading, slight figure in a dark jacket and navy blue beret moved up to walk beside her. It was Greyhound.

"Keep walking and don't look at me," he said.

She remained looking straight ahead and threaded her way through the other people walking along avenue de Villars.

"There is an overweight German Gestapo agent in a black leather overcoat following you."

"Yes," she said. "I know. He's been there for the past few days. A couple of times before I've managed to lose him."

"Hmm!" The little man gave a grunt of satisfaction. "See if you can do it again. Where are you heading?"

"To the railway station; gare d'Austerlitz."

"I'll meet you at the entrance to platform three," the Gypsy said. He moved off to the side and crossed the road, disappearing into the traffic.

Going in and out of several shops, Kirsteen had no difficulty losing her "tail". He seemed very inefficient, she thought. She wondered how he explained his failures to his superiors. Once at the busy gare d'Austerlitz she breathed easier. There were many uniforms everywhere, including Gestapo, but everyone seemed to be intent on getting somewhere and she knew that so long as she gave the same impression she was not likely to be questioned. She headed for the entrance to platform three.

Greyhound saw her first and gave a loud greeting.

"Marie! There you are! How wonderful to see you."

He rushed up and gave her a quick kiss on each cheek. Then, taking her arm, walked her off towards a refreshment room. There they managed to find a table to themselves and sat each nursing a cup of ersatz coffee. Keeping her voice low, Kirsteen quickly told Greyhound of her recent adventures.

"So that's what happened to you," he said. "I wondered how you disappeared from Falaise."

"You were there, then?"

He nodded. "Oh, yes. But I'm afraid Stonehenge wasn't. He never showed up."

"Did you see anything of Paulette?" she asked.

Again he nodded. "Yes, I did. According to the hotel owner she seemed genuinely surprised when you disappeared. She told him she'd gone out early looking for 'a friend' -- presumably Stonehenge -- and when she came back you were gone."

"Hmm." Kirsteen wondered whether she could believe that.

"He said that she hung around for a couple of days and then took the train to Paris."

"She certainly didn't wait long for Stonehenge."

"No."

"Unless, of course, he *did* show up and made contact with her."

The Gypsy was quiet for a moment, thinking it through. Slowly he shook his head. "I don't think so. Of course it's possible, but I have a feeling for these things. I'm certain he was nowhere near Falaise after all."

Kirsteen glanced at her watch.

"You have to go?" Greyhound asked.

"I'm going back to London tonight," she said. "I must catch a train out of here in half an hour. I've still got some time "

"You're going home?" He was surprised. "For good?"

"I don't know," she said. "I really doubt it. I was called back. I'm pretty sure I'll in Paris again within a few days." Kirsteen drank some of the coffee and made a face. It was bitter. "Why do you think the Gestapo came and picked me up?" she asked.

Again he was silent for a moment as he thought it through. "I don't think it was your redheaded friend who turned you in. More likely the hotel owner. Though what his motive would be I don't know. No, I suspect there's more at work here than we realize. Casey . . . Marie, if you get back here I'll meet you at the café on the corner of rue du Marignan, three o'clock, one week from today. You know the place?"

Kirsteen smiled. "Very well. It's where I had my first cup of coffee -- if you can call it that -- when I first arrived here a little over a week ago."

"If you're not there I'll keep going back there every day at that time for another week."

"Very good. Thank you Grey-- . . . thanks Claude."

Kirsteen left the train at a local stop just north of Le Mans. She walked through the village and out on a small country road. By this time it was dark and she felt confident that no one was following her. A quarter mile from the last cottage she left the road, pushed through a sparse hedgerow, and set off across the fields. She had unscrewed the cover from the top of one of the large buttons on her overcoat to reveal a small pivot-compass, which she was able to study in the light of a miniature flashlight. She had studied large-scale maps of the area for days before she had come to France and felt she knew this part of the country as well as anyone.

By ten o'clock Kirsteen was safely ensconced in the undergrowth at the edge of the woods, by the field where the Lysander had dropped her off nine days before. She had an hour to wait.

At eleven o'clock she ran out into the middle of the field and stood trying to determine the wind direction. There was very little wind and she wet her finger and held it up high, trying to tell which side of it felt cold. She decided that what wind there was blew parallel with the side of the woods; an excellent direction. It would give the airplane a long run in and out with no great obstacles to surmount.

Kirsteen strained her ears but could hear nothing. She crouched close to the ground, feeling naked and vulnerable away from the cover of the trees. The thought passed through her mind that she had the day wrong. Quickly she went back in her mind over the happenings since the radio broadcast. No, this should be the night, she thought.

At twenty past the hour she thought she heard something. Raising her head she strained to hear more clearly. It sounded like a motorcycle, pop-popping along a country road. Damn! she thought. Supposing it's a German patrol?

Suddenly she realized what she was hearing. Somehow the pilot was making the Westland Lysander's engine sound like a motorcycle, as he came low across the adjoining fields. Jubilantly, Kirsteen sprang up and stuck a small flare into the ground. She lit it and then ran as fast as she could in a downwind direction. When she felt she'd gone far enough she stuck another flare into the ground and lit that. She then ran off to one side and waited.

The big black airplane seemed to come suddenly out of the darkness, swooping down on the field and kissing the grass just a few feet away from the first flare. As it rolled towards the second flare Kirsteen ran at full speed towards it. She grabbed the rungs of the ladder on the side of the plane and beat three times on the paneling with her other hand. At the signal the pilot gave the great Bristol Mercury-XX engine the throttle and, without stopping, the aircraft climbed back up into the air while Kirsteen struggled up the ladder and into the rear cockpit. The pick-up had taken less than three minutes.

Thankfully Kirsteen pulled the "greenhouse" cockpit cover closed and let out a great sigh of relief. She had done it.

"Good job!" The pilot's voice sounded in her headset as she put on the leather flying-helmet. "For a minute there I thought you'd given up on me and gone back to Paris. Sorry I was late. Ran into a little flak over the coast." It was the same pilot who had brought her to France, Wing Commander Fielden.

"Oh, I wasn't going to give up, Mouse," Kirsteen said, still breathing hard. "I'd have waited till sunrise if necessary. By the way, I thought I was hearing a motorbike for a minute. How did you do that?"

'Mouse' Fielden chuckled. "It's something I've perfected, just in case there are ever any German patrols out listening for aircraft. With these big radial engines it's not too difficult, if you lean down the mixture just right. Makes it 'pop' a bit, and sound like a motorbike."

The flight back to England was uneventful and Kirsteen bid farewell to her pilot at Tempsford and got into the black Humber car that was waiting for her. In no time she was in London and back in her own flat in Duke Street.

She'd no sooner taken off her coat and put the kettle on for a decent cup of English tea than the telephone rang.

"Welcome home, Casey," said a voice. She felt a thrill recognizing Winston Churchill and knowing that he -- the Prime Minister of England -- was calling her at home on her own telephone. "Say nothing for the moment, just listen. I have to be up in the North of England tomorrow but I would like to see you the day after. Come to Storey's Gate at ten in the morning. We'll talk then."

There was a click and he was gone.

Kirsteen drank two large cups of tea then stripped off and languished in a hot, soapy bath. By the time she tumbled into her own comfortable bed she was finding it hard to remember that just hours before she had been in a dirty little apartment in enemy-occupied France. She slept till almost noon the following day.

Winston Churchill was looking spry and had a mischievous gleam in his eye when Kirsteen walked into the underground War Cabinet Room. She couldn't help commenting on it.

"You look very bright this morning, sir. Good news?"

"There have been a few things to brighten an otherwise dreadful war, my dear," he said. He waved her to the seat beside him. "Among other pieces of news, I have just been informed that French General Henri Giraud, who has been a prisoner of the Germans since May of 1940, has managed to escape from occupied France. That alone is worth celebrating. There has been other good news though I'm afraid not of a nature I can share with you, Casey."

"I understand, sir," she said. "I'm glad you're looking so well."

"Well, thank you, my dear." He reached for one of his cigars. "I try not to light up one of these till noon, but I think today I might be excused if I do. There are precious few things to celebrate these days so we might as well make the most of the small items."

He was soon filling the room with blue smoke as he leaned back in his chair and pulled a small pile of files into the center of the desk. He flipped open a notebook and laid a pen on top of it, ready to take notes if he needed to.

"Now then, Casey. Tell me your story."

When Kirsteen had finished Churchill was well along on his cigar. In silence he studied the long ash that had formed, as though giving himself time to absorb all that Kirsteen had said.

"You were lucky in your encounter with the Gestapo," he said finally, laying down the pen he had been using. "Others have not been so lucky."

"I know." Kirsteen nodded.

"Very well." He shook himself like some great dog and sat up straighter in his chair. "Tell me more about what you found in Paris. The general attitude of the French; their acceptance, or not, of the situation. We get many reports but I'd like to have your views, Casey, if you don't mind. Did you notice any change of attitude during the time you were there? I know you weren't there for long, but the situation is very fluid."

Kirsteen told the Prime Minister of all she had seen and observed; of how surprised she had been at the almost 'normality' of life. There were obvious hardships -- food, clothing, transportation were obvious -- but it seemed that Parisians were determined that life should go on as near to usual as possible. She told him of seeing well-dressed Frenchmen and women, as well as Germans, in the fancy restaurants, which seemed to keep well stocked through the black market.

"Was there an awareness, on the part of the people, of the Resistance, do you think?"

"Oh, yes!" Kirsteen didn't have to stop and think. "Yes, the average Parisian knows that there are many fighting the occupying Germans in their own way, and they very much approve. I think many would assist anyone in need of help."

"You say 'many' rather than 'most'?"

Kirsteen was silent for a moment. "Yes. Yes, and I did that deliberately. There are many who would aid the Resistance or an escapee or downed flyer . . . but there are also many who would turn them in. Food especially is becoming hard to get. There are certainly many who would turn traitor if it meant getting an extra loaf of bread for their family."

Churchill nodded. "And who is to say that we might not do the same in their position?" he said. "These are hard times to judge. Now, your two Resistance groups -- what work do they do?"

"Gaston has told me that his group have several times sabotaged trains scheduled to take hundreds -- even thousands -- of forced workers to Germany."

"Good. And the other group; the priest's?"

"I believe they have some big operation planned that they're working toward, but they haven't yet finalized it."

Churchill nodded thoughtfully.

"My friends report that there is evidence of the Germans getting ready to move into the

Free Zone," Kirsteen continued. "They think that by the end of this year there will no longer be a Free Zone as such."

"I've heard other reports to verify that. Now what about your short time in Normandy, Casey? What a shame you didn't manage to get into the Forbidden Zone after all."

"Yes, sir." Kirsteen thought back to the train ride north. "The train we took had only two passenger cars, but three goods cars. I believe they held military equipment."

"And they were going beyond Falaise, I take it?"

"Oh, yes." Kirsteen had noted words stenciled on the outsides of the wagons. "They were going through to Caen."

Churchill made a note in the book in front of him.

"You've done extremely well, Casey. I'm very pleased.   Are you willing to return to France?"

"Oh, yes, sir. Definitely. At last I feel I'm doing something really useful, even if I'm not getting all the results I want."

"You mean because you haven't yet located Stonehenge?"

"Right, sir."

The Prime Minister put down his cigar and sat back in his chair, pursing his lips. "Don't be hard on yourself," he said finally. "I never expected you to go over there and find him right away. We have had agents trying to locate Stonehenge for many weeks now. I'm quite happy knowing that you're there, Casey, and looking out for my interests; for the interests of Britain. I know that what information I get from you is reliable. And I thank you for it."

Kirsteen wasn't sure whether she should thank him or not so she said nothing.

"Keep on trying to locate Stonehenge. I've a feeling that you are going to be successful where all others have failed. Now, I have someone who might have news for you on this score."

She was surprised when Churchill stood up.

"Come with me, my dear," he said.

They went out of the War Room and along a narrow corridor leading to a maze of other passageways and doors. The Prime Minister seemed to know exactly where he was going. He led her to a door marked "No Entry" and opened it.

"Just keep with me," was all he said.

The door led to another parallel corridor though with few doors off of it. At the first one they came to Churchill tapped lightly and went in.

Kirsteen was right on his heels. She found herself in a small office with two desks and three filing cabinets. There were the inevitable war maps on the walls. On top of one filing cabinet was a lit gas ring holding a simmering tea kettle. Two or three mugs, a spoon, a small container of sugar and a jar of Camp coffee stood close by. She was sure there were similar set-ups in all the other offices.

One desk was empty but at the other sat a skinny, middle-aged woman with grey hair piled on top of her head in a bun. She was wearing WRNS uniform with the rank of Lieutenant. She came to her feet as Churchill and Kirsteen entered the room.

"Sit, sit, sit!" Churchill said, flapping his hand up and down. "I'm not staying. I've just brought someone for you to talk to. Remember I told you of Casey? I want you to fill her in on the whole Stonehenge incident. She has full secrecy clearance." He turned to Kirsteen. "Casey, this is one of MI6's best agents. You can call her Molly. I think you'll find what she has to say interesting."

Minutes later Kirsteen was sitting at the desk opposite the older woman, listening intently to what she had to say.

16: RETURN TO FRANCE

Molly had been an operative for several years, she told Kirsteen. She apparently assumed that Kirsteen was also an MI6 agent and the younger girl didn't tell her otherwise. Molly had joined the Secret Intelligence Service, then under Rear Admiral Hugh "Quex" Sinclair, back in 1938 she said, and had been in Germany for the eleven months leading up to their invasion of Poland on September 1, 1939. She had transferred from Germany to France only a week after German troops marched into Paris and past the Arc de Triomphe, on June 14, 1940. She had been active in Paris and all over the Occupied Zone, establishing escape routes for downed flyers and others who needed to get out of France.

"I mainly work under Commander Kenneth Cohen who, I'm sure you know, heads the French section of the SIS that liaises with the Vichy."

"Have you done any sabotage work?" Kirsteen asked, fascinated.

"Oh, yes." Molly gave a little sigh and nodded her head. "Most recently in Rouen, where we were able to completely disrupt the big rail center and marshalling yards, destroying six locomotives in the process. I've also been instrumental in blowing up goods trains and bridges. But that's not my favorite sport."

"I've just come back from Paris. Though I've only been over there for a little over a week."

"So the Prime Minister was telling me. But you're doing very important work, I understand."

Kirsteen gave a little laugh. "That's what he told me. It doesn't seem half as exciting as what you've been doing though."

"Excitement isn't everything," Molly said, her mouth a hard line. "I'd far rather be without it."

"I've been strictly in Paris . . . except for an over-nighter in Falaise," Kirsteen said. "What's going on in the rest of France?"

Molly got up and moved to the gas ring on top of the filing cabinet. She poured two cups of Camp coffee and brought one to Kirsteen.

"The so-called Free Zone isn't as free as we might believe," she said. "Most, if not all, the rivers are being used like canals, with assault boats, torpedo launches, ammunition barges and the like moving up and down them, into and out of the Free Zone as well as the Occupied Zone and the Forbidden Zone. There's a lot of armor gathering. I think the Germans intend to move into Midi and the South very soon."

"That's what I was telling Mr. Churchill," Kirsteen agreed. "But what's this he said about you and Stonehenge? Have you heard something about him?"

Molly took a long drink of the bottled coffee before replying. "I was captured by the Gestapo about three weeks ago. They took me to 74 avenue Fochs for preliminary questioning and then on to their rue des Saussaies facilities where they tortured me. Happily I did not give away any information." She took out a pack of Craven A cigarettes and lit one. Kirsteen saw that her hands did not shake in the slightest. "I was placed in an underground cell, about six feet by five, as far as I could gauge. Not too much room." She gave a wry smile. "I was left for two days without food or water then dragged out and beaten. They raped me -- five of them; silently and intently. They did it three days in a row. It was . . . not nice." She dragged hard on the cigarette.

Kirsteen swallowed but said nothing, allowing Molly to tell her own story.

"I was wondering how much more I could stand when I managed to escape. It was a silly thing; I'm sure the guard is paying dearly for it now. They had beaten me unconscious, dragged me back to the cell and dumped me on the floor. The guard must have gone off to get something before coming back to lock the door. Anyway, I came around and slowly realized the door was ajar. It took all the energy I could summon but I crawled out of there and down the corridor. I got only as far as an SS-Obersturmbann-führer's office on the floor below but I knew that he was away in Berlin for a fortnight, so I crawled in there and curled up in his supply cupboard." She stopped and lit a second cigarette from the first. "I heard the panic and the shouting and running around, but no one thought to look in the office. I stayed there for twelve hours, till I'd regained a bit of my strength, then I got out of a window and managed to hide in the back of a *Küblerwagen*. I finally ended up in Monmartre."

"But -- what about Stonehenge?" Kirsteen asked.

"I'm coming to that, Casey. Sorry for the long preamble." She finished her coffee and seemed to get her strength back. "While I was in the cell in rue des Saussaies who do you think was a cellmate? Stonehenge!"

"What!"

"Yes. I never saw him, of course, but we used to communicate by tapping on the wall in

Morse code. There were others there too, though some too far away to be heard well. But yes, I remember Stonehenge. He must have been right next door to me. One of the first things we did was to exchange names. I was thrilled because I had heard of him. He said he'd been betrayed by a fellow Resistance worker, though he didn't say who."

"And he was still there when you left?"

"No. I believe he was transferred to the building off avenue Kléber. Leastways, he said he was being transferred and guessed that was where it would be. That was three days before I managed to get out."

Kirsteen was amazed. That meant that Stonehenge was in all probability in the Hôtel Majestic Gestapo Headquarters at the same time that she was. If only she had known. Though what could she have done, she wondered?

"And that's all I can tell you, I'm afraid," Molly said. "I hope it helps."

"Yes. Yes, it does. Thanks, Molly. I ... I ..."

Molly smiled and shook her head. "It's all part of this damn war," she said. "But I'd do it all again to help us win."

The Westland Lysander came in low and swept across almost brushing the tops of the trees.

Kirsteen felt the big plane suddenly pull up again and climb. It banked and started to go around.

"Something wrong?" she asked over the intercom.

She had a new pilot, Squadron Leader Lewis Hodges. She had found him quiet and intense, not as given to talking as Mouse.

"Bloody Jerries have plowed up the field," he said. "I'd heard they've been doing that. Any field that might serve our purpose gets plowed. I'm afraid you're going to have to jump."

Kirsteen's heart pounded and she felt the sweat break out and trickle down her armpits. But she gritted her teeth.

"Okay. Tell me when to climb out."

The Squadron Leader lined up again and came in as low as he could. He was heading into a stiff breeze, which helped bring down the ground speed. Kirsteen silently gave thanks for it as she clung to the bottom of the ladder. Next thing she knew he reached out and loudly banged the outside of the fuselage beneath the cockpit. At the signal she jumped.

Kirsteen had been unable to see the ground at all and hit sooner than she expected. Luckily the freshly-turned earth was soft and she did no damage. She gave another silent prayer for the pilot; he must have held the airplane almost on the ground judging by the short distance she fell. She heard it climb up and away as she scrambled over the furrows to the safety of the near-black trees.

"*Es ein englisch Whitley wast.*"

"*Nein! Es ein Hudson wast.*"

Kirsteen jumped at the sound of the German voices. She realized that they came from the side of the field bordering the road to her left. The night air and the breeze carried the voices so that they sounded closer than they were. It was two German soldiers arguing as to the type of airplane that had just flown over.

"It was smart to have these fields plowed," continued the first voice. "You see he wasn't able to land."

"He'll find somewhere, don't worry," said the other.

"Well, so long as it's nowhere near me!"

They both laughed and then moved off. Straining her eyes, Kirsteen made out the two figures as they climbed onto the bicycles they had been wheeling and slowly pedalled away down the road. She gave them plenty of time to get away.

As she reached the edge of the woods, at the roadside, Kirsteen stopped to examine her shoes. She took them off one at a time and wiped the mud from them, using grass and leaves. A small stream ran along the hedgerow for a short distance and she made use of the water to ensure that the shoes were completely free of the field's mud. Then she set off for the railroad station.

It was as easy getting on the train as the last time she had arrived and in no time she was sitting in the corner window seat of a small compartment, a snoring old man, who smelled strongly of garlic, sitting beside her.

This time Kirsteen was not too surprised when the train ground to a halt outside Paris and the Gestapo officers started their inspection. The old man beside Kirsteen woke with a start. He looked around for a moment as though he'd forgotten where he was, then grinned a toothless smile at Kirsteen.

"Bosch inspection time," he said.

She smiled back and nodded.

The door slid open and an SS-Haupsturmführer pushed his way in. Unlike the inspecting officer on Kirsteen's first trip this one was thorough. He demanded to see papers and then asked everyone to remove their shoes.

"What?" Kirsteen couldn't help herself.

The German glared at her. "Take off your shoes!" he said.

She did so and handed them to him. He examined them carefully, particularly the undersides and where the heels met the soles.

Finally, seeming to be satisfied, he handed them back and went out.

"What was that all about?" Kirsteen asked the old man.

A middle-aged woman, wearing a coat made of cat-skin, on the far side of the compartment replied. "He's looking for mud," she said. "The area around the river Cher is very muddy. People come in from Midi, sneaking across the Cher or the Loire rivers without passes."

"Oh! I see." Kirsteen gave up a silent prayer for whatever had possessed her to so scrupulously clean her shoes of the mud from the plowed field.

As Kirsteen neared the avenue de Villars she was startled when two men on bicycles suddenly came pedaling rapidly towards her calling out: "*Rafle!* Rue Macé! *Rafle!* Rue Macé!"

She knew it was an alarm. The Gestapo had started to make raids on blocks of houses, suddenly and unexpectedly barricading off whole streets and inspecting the papers of everyone entering or leaving. The word *rafle* became a synonym for fear and uncertainty. To support one another, citizens would run around when a street got blocked off, letting everyone know where the Gestapo were. Kirsteen crossed the road to take the long way around to avenue de Villars.

Madame Delestraint was sweeping the steps when Kirsteen arrived at number seventeen. She coughed and wheezed as she languidly moved the broom.

"Good day, Madame Delestraint," Kirsteen greeted her. "How are you?"

The old woman stopped sweeping and leaned on the broom.

"What d'you want?"

"W-why, nothing." Kirsteen was surprised at the old woman's challenging tone. "I'm just going up to my room."

"You don't have no room here, Mademoiselle."

"What? Why of course I do! I gave you two weeks rent in advance." Kirsteen was bewildered. What was happening?

"Do you have a receipt?"

"No, of course I don't have a receipt! You didn't give me . . ." She saw the slightest smile on the old woman's face.

"Like I said, Mademoiselle, you don't have no room in this house. Someone else is now living where you used to be."

"But - but, Madame Delestraint . . ."

The old woman gave a final flick with the broom then turned and went into the house, slamming the door behind her.

For a long time Kirsteen stood on the doorstep wondering what had happened. She knew the old woman was temperamental but she was always sweet on Gaston, and Gaston had said he'd keep an eye on Kirsteen's room. Apart from anything else, she thought, she'd left her gun and codebook safely -- so she thought -- hidden away in the ceiling of her room. She had to get them back, whatever happened.

Slowly Kirsteen turned away from the closed door, descended the steps and headed towards the *Rescoe* on rue Vaneau, where they used to meet. Perhaps Gaston would be there and she could find out what had caused Madame Delestraint to throw her out.

She spotted Antoine as soon as she went in. He was sitting in his usual position, facing the door, but he was alone. Quickly he waved her over.

"Good to see you, Marie," he said. "I've been coming here every day for the last three days in case you showed up. I guess you've found out what happened to Gaston?"

"Gaston? No! What? Tell me." She thought the old soldier had aged ten years in the few days that had passed since she had last seen him.

He gave a weary shrug and sighed. "Much has happened since you left for Lyons. Everything at once, it seems. They picked up Gaston. And Paulette and Norbert and Collette. Why they didn't take me I don't know."

"When did this happen?" Kirsteen was shocked. She had known that the Gestapo knew about them all, of course, but Gaston had not seemed too concerned when she left for London.

"The very next day after you went back to Lyon. They were all picked up at about the same time. It was something to do with the murder of the German officer."

"What murder of a German officer?"

He sighed again. "Agh! It seems everything came to a head the day after you left, Marie. A Gestapo officer was shot in the back as he was entering the new Franco-German exhibition, *La Vie Nouvelle*, at the Grand Palais. At about the same time a policeman was shot on the boulevard Magenta and a home-made bomb was thrown into a Wehrmacht canteen on avenue Suffren, killing three Germans and wounding two others."

"What!"

"That very afternoon General Schaumburg announced that known Communists, Jews, and other 'collectively responsible persons' would be picked up and immediately shot. And if the culprits for the incidents didn't give themselves up within three days twenty Communists and Jews would be executed each and every day until they did!"

"My God!" Kirsteen gasped. "Did anyone turn themselves in?"

The old soldier shook his head. "No. Not so far. Today is the third day. But no one really expects them to. They did shoot a number of people but things seem to have quieted down. I guess the Germans realize they won't be able to keep executing people every day indefinitely."

"Were Gaston and the others picked up as a result of this? Are they likely to be shot?"

"I don't think so. Why they were picked up, exactly, I don't know. It may or may not be related, but they're still alive, according to my source in the rue des Saussaies."

"You say Paulette was also picked up?"

He shrugged again. "I presume so. I certainly haven't seen anything of her since the others were all taken. In fact I haven't actually seen her since the two of you went off to Falaise."

Kirsteen thought for a moment. "Did Gaston tell you of my encounter with the Gestapo, before I left?"

"No. He probably didn't have time."

Quickly she filled him in.

"So they knew all about us?" he mused, when she had finished. "But I still don't understand why they didn't pick me up."

"They probably decided to leave one member of this *Réseau* free in the hopes you'd lead them to others."

He nodded. "Yes. That makes sense. Though they'll be disappointed. As I said, I've spent the whole time here."

Kirsteen had a quick look around. "That must mean they are watching you even now," she said, uneasily.

Antoine spread his hands. "Of course! But that's not too unusual. There's a man over near the door, sitting alone at a table and pretending to read a copy of *Paris-Soir.* He's been here every day that I've been here. Of course he's Gestapo. But he's not doing anything; just keeping an eye on me."

"Well, at least they'll now know that I'm back. Now what about you, Antoine? What are you going to do with Gaston and the others gone?"

"I was wondering if I might join up with this other group you know of? The canon's? What do you think?"

"I think it's an excellent idea," Kirsteen said. "I'll speak to him as soon as I can. But first,

Antoine, where can I get a room?" She told him of her eviction by Madame Delestraint.

He snorted. "I'm not surprised. I never trusted that old hag. I'm sure she also rented Gaston's room as soon as he was out the door. I would suggest you make your way over to the Leycurases. Do you know of them?"

Kirsteen nodded. "Yes. In fact I've met them, briefly. That's a good idea, Antoine. Thanks."

"You will, of course, be cautious in going to them, Marie?"

"Of course. Don't worry. I'm sure I'll be followed from here but I have had some experience at shaking off a tail. I won't lead anyone to the Leycurases."

In fact she found that she had a tail as soon as she left the *Rescoe*. A second man had apparently been stationed outside. He was a young man wearing a black coat that looked too large for him. He wore a wide-brimmed hat pulled down over his eyes. Kirsteen smiled to herself. He must have enjoyed American gangster films before the war, she thought. She walked briskly to the end of the block and crossed the road. Her tail followed. At rue Oudinot she spotted a vélo-taxi and waved it down. As she maneuvered herself into the small boxseat behind the bicycle she glanced back at the German. He was frantically looking up and down for a similar conveyance. As Kirsteen's driver pulled away from the curb she saw the young man wave down an elderly, well-dressed woman on a bicycle and commandeer it from her. She was left fuming on the sidewalk as he pedaled away, trying to catch up with the vélo-taxi while holding onto his large hat.

Kirsteen felt happier when they got in amongst more traffic. There were any number of vélo-taxis; some pulled by bicycles and some by tandems. There was very little motor traffic. She directed her driver down one side road then back up another. The German stoically pedaled after them.

"Quickly! Down there and keep tight to the right," Kirsteen said. The vélo-taxi swung along an avenue, moving past other traffic and easing over to the right side of the road. As they moved behind a large horse-drawn cab Kirsteen leaned forward and tucked 100 francs into the driver's back pocket.

"Thanks a lot," she said. "Don't bother to stop."

She swung her legs over the side and jumped off, running off to the side and into an open shop doorway. She moved quickly through the shop and then around to the window, where she peered out. She saw the German gallantly following the vélo-taxi and then, as they both broke out of traffic into the middle of the road again, he apparently noticed that the cab was now empty. He immediately stopped pedaling and jammed on his brakes. An old man on a bicycle, following close behind him, banged into him and they both fell to the pavement. Kirsteen seized the opportunity to get out of the shop and run back the way she had come.

After two changes on the *métro* Kirsteen felt certain she no longer had anyone after her. She emerged from the underground railway just a few short blocks from the Leycuras antique shop on rue Bièvre. Double-checking that she had no follower she entered the store.

Monsieur Leycuras was with a customer; an elderly woman wearing expensive clothing and fine jewelry. She spoke with a terrible French accent and Kirsteen knew she was German.

"It's so difficult deciding on accessories," she said, studying an ornate silver chafing dish. "Do you think this will go with the cutlery I bought from you yesterday, Monsieur Leycuras?"

The suave, urbane dealer smiled his widest smile, stroked is mustache and nodded enthusiastically. "But of course, Frau von Stülpnagel. I would never steer you wrong. The one complements the other to perfection." He glanced up at Kirsteen. "Be with you in a moment, Mademoiselle."

"Oh, that's all right," said Kirsteen. "I'm in no hurry. I can browse for a while."

It was half an hour later that the German General's wife left the store, weighted down with expensive antiques. Leycuras watched her go. He chuckled softly.

"She paid three times what I would normally charge and still thought she was cheating me!"

Kirsteen laughed. "That's wonderful. At least *you* can make a profit off the invaders."

"Don't be too quick to judge, Marie," he said. "Half of what I take in I give to the Resistance movement."

Kirsteen was surprised that he remembered her name, since they had only met briefly several days before. "I'm not judging," she said. "I'm really glad that someone *can* make a profit from them."

"And how may I help you, Mademoiselle? You have a package to bring through?"

"Actually, I'm the package, in a way." She quickly told him of Madame Delestraint's treachery and her subsequent need for a room.

"No problem." He smiled his broad smile again. "We are not expecting any packages for at least a week -- though you never know when an emergency may come about -- so you may certainly stay here temporarily. Come into the back. Victoire is home and she must meet you."

17: BACK ON THE TRAIL

Victoire Leycuras complemented her husband in that she too wore expensive clothes, was very conscious of her appearance, and had a great familiarity with antiques and their potential owners. In lieu of the heavy gold watch-chain of her husband's she wore a double strand of gleaming pearls; gold bracelets and rings adorned her skinny wrists and fingers. Her hair was the same charcoal gray as Godefrois's. It must have been long, thought Kirsteen, for it was plaited and coiled up about her head in the Austrian style. She had a high voice that could begin to grate after a while and she seemed to have a Gauloise cigarette permanently attached to her lower lip with at least an inch of ash hanging perilously from it at all times.

She welcomed Kirsteen and led her through to the back room, which was the Leycuras's dining room. Going to the far wall she pushed against a section of wainscoting and a hidden door swung open.

"You'll be staying in here, child," she said. Kirsteen resented being called "child" but bit her tongue and said nothing. "It's a private chamber left over from a century ago. We don't know what it was originally for but it's certainly come in handy recently. There is everything you need: bed, table, chairs, toilet, food cupboard."

"This is where you keep the people you help pass through?" Kirsteen asked, ducking her head slightly to pass through the undersize door.

"Yes, child. It's amazing; we've had as many as ten people living in here for a full fortnight."

"That was unusual," put in Godefrois. "There was an intense crack-down by the Germans going on at the time. Normally we only handle one or two at once."

"Make yourself at home, child," Victoire said. "Godefrois and I have to go out this evening -- some dreary reception at the home of General Karl-Heinrich von Stülpnagel. He only arrived in Paris at the end of February."

"He took over from his cousin, as German Military Commander, when Otto was relieved of his command," added Godefrois.

"Relieved?"   Kirsteen   said.   "What happened?"

"They said that Otto had lost his nerve because he expressed his distate at executing

Jewish hostages," Godefrois explained. "But I understand there had been some political powerplay going on for some time, between the Abwehr and the SD -- the Sicherheitsdienst. Himmler's and Heydrich's people battling again."

"This Heinrich von Stülpnagel is actually quite nice," Victoire said. "Compared to Otto anyway. The man is something of an intellectual, which is refreshing in a German!"

There was a curfew effective at midnight; the last *métro* running at eleven o'clock. It did not pay to be caught out after curfew or the rest of the night would be spent in a prison cell, put to work polishing German army boots. Kirsteen let herself out of the back door of the Leycuras shop at fifteen minutes after ten. She moved quietly but quickly along rue Bièvre, heading for avenue de Villars. She had to retrieve her gun and code book.

Kirsteen's plan was to get into one of the houses on the avenue -- it didn't really matter which one -- and go up through their top bathroom ceiling exit to the roof, then climb along to number seventeen. It would be just the reverse of the journey she had made with Paulette when she thought the Gestapo was after them.

It seemed like a good plan until she got to the row of houses. The end building had been converted into offices and was securely locked up. The second was a rooming house, like Madame Delestraint's, but had what looked to Kirsteen to be a building manager, or the owner, sitting on the top step reading a copy of *Signal* in the light coming from the hallway behind him. As Kirsteen approached he greeted an elderly couple who entered the house then, as though he had been waiting for them as the last ones in, he got up and went inside, closing the door and locking it securely.

The next house -- six down from number seventeen -- looked promising. Kirsteen darted up the steps and into the entrance hall, quietly closing the door behind her. There was no one in sight so she moved forward to the bottom of the stairs. Just as she put her foot on the bottom tread a voice sounded behind her.

"Can I help you, Mademoiselle?"

She spun around to find a dwarf, clutching a blanket about his shoulders, standing in the now open doorway closest to the street entrance. She hadn't heard him come out of his room. He eyed Kirsteen suspiciously.

"I-I'm looking for a Madame Delestraint," Kirsteen improvised.

The dwarf seemed to relax a little.

"Ah! Madame Delestraint. That one!" He shook his head as though he gave up on the woman. "You've got the wrong house, Mademoiselle. You want number seventeen; six houses along."

"Oh!" Kirsteen acted surprised. "Oh, I'm so sorry! I thought this was the house she said."

"What is your business with Madame Delestraint?" He raised his heavy eyebrows.

"My business is personal," Kirsteen said and went outside again. The dwarf followed her to the door and stood watching as she moved off along the sidewalk. She was afraid he was going to stand there and watch her all the way, but by the time she'd got past the next two houses he had gone back inside and closed the door. Kirsteen breathed a sigh of relief.

At the next building she came to she hung back for a moment, pretending to look in her handbag as though searching for a key. When she was sure there was no one watching her, and no one in the entrance hall of the building, she once again slipped inside and, with a glance at two closed doors she passed, moved up the stairs. Once around the first landing and onto the second flight Kirsteen breathed a little easier. The building seemed to be in an even worse state of repair than number seventeen and many tenants had stuck their rubbish and cast-offs outside their doors, partially blocking the hallways. She stepped over broken chairs and old rolled-up rugs. Some of the stairs creaked but no one seemed to notice. There were the sounds of voices coming from behind many of the doors she passed and even, behind one, the slightly syncopated notes of someone practicing on an out-of-tune piano. It didn't take her long to get to the third floor and then along the hallway to the end bathroom. The layout was exactly the same as at Madame Delstraint's; all the houses in the row were identical. She gave a silent prayer of thanks as she closed and locked the bathroom door.

There was no cord hanging from the trapdoor and Kirsteen had to balance on the hand basin and reach across to get a finger into the hole and pull it open. She almost fell when the trapdoor finally did come free and swing down. Then she saw that it had no folding stairway.

Kirsteen remembered seeing an old ironing board leaning against the wall outside one of the doors on the second floor. Cautiously she opened the bathroom door a crack and peered out. All seemed quiet in the hallway. Quickly but quietly Kirsteen descended to the floor below and located the ironing board. She returned with it to the bathroom.

It was tricky and Kirsteen couldn't help thinking that the scene belonged in a French comedy film. She leaned the ironing board against the wall then climbed onto the sink. Stretching across, she was able to place her other foot on the sloping board for balance and reach up to grasp the iron downpipe from the water closet of the toilet. From there she swung out and at the same time lunged upwards to grasp the edge of the open trapdoor. Hanging from the edge, Kirsteen was then able to "walk" up the ironing board and swing one leg across to the toilet downpipe, enough to give herself a hoist upward. Next thing she knew she was lying across the trapdoor entrance, gasping into the dust of the attic.

The going got smoother after that. Kirsteen closed the trapdoor behind her and dragged an old trunk across on top of it. The attic was pitch dark but she found, by bumping into them, that there were a large number of objects stored up there. She encountered trunks, boxes, chests of drawers, standard lamps, a barrel or keg, a dressmaker's dummy and a child's rocking-horse before she found the sloping door to the roof. It was locked but a rusty key was in the lock. With difficulty Kirsteen turned it and dragged open the door.

The stars seemed bright after the pitch black of the attic and Kirsteen breathed deeply of the chill night air. She stepped out onto the roof.

It took a moment to orient herself as to the direction in which she faced. When she had established where the roof ledge was that overlooked avenue de Villars she was able to tell which of the gradually rising rooftops was that of number seventeen. It took only a few minutes to move across, climbing from house to house, and edge her way along the top of Madame Delestraint's building to the roof-door into the attic. She was delighted to find that it was not locked; probably left wedged closed by Paulette, in case of emergencies. This was an emergency.

Within ten minutes Kirsteen was standing in the familiar top floor bathroom of Madame Delestraint's house. She eased open the door and peered out. All seemed to be quiet on the third floor. There, halfway down the corridor, was the door to her old room and, opposite it, the door to Gaston's. Now the question she asked herself was, was anyone in her room?

She stood outside the door and listened, reminding herself of how the nosy Madame Delestraint used to climb the stairs to listen. No sounds came from inside her old room; it seemed it was empty, at least for the moment. She tried the door handle. It was locked.

Dropping to her knees, she took the lock-picking tool from her belt buckle and carefully unlocked the door.

Holding her breath, Kirsteen gingerly opened the door and peered in. She let out her breath again as she saw that the room was indeed empty. She quickly went in and closed the door behind her, flicking on the light and praying that the new occupant wouldn't suddenly come home while she was there.

There were a man's clothes strewn across the bed and a pair of boots in the middle of the floor. She wasn't concerned with who now rented the room, only with getting her gun and code book, so quickly she pushed the table over under the light and climbed onto it. It took only a few minutes to ease the lightbulb-holder down away from the ceiling and to reach up through the plaster to locate her property. As she let herself out of the room again, gun and codebook in her pockets, she breathed a sigh of relief.

I wonder if Madame Delestraint did indeed also rent out Gaston's room, Kirsteen wondered? She glanced at her watch. There was still plenty of time to get back to the Leycurases before curfew. On tiptoe she moved across to the door on the other side of the hallway and listened for any sounds. Once again there was nothing and once again she picked the lock.

Apparently Madame Delestraint had not rented the room after all. She's probably keeping it, hoping Gaston will return, thought Kirsteen as she entered. That would seem to indicate, then, that it wasn't the old Frenchwoman who had turned-in the members of the *Réseau*. The Gestapo must have operated on their own initiative. However, the Germans had obviously searched the room. The drawers had been pulled out of the chest; their contents tipped onto the floor. The wardrobe stood open. Kirsteen wondered if they had found Gaston's gun hidden in his boot. The bedclothes had been pulled off the bed and the mattress was askew.

Quickly Kirsteen moved to the foot of the bed and felt under the mattress. The package of papers was gone. Had the Gestapo found them, she wondered? It seemed probable. That might be damning evidence against Gaston.

She had a last quick look around before turning to go. Just as she was about to move to the door something caught her eye. It was the tiniest corner of something stuck behind the wardrobe, against the wall. Moving quickly across the room, Kirsteen pulled out the brown-paper wrapped package that had previously been under the mattress. She gave a sigh of relief. Gaston must have just had time to slip the package out of the bed and tuck it behind the wardrobe before the Gestapo invaded his room. She straightened up and turned to find a German soldier standing in the doorway pointing a Luger pistol at her.

18: ON THE RUN

The man was an SS-Scharführer and the gun was a Luger P-08. Kirsteen eyed the muzzle carefully. It did not waver.

"So! We knew someone would come here."

Kirsteen said nothing but studied the man. The sergeant was middle-aged; obviously a career soldier who would obey to the letter any orders he had been given. His faced was expressionless -- where did the Gestapo find so many expressionless men, she couldn't help wondering? -- his lips thin and drawn tight and his eyes narrowed.

"What do you mean?" she asked. "I was looking for my friend Gaston."

"I'm sure," he sneered. "And for what purpose?" His eyes fell on the brown-paper covered package in Kirsteen's hand. "And what have we here? Open it, please."

Kirsteen thought quickly. She was holding Gaston's papers, which she was sure were forged. But far more damning and frightening, she had her code book in her pocket; something which would immediately identify her not just as a Resistance worker but as a spy. And spies were shot.

"I said open it, Mademoiselle!" He raised the Luger a fraction and tightened his grip on it.

All Kirsteen's training came into play at that moment. She raised the package as though offering it to the German. In response he took a half step forward and his pistol-holding hand drooped slightly. Kirsteen's other hand was in her pocket, and had found her Walther. Even in this predicament she could not bring herself to kill the man, but she did shoot.

With a sharp report the automatic fired through her coat and the bullet hit the sergeant in the upper thigh. His eyes came wide open as he dropped the Luger and fell to the ground with a cry, clutching his leg. Quickly Kirsteen stepped forward and kicked the Luger away into the far corner of the room. She stepped over him and to the door.

"Aah! Mein Gott!"

The shock of surprise was probably as effective as the bullet itself, thought Kirsteen as she ran out of the room, closing the door behind her.

"What's going on? I heard a shot. Marie! What are you doing here?"

Kirsteen spun around. It was Madame Delestraint, standing at the top of the stairs, catching her breath after what had probably been a hasty climb. There came a cry from the room as the German heard the old woman's voice.

"Stop that woman! Stop her!"

To Kirsteen's surprise Madame Delestraint raised a shotgun she had been leaning on, like a stick. It looked to be a very old one, but it could still be effective, and lethal. Kirsteen hesitated.

"What's going on?" repeated the French woman. "Stay where you are."

Again Kirsteen acted on her training. She didn't want to shoot the old woman but she took a step towards her.

"I'll fire!"

Kirsteen didn't wait to see whether or not she would. She suddenly ducked down and charged, hitting the older woman in the mid-section and knocking her off balance. The shotgun flew up in the air and exploded, blowing a hole in the ceiling of the hallway. Madame Delestraint, with an anguished cry, fell backwards and rolled down the stairs, bouncing against the banister rails as she went. Kirsteen didn't wait to see how she fared; she spun around and ran as fast as she could to the bathroom, climbing up the still-open ladder to the attic. In no time she was across the rooftops and descending the house she had used to get up to the roofs. She was out of avenue de Villars before the *Küblerwagens* arrived and the area was sectioned off.

"That was very brave of you to go and get Gaston's papers like that." Godefrois poured himself another glass of wine and offered to top-off Kirsteen's glass. She waved the bottle away.

"I just thought that if he'd been surprised, as I'm sure he was, he wouldn't have had time to hide his things. I thought I'd better get them before the Gestapo went back for a thorough search."

They sat in the Leycuras's living room, having a last drink before bed. Kirsteen had told them of her evening's escapade, though without mentioning her own gun and code book. She led them to believe that it was a gun of Gaston's that she had used to shoot the German.

"Nonetheless, child, it was brave of you." Victoire leaned forward to help herself to the wine. A long ash on the Gauloise cigarette in her mouth threatened to fall and spill down the front of her expensive gown. "I'm afraid our evening was dull by comparison. Von Stülpnagel's wife can barely speak French and all she could discuss was German fashions in the thirties and the American films of Marlene Dietrich! Happily she's only here visiting her husband for a few days. German families are not allowed in Paris. She's living in their home at Bad Pyrmont." The ash finally fell, unheeded, sprinkling into oblivion down the gold lamé dress. Fascinated, Kirsteen watched as Victoire instinctively took the cigarette from her mouth and, too late, flicked what remained of the ash into an ashtray. "At least the other guests were interesting. Eberhard Kessel was there -- he's from the University of Berlin -- and so was Professor Max Braubach and his young wife. Max is the Historian at the University of Bonn. Very nice young man, though his wife has no dress sense." She puffed new life into the Gauloise. "And at least Heinrich's cellar was acceptable."

Godefrois nodded. "Considering that he's simply appropriated half of Louis Nouveau's wines it's not surprising. Well, it's after midnight and I've a full day tomorrow." He drained his glass and stood up. "Good night, Marie. Again, well done!"

Kirsteen retired to the secret quarters behind the paneling. It took her a long time to get to sleep. She lay in bed thinking over the events since her return. Every-thing seemed to be moving so quickly. She'd only been back for twenty-four hours and already she was on the run after shooting a German. If she was to continue moving around she'd have to disguise herself. Perhaps she'd cut her hair and bleach it. She shuddered at the thought but made a mental note to ask Victoire for bleach.

And where were they holding Gaston and the others? She had to find them and perhaps even try to rescue them, if that was possible. But, more importantly, she had to get in touch with Stonehenge, if he really was at the Hôtel Majestic. She decided she'd try to contact the canon in the morning. Perhaps he could help.

She smiled to herself. If Matron could see me now, she thought. Queen Charlotte's Hospital was a far cry from Gestapo Headquarters in occupied France!

Kirsteen slipped out of the back entrance to the antique shop and walked along the alleyway to the road. She peered out onto rue Bièvre. There were a number of people hurrying along and she quickly moved out to mingle with them. As she reached the corner of the block she almost bumped into Antoine, leaning against a wall, trying to look inconspicuous reading a newspaper, *Le Petit Parisien*.

"Antoine! What are you doing here?"

For a moment he looked at her wide-eyed, then recognition came.

"Marie! It's you. What have you done with your hair? I didn't recognize you."

She took his arm and they started walking with the other pedestrians.

"I thought it better to change my appearance somewhat, so I cut it and bleached it." She filled him in on her escapade of the previous evening.

"*Mon Dieu!* You killed a German?"

"No, I didn't *kill* him, Antoine. I'm sure he's fine. It was basically just a flesh wound."

"But you got Gaston's papers. Thank God! I knew of them, of course, and was wondering myself how to get them. But you just went in there and took them! You're amazing, Marie."

Kirsteen blushed and shook her head. "It didn't seem anything special, Antoine. I'm sure any of you would have done the same for me. I'm keeping Gaston's papers at the Leycurases, by the way."

The older man stopped dead, causing a couple walking close behind to almost bump into them. Grumbling, the couple pushed past.

"What's the matter, Antoine?"

"It's why I came to try to find you this morning . . . the others. At dawn Norbert and Colette were shot. Gaston, so far, is still safe."

"Oh, no!" Kirsteen felt a sudden hollowness in the pit of her stomach. She thought of the young, eager, blond-haired Norbert -- little more than a boy -- with his persistent frown, and of the petite, elfin-like Colette. Both shot. "But why, Antoine? Why? They weren't dangerous."

"It was part of General Schaumburg's reprisals. He didn't care who he took. It's pure luck it wasn't Gaston as well."

They stood there for a long time, other pedestrians cursing as they pushed around to get past. Antoine kept brushing irritably at his moustache, as though it offended him for some reason. He was obviously very upset, thought Kirsteen. Finally she took his arm again and they moved on.

"Where are they holding Gaston?" she asked gently.

"Rue des Saussaies. I can't get too much information from my contact there; security has really been tightened up since the assassinations. I understand he's being held in one of the basement cells but will soon be transferred either to a police cell or, more likely, sent off to Germany to one of the slave camps."

"We have to get him out."

He said nothing but she felt his arm tighten where she was holding it.

"Where are we going?" Antoine suddenly asked. He had obviously not been paying any attention to where Kirsteen was steering him.

"We'll take the *métro* to Notre Dame. You need to join up with the canon, and perhaps his group will have some ideas about getting Gaston free before it's too late."

The huge cathedral on the Ile de la Cité was a comforting sight. They decided to walk through it before going on to the Canon's little church. There were many military uniforms about but all seemed to be playing the part of tourist. In twos and threes Wehmacht, Luftwaffer, Waffen-SS, even a few Kriegsmarine personnel, wandered the great cathedral staring up into the stained glass windows, pointing out the "flowering stone" of the gothic arches and taking photographs of the flying buttresses and the gargoyles.

Kirsteen and Antoine admired the length of the nave and looked at the double aisles. They paid their respects to Notre-Dame de Paris and walked around the ambulatory to see the choir stalls. Then they passed on out to the place du Parvis-Notre-Dame. There, under the great equestrian statue of Charlemagne, they saw Canon Bizien standing talking with two

Wehmacht soldiers. As they drew near they heard that he was filling them in on some of the history of the church. One of the German soldiers apparently understood French and he translated for his friend all that the cleric said.

Finally the two soldiers and Canon Bizien parted company and the cleric headed towards where Kirsteen and Antoine stood. As he neared, the white-haired Canon smiled, nodded, and moved out to pass them.

"Canon Bizien! It's me; Marie," Kirsteen said.

He stopped and stared at her. Slowly a smile spread across his face. "Why, what have you done to your hair, Marie?"

"Do you like it?"

He studied her for a moment then slowly shook his head. "I'm afraid I have to say no. I think you look much better as a brunette." He chuckled to himself. "But then I could never keep up with the changing of fashions with young women."

Kirsteen introduced Antoine and said that they were on their way to see him. The three of them started a slow stroll around the great *parvis* so that they could talk freely. Kirsteen told the canon of her previous night's exploits and of the execution that morning of Norbert and

Colette. She asked if Antoine could join his group and if they might be able to help rescue Gaston.

"We'll be happy to have someone of your caliber, Antoine," he said, smiling his cherubic smile at the old soldier. "And if it's possible to get your friend out of the Gestapo's clutches, believe me we'll do our best. Now, I suggest we all get together tonight and formulate a plan."

"You can get your people together that quickly?" Antoine asked.

"Oh, yes. Yes. You see we already had a meeting planned." The cleric laughed and the others joined in. "At the church -- my church -- at eight o'clock.   You know the robing room, Marie?"

"Of course."

"From there up into the bell tower. You will be careful, of course?"

"Of course," she assured him. "We'll see you then."

19: MISCHIEF

It was a cool night but with eight people squeezed into the small space it seemed warm in the bell-tower of Saint-Denis church. Kirsteen sat between Antoine and Lucie; she'd taken care not to be anywhere near Michel. The skinny, unshaven Frenchman perched on the parapet overlooking the street below, sometimes looking around at the group and sometimes gazing intently down at the rue Michel-Ange.

Canon Bizien sat opposite Kirsteen, his back to the small parapet surrounding the bell, with Hélène on one side of him and Elise on the other. Albert sat between Hélène and Lucie.

"Marie, why don't you start by introducing Antoine to everyone?" the canon asked.

Kirsteen did so and then went on to tell them of the Gestapo raid that took Gaston, Norbert and Colette and ended with the deaths of Norbert and Colette.

"They had no warning?" Albert asked.

"None," Antoine answered. "It seems the Gestapo knew of us -- according to what Marie says -- and suddenly decided to scoop us in; with the exception of me. The executions were just the result of bad timing; tying-in with the Kommandant von Gross-Paris's strike back for the killings of a few days ago. '

"So your leader, Gaston, is the only one still held?"

"Unless they also picked up Paulette," Kirsteen said. "We've more or less assumed they did, since she seems to have disappeared, but we're not absolutely sure."

"My contact at rue des Saussaies didn't know anything about Paulette," Antoine added.

"There is something else," Kirsteen said, looking around at all their serious faces. "I have information that Stonehenge was being held at rue des Saussaies but was then transferred almost certainly to the Hôtel Majestic."

No one asked where she got the information.

"What do you want to do?" Hélène asked.

Kirsteen shook her head. "I don't know, exactly.   Certainly check it out as soon as possible. See if he really is there. Then, hopefully, get him out."

"What's it like at rue des Saussaies?" Lucie asked.

"Huh! You wouldn't want to know!" Michel grinned at the young blonde, displaying the gap of his missing front teeth.

"But I do want to know," she insisted. She looked around at the others. "Has anyone been there?"

Albert spoke up. "My brother was there for a time -- which is why I'm here now. I spoke to him briefly before they took him off to Germany in one of those cattle trucks. He told me of a basement and a sub-basement of cells where they torture prisoners. Terrible tortures. My brother was lucky . . . they only pulled out his fingernails and broke the bones of his fingers and toes."

"And that was lucky?" Elise asked with a shudder, pushing her spectacles up her nose.

"The truly lucky ones are the ones who die," Michel said.

"All right!" Canon Bizien spread his hands and looked around at all of them. "It's not pleasant what can go on there. All the more reason we should try to get people out. Though that's supposedly impossible."

"We can't not try," Kirsteen said.

"*I* intend to try," Antoine added.

"I didn't say we wouldn't try," the canon said. "We must work out a plan. But meanwhile, much as we feel for Gaston -- and I recognize also that Stonehenge is Marie's special project -- we do have our other task, that we've been working up to for the past few weeks."

"Oh?" Kirsteen was interested. "May we know what that is, Pierre?"

The old cleric was obviously pleased with himself, she thought, as he leaned forward, his eyes gleaming.

"Marie; Antoine. You are now members of our group, if it so pleases you. We have been planning a strike that will cripple an important aspect of the occupying forces and, in so doing, will proclaim our determination to survive to the French people."

"A railroad?" Antoine asked, eagerly. "You're going to blow up a railroad?"

"No. This is more devastating in many ways, and certainly unique," the priest said. "We're going to sabotage the gigantic Radio Paris transmitter that they use to jam Royal Air Force radio traffic."

"It's several miles southeast of the city," added Hélène. "Albert is going to lead us." She looked adoringly at the plump, ruddy-faced butcher, who grudgingly smiled back at her.

"Pierre claims he's too old to lead us himself," he said, smiling also at the cleric. "Though I think he could leave us all miles behind, with his energy."

"When are you going to do this?" Antoine asked.

"Tomorrow night," Bizien responded.

"You have the explosives?" Kirsteen asked. She had covered such things in her training.

"They were dropped by the R.A.F. three weeks ago. We have already used some for destroying a supply warehouse. Albert is our explosives expert. And Elise is showing surprising expertise in this direction."

"I think it's exciting," the skinny brunette said, tugging her big beret down more over one ear. "And Albert is very good at teaching things."

Kirsteen couldn't help but notice the evil look thrown at Elise by Hélène.

"Excellent!" Antoine cried. "Count me in."

They discussed the plan they had put together. Kirsteen noticed that Michel had volunteered to stay at the church with the canon, manning the radio in case of emergencies, though what he would be able to do she had no idea. Albert and the three women -- now supplemented by Kirsteen and Antoine -- were to go to the transmitter.

"I drive my father's delivery van," Lucie said to Kirsteen. "We've managed to accumulate some petrol for this, or he'd never let me have it. I'm a pretty good driver!"

"I'm sure you are." Kirsteen couldn't help smiling at the young girl's enthusiasm.

After a day spent lying low in the Leycurases' secret apartment Kirsteen was happy to be out again, even if it was lying flat in the bottom of an old Renault delivery van, covered by a pile of smelly, moldering, flour sacks. Albert sat up front beside Lucie, who drove with a determined look in her eye and her jaw set tight. Elise, Hélène, Antoine and the explosives were hidden in the back with Kirsteen.

It was nine o'clock in the evening and what little traffic there was had almost completely disappeared, though there would be a scurrying around later on, nearer curfew. They headed onto quai de la Gare, southeast through Paris, past the gare d'Austerlitz and out towards Ivry-sur-Seine.

Kirsteen was feeling every bump, and beginning to think that Lucie was purposely finding them, when suddenly the van slowed.

"Keep down and keep quiet, everyone," Albert said. "We're being waved down by an SOL man. Lay low and keep quiet."

Kirsteen knew that the SOL was the *Service d'Ordre Légionnaire*, founded in the spring of 1941 by Joseph Darnand, a zealous

Fascist. It was now thirty thousand strong, she'd heard, made up of the dregs of French criminal society, hoodlums and criminals; a veritable French Gestapo. They were hated even more than the German Gestapo. Darnand directed them specifically against the Resistants. They had started in Vichy but were gradually spreading their reign of terror into the Occupied Zone. They had only recently started to operate in Paris, alongside the Germans.

"Where are we?" Elise asked.

"Just about to make a left onto boulevard de Masséna. Ssh!"

The van came to a jerky stop and Lucie wound down the window. Through a gap between two flour sacks Kirsteen saw a thin-faced man in a scruffy uniform thrust his face close to Lucie's.

"Destination?" he barked.

"I-it's not curfew yet," Lucie responded, timidly.

"I asked for your destination," the man snarled.

Albert nudged Lucie and leaned across towards the window. "We're just trying to get some last deliveries completed before curfew," he said. "No one destination; just around in a big circle really, then back to the center of town."

"Hrmph! Let's see your papers." The man wiped his nose on the back of his hand.

Lucie and Albert dutifully proffered their papers.

"What's wrong, officer?" Albert asked.

Kirsteen smiled to herself at his use of the word "officer". That's smart, she thought. He'll like that. Sure enough the man seemed to grow less assertive. He handed back the papers.

"Nothing you need worry about," he said. "Just routine. Be on your way, and mind you're off the streets by curfew."

"Yes, officer. Thank you, sir." Lucie was a quick study. She wound up the window and they were on their way again.

"Phew! We can do without any more of that," sighed Hélène. "Just think, if he'd looked in the back here!"

Without further incident they drove through the outer suburbs of Charenton and the working-class district of Fontenay-sous-Bois and, in a short time, were driving past the huge radio transmitting tower of Radio Paris, on the southern edge of the Bois de Vincennes. Despite its size it was difficult to make it out, silhouetted against the dark, almost moonless sky.

Lucie drove the van past the site and turned up a side road, away from it. She finally parked under some trees on the side street.

"All right," Albert said. "We've checked this out thoroughly. Now, Elise and I will go out first." Kirsteen heard a sniff from Hélène. "Give us five minutes then you, Marie, and Lucie follow. Five more minutes and then Antoine and Hélène. Keep close to the houses on this side of the street. There's not much of a moon tonight so we don't have to worry about that."

They divided up the explosives, each of them tucking a flour sack under his or her coat.

"Remember," Albert added, "the shop on the corner of the street is empty. I'll pick the lock and we'll all meet inside."

"You sure you'll have no trouble with the lock?" Antoine asked.

"Don't worry. We've been over this ground a dozen times. I've checked out the lock before -- and even oiled it," Albert chuckled.

He and Elise slipped away into the darkness and the others checked their watches. Five minutes later Kirsteen and Lucie left. It was a dark night and they held hands as they moved across the sidewalk and started walking down the street, keeping tight against the sides of the buildings.

"I wish the moon wasn't quite so hidden by clouds," whispered Lucie. "I really don't like the dark."

Kirsteen gave her hand a squeeze. "Don't worry. It's not far. And it's better to be a bit scared of the dark than to be visible to anyone who happens to look out of a window."

In a short time all six of them were huddled on the floor of the empty store, peering out of the grimy window across toward the radio tower. There was a wire mesh fence around the tower which was, in turn, inside a wrought iron fence around the whole radio station complex.

"The outer fence is no problem," Albert said. "It's more decorative than anything and it's not high. We can get over that all right."

"And what about the inner fence," Kirsteen asked.

"I'll cut a hole in that, closest to the southwest leg of the tower. That's the nearest one. Once through that hole we move quickly across to that junction hut in the middle of the base."

"Is there any high voltage?" Lucie's voice wavered a little. Again Kirsteen reached out and gave her hand a reassuring squeeze.

"No," Albert said. "You needn't worry about that. There's nothing at ground level, where we'll be, that can harm you."

"What about sentries?" Antoine asked.

"That's something we weren't sure about. We've seen a man patrolling a couple of times when we've been here checking things out, but not every time."

"It just doesn't seem consistent," Elise added. "Which doesn't help."

They lay there for ten minutes, studying the tower. There was no sign of activity anywhere near it.

"Okay. I think we're in luck," Albert said.

"I can hardly believe it," Kirsteen said, feeling uneasy. "You'd think the Germans would know that this is a potential sabotage target. I can't believe they don't have anyone patrolling."

"Well, see for yourself," Hélène said. "We've been watching for hours and there's no one there."

"Not to be picky," Elise said, "but ten minutes isn't exactly 'hours'. I'm with Marie. I don't like it."

They had lain there for another five minutes and were finally thinking of making their move when Kirsteen let out a gasp. She gripped Albert's and Lucie's arms; the two people beside her.

"Look! Look there, just to the left of the junction box. See?"

Everyone strained to see.

"No. No, nothing," Antoine said. "What . . ."

"Look! There!"

They all saw it; the brief but unmistakable red glow of a cigarette. Someone was sitting on the ground, leaning back against the hut-like structure at the base of the tower, smoking a cigarette.

Albert cursed and turned to sit on the floor with his back now to the window. "Damn! There *is* a sentry. Well done, Marie! We could have walked into that one."

"So what do we do now?" Hélène asked.

"Let's just think it through. Pierre did bring up this possibility, don't forget."

"And what did he suggest?" Kirsteen asked.

"Kill him," Elise said simply.

Kirsteen was surprised. Somehow she had difficulty seeing the gentle priest recommending someone be killed, even if it was a German. "Really?" she asked. In the darkness she could just make out Harold nodding.

"There's no real alternative," he said, "unless we can somehow overpower him and incapacitate him."

"Well, let's put our minds to that," Kirsteen said. As it happened it didn't take long to come up with a plan. "If this doesn't work, then we'll try to think of something else," she said.

20: SABOTAGE

Albert slipped out of the shop and made off to the north, crossing the street and climbing over the low outer fence to the rear of where the sentry was enjoying his smoke. At the same time Lucie went south, crossed the street and then started to walk slowly along beside the fence. She made a point of coughing a couple of times and then of singing softly as she walked. When she got nearly level with where the sentry sat she stopped and cried out.

"Damn! I've laddered these stockings. The only silk stockings I've got. Damn!" She lifted the hem of her skirt and examined her leg.

From the shop Kirsteen and the others watched the little charade. They were gratified to see the red cigarette end be flipped away and, soon after, a figure emerged from the darkness under the tower. A German soldier came to the wire mesh fence.

"Mademoiselle? Hello! Can I help you?"

Lucie jumped as though she had no idea he was there.

"Who is that?"

"Mademoiselle.   One   moment."   The German went around to the gate in the fence and unlocked it. He came out, leaving the gate open, and moved across to the outer fence and Lucie. He had a rifle slung over his shoulder.

From inside the shop it was difficult, in the near- darkness, to see everything that was going on but the group did make out the figure of Albert as he moved rapidly across to the wire fence and around to the gate. Meanwhile the soldier was talking to Lucie.

"I've got a run in my stocking," she said. "See?"

She again lifted her skirt and the soldier leaned forward. "One moment, mademoiselle," he said. He laid down his rifle and climbed over the fence to stand beside her. "Now, that's better. Let me see what the problem is, eh?" He knelt down.

Kirsteen could imagine the smile on the man's face as he thought he was about to enjoy an entertaining interlude in his dreary sentry duty. He ran his hands up Lucie's leg. At that moment Albert moved quickly and silently across the grass from the inner fence, picked up the guard's rifle and, leaning out over the fence, clubbed the soldier over the head with it. The sentry fell to the ground.

"Well, you took your time!" Lucie said, stepping back and smoothing down her skirt.

The others quickly ran across the road from the shop and together they lifted the guard and carried him back inside the inner fence.

"Well done, Lucie," Kirsteen said. "You certainly got his attention."

"I was afraid for a minute that Albert would be too late and I'd get more than his attention," she said. They all laughed.

"All right," Albert said. "Let's get on with the job." He had tied the guard's feet and hands together with the sling from the man's own rifle. "You all know what to do. Let's go!"

Quickly Kirsteen and Lucie moved to the base of one of the legs of the tower. They took the explosives out of the flour sacks and wedged them firmly in place at about chest height, where a cross-brace came into the main joist. Kirsteen taped the timing device to the same brace and wired it into the charge, setting it to explode in thirty minutes. The others worked similarly at the other legs. Albert moved across to the small building in the center of the area, against which the guard had been resting. He forced the lock on the door and went in. By the time everyone had finished planting their materials Albert emerged and closed the door again.

"What do we do with the guard?" Kirsteen asked.

"I'm for leaving him here, to be blown up with the rest of it," Hélène said.

The others murmured and shook their heads.

"We can't do that, even if he is a German," Elise said.

"Let's drag him over to the outer fence," Kirsteen suggested. "At least he'll be away from the blast."

Ten minutes later they were all back in the van heading for the center of Paris.

"Those were thirty minute fuses," Albert said. "We'll be well on our way home by the time they go off. Even if they cordon off the surrounding area, we'll be well clear of it."

By the time they got back into the center of Paris Kirsteen was breathing easier. She had taken part in her first act of sabotage and had found it exhilarating. And now that it was over, perhaps she could get on with her search for Stonehenge.

News of the demolition of the radio tower was all over Paris the following morning. Kirsteen had breakfast with Godefrois and Victoire and it was all they could speak of.

"They say it was a small British Commando group that parachuted into the Bois de Vincennes and were later spirited out by Resistants," Victoire said breathlessly.

"The tower was toppled and the relay station underneath it was totally demolished," Godefrois added. "It'll be months before they can get it back to anything like its original strength."

"Were there any casualties?" Kirsteen asked, innocently.

Victoire nodded. "It seems there was a guard there who was overpowered by six of the men and then lashed to the foot of the tower. They say he would have been blown to pieces if he hadn't managed to break free and get out just seconds before the explosions."

Kirsteen smiled. "Six men, you say?"

"That's what *Pariser-Zeitung* says. Of course that's a German newspaper but I understand *Paris-Soir* is running much the same story." Godefrois finished his breakfast and stood up. "You must excuse me, Marie, Victoire. I have to be at the office of the Militärbefehlshaber at Hôtel Majestic first thing. Something to do with Dr. Verner Best wanting me to verify my silver inventory." He grunted. "Hrmph! Coincidentally he also wants to buy some silver place-settings for his German villa. He is hand-in-hand with German Ambassador Abetz in stealing France blind of its art treasures! I should be grateful he's dealing with me directly, I suppose. With any luck I should be back by lunch time."

As soon as she could Kirsteen also excused herself and went to debrief with Canon Bizien's *Réseau*. They were all there when she arrived and everyone of them -- with the exception of Michel -- looked pleased with him or herself.

"Good morning, Marie," the canon cried. "Congratulations! You did well; as did everyone. What a success!"

"Lucie did a great job of driving and Albert was an inspiring leader," Kirsteen said, smiling at them all. "Have you heard the German version of what happened?"

They all laughed. "Yes! British Commandoes!"

"I guess we should be thankful," Elise said, thoughtfully. "If they acknowledged it was Resistants who'd done it they'd be taking reprisals."

They were quiet for a moment.

"That's true," Lucie said. "And, of course, they may still do that. There's no logic to much of what the Germans do."

"How did it go here, last night, Pierre?" Kirsteen asked.

The canon shrugged. "It was quiet, I'm glad to say. Michel monitored the RAF frequency and we listened to the BBC French Language broadcast. There was nothing important to us."

"You don't still transmit from here, do you?" Kirsteen asked.

"No! No, not since the Gestapo visited. But we can still receive and monitor from the bell tower here."

"By the way, Pierre, where is Claude these days?" Kirsteen asked. She had missed the Gypsy and had expected him to be in on the sabotage raid the previous evening.

"He's run off again," Michel snorted.

Kirsteen looked at him. "What do you mean?"

The canon shook his head. "No, no, Michel! It's all right, Marie. Claude has other jobs he has to do, it seems. He has to have his own priorities, of course. Michel just doesn't understand that."

"No, I don't!" Michel turned his back on them all.

Kirsteen didn't mention that she was due to meet with Greyhound that afternoon, at the café on rue de Marignan. She looked forward to it. Perhaps he had news of Stonehenge, or even of the mysterious Paulette, she thought.

A quarter of an hour before their three o'clock meeting time Kirsteen was settled at a table, under a "Dubonnet"-bedecked umbrella, nursing a cup of *tilleul* and watching the people go by on the rue de Marignan and the avenue des Champs-Elysées. The corner café was ideally placed for people-watching, she thought. She had a copy of *Signal* on the table in front of her and idly flicked through its pages. *Signal* was a fortnightly illustrated magazine put out by Goebbels's ministry of propaganda. There was a French language edition, popular because of its high-quality color photographs.

She watched a blonde young woman wearing trousers and riding a man's bicycle pedal past her and disappear into the mass of bicycles and vélo-taxis. She saw two or three *voitures à gazogène*; natural-gas-propelled cars. There were also converted cars that burned the wood that powered them in wash-boilers bolted to their trunks. A German motorcycle and sidecar swept past closely followed by two *Küblerwagens*.

An elaborately decorated vélo-taxi, pulled by twin young men on a tandem, deposited a German Wehrmacht Oberstleutnant almost at Kirsteen's feet. He clicked his heels at her, with a tight smile, and then threaded his way through the tables to join an overly made-up, dark-haired, young woman at the rear of the café.

At three o'clock exactly Greyhound appeared beside Kirsteen. She jumped. Although she'd been watching the people so closely she just hadn't seen the Gypsy until he was right there beside her.

"And how was your trip?" he asked, as he dropped into the seat opposite her.

"Goodness! You gave me a start! How d'you do that?"

The dark-skinned man smiled and glanced quickly to either side. "I guess you could say it's a gift," he said with a shrug. "I've been told my ancestors were Witches and they learned the art of making themselves invisible."

Kirsteen laughed. "Oh, Claude!"

A waitress appeared and Greyhound ordered a coffee. When the woman had gone he leaned forward and repeated his question.

"The trip was fine," Kirsteen said. "No incidents. I'd say it was a piece of cake but I don't want to get complacent."

"And how is the old 'homestead'?"

She knew, of course, that he meant England. "The same as ever. Everyone settling in for what they now accept may be a long term event."

"Well, thank God they've got Winnie to inspire them."

"He seemed very tired . . ." Kirsteen bit her tongue.

Greyhound looked at her sharply. "What d'you mean? How did you see him?"

"I-I mean he *sounded* very tired. He was on the radio."

"Ah! Ah, yes. Thank you." Greyhound accepted his coffee from the waitress and Kirsteen let out a breath of relief. She must really watch herself, she thought. Even though Greyhound was on the same side, *no one* was to know of her relationship with the Prime Minister.

She pushed back the headscarf she had been wearing and saw Greyhound's eyes go immediately to her hair. A look of puzzlement passed across his face but he said nothing.

"It's a long story. I'll tell you later," she said. "Have you learned anything while I've been away?"

"Not much, I'm afraid. Your friend Paulette is still missing, though I did hear rumors of a redhead answering her description being seen at avenue Kléber."

"You mean she's been taken-in by the Gestapo?" Kirsteen asked.

He shook his head. "No. From what I heard she was at the hôtel in the company of a Gestapo officer and it was pretty obvious she wasn't in any sort of custody."

"I see." Kirsteen sipped the strange-tasting *tilleul*. It really wasn't too bad when you got used to it, she thought.

"But, as I say, I can't swear it was Paulette."

Kirsteen surprised herself by ordering a second cup of *tilleul* and then went on to tell Greyhound all about how she came to shoot the SS Sergeant and that she was now hiding out at the Leycurases'. She also told him of the attack on the radio transmitting tower.

"I heard about that. That's good work, Casey -- I mean, Marie."

"I'm really not sure what my next move will be," she said. "I've got to keep a low profile, of course, but hopefully the blonde hair will help somewhat. I was given information that seems to indicate Stonehenge may be in the Hôtel Majestic. If so I have to get to him. And I think I'll see if Canon Bizien has any ideas on rescuing Gaston."

"Don't worry too much about Gaston," Greyhound said, his dark eyes locked on hers. "You must remember what we learned: make your priorities and stick to them. Your number one priority, I believe, is Stonehenge. It's too bad Gaston got picked up but you mustn't risk getting yourself arrested trying to rescue him. The Stonehenge mission is much more important."

She sighed. "You're right, of course, Claude. And thanks for reminding me. It's just hard when someone you like . . ."

"I know. But these are hard times. Remember those priorities." He got to his feet. "Well, delightful as this coffee is, I must go. Take care, Marie. You're going to be all right, somehow I sense it. But don't go taking chances."

"When will I see you again?"

He gave his familiar shrug and a smile spread across his face. "When you least expect it, probably." He gave a quick nod and then was gone.

21: THE CELLS OF HÔTEL MAJESTIC

The best approach was the direct one, Kirsteen told herself as she rode in the vélo-taxi along avenue Kléber. She alighted at the green and peaceful-looking place des Etats-Unis and strolled casually toward rue de Belloy. The end of the street was barricaded off with barbed wire and a Gestapo sentry was checking the papers of everyone who went into and came out of the small street. As she glanced past the sentry-box she could see the Hôtel Majestic looking nondescript and inconspicuous, set back slightly from the road. She didn't want to stop and stare but she noted an art gallery across the road from the hôtel and office buildings and private residences on either side of it.

A large black Mercedes limousine glided up to the barrier and Kirsteen stepped to one side to allow it to pass. The barricade guard moved to the chauffeur's side and inspected papers, then stepped back, raised the barrier and saluted the occupant of the car. On the spur of the moment Kirsteen moved quickly forward and, keeping abreast of the vehicle's rear wheels, on the far side away from the sentry, walked forward with the car as it moved on past the barricade and into the street. She looked straight ahead, expecting any moment to hear a shout. Nothing happened and she quickly moved away from the car and up onto the sidewalk, hurrying forward and into the art gallery. She breathed deeply. She had got past the first hurdle.

"*Mademoiselle?*"

An unctuous, short, fat man in a black suit that was too tight for him slid toward Kirsteen and smiled an insincere smile. He smelled of garlic and cheap cologne. Kirsteen gave a rapid glance around the gallery and then spoke haughtily over the head of the man.

"I'm redecorating the Herr General's apartment. He suggested I stop by and see what you have," she said. "I'm only browsing so please don't bother me."

She was surprised at her own audacity but her ploy seemed to work. The slick-haired man gave a slight bow and backed away. Obviously, she thought, she was not the first to take that attitude with him.

She really wanted to check-out the Hôtel Majestic so she positioned herself where she could look out of the window and across the street, pretending to study the eclectic collection of paintings on easels before her.

She recognized the entrance from when she had been taken in there after her arrest in Fallaise. She tried to remember the layout inside. There had been a reception desk and then the wide, sweeping staircase going up to the right. She thought there were elevators to the left but wasn't sure.

If Stonehenge was being held here, where would he be? It was ridiculous, she thought. He could be anywhere. In fact there was no guarantee even that he had been transferred here. He might still be at 11 rue des Saussaies or, worse yet, on his way to Germany. She sighed.

"Mademoiselle is having difficulty deciding?"

She started at the voice and turned to see the fat man in the black suit studying her. He was wringing his hands as though washing them. He smiled his insincere smile.

"I beg your pardon?" she said.

"I could not help noticing that you have been staring at these same paintings for some time, Mademoiselle. I was wondering if I might be of some assistance?"

"No. I -- I mean -- the General . . ."

"And which General is that, Mademoiselle?" He was still all smiles.

She ignored the question. "I don't see anything that really captures my attention. Perhaps if a look further." She turned away from him and strolled around the gallery walls. She wished she had thought things through a little more. How was she to get into the hôtel and, once inside, where would she start looking for Stonehenge? Then she remembered the NCO at the reception desk when she had been taken in there. The officer with her had signed them in. Perhaps someone had signed in Stonehenge? But then, under what name? She bit her lip.

"Your papers, please, Mademoiselle."

For the second time she looked up with a start. A Gestapo officer stood looking at her. Behind him, half hidden behind the black uniform, she caught a glimpse of the oily art gallery manager -- still smiling and still wringing his hands -- studying her from under his hooded eyes.

"My - my papers?"

"Yes, Mademoiselle. The same ones I presume you showed at the gate when entering this street."

"How do you know I don't live on rue de Belloy?" she asked, although she knew she was merely delaying the inevitable.

"Your papers!" Any previously deferential tone disappeared.

With a sigh, Kirsteen pulled her papers out of her bag and handed them over. The officer studied them, looked up at her and then back at the papers.

"Why are you blonde?"

"A woman's fancy," she said, fighting to keep her voice steady. "It's not unheard off for a woman to change the color of her hair, is it?"

"Not under certain circumstances, no." He clucked his tongue for a moment. "You will come with me!"

He gripped her arm in a vice-like pinch and propelled her across the art gallery and out of the door. She caught a glimpse of the complacent proprietor smiling broadly and working his hands double time. He had definitely scored brownie points, she thought.

As she was man-handled up the steps to the hôtel and pushed through the front doors Kirsteen had a fleeting feeling of success that she had now achieved her second objective; she was inside the building. But any feeling of elation was very rudely squashed.

She was taken through a door behind the reception desk, down a flight of stone stairs and along a cold, dimly-lit corridor. She soon found herself locked in a small, airless room that had probably been a storage room originally. The door had been replaced with a metal one and there were bars at the one small window high up in the end wall. The room was completely bare and smelled musty and unclean. She could see a variety of stains on many areas of the floor; some smelled strongly of urine, others looked dark and ominous.   Unintelligible scratches and a few hand prints smudged the dirty walls.

For nearly two hours nothing happened. Reluctantly she gave up standing and sank down on the cleanest patch of floor she could find. She had hardly rested there ten minutes when she heard footsteps approaching along the corridor. The metal door screeched open, dragging across the concrete of the passageway floor. As Kirsteen scrambled to her feet she saw two men standing in the doorway staring at her. One was the arresting officer. The other was the SS-Scharführer she had shot in the leg at Madame Delestraint's. She was gratified to see he was leaning on a crutch.

The two men stared at her for several moments then turned and slammed the door. The echo reverberated as background to the sound of their jackboots marching away.

So they know who I am, Kirsteen thought bitterly. Well, she had hardly expected otherwise. Her papers still showed her as Marie Nègre, schoolteacher from Lyons. She presumed they would dig out her file, started when she had been brought in from Falaise. With thoughts of that she remembered the good-looking Brigadeführer who had rescued her from the lecherous officer who first interviewed her. What was his name, she thought? Artur. Artur Ebernach. He had certainly been handsome. She found herself smiling despite her circumstances.

It was several hours later, and dark outside, when a stocky, muscular SS-Hauptscharführer, jacketless and with his shirtsleeves rolled up, entered the room. He carried a wooden chair and a clipboard. Seating himself he consulted the papers on the board.

"You are Marie Nègre?" he asked in German.

Kirsteen did not answer. He repeated the question in French.

"I am."

"What are you doing in rue de Belloy?"

"Looking for a painting for my apartment."

"Which is where?"

"Seventeen avenue de ..."

"Liar!" he snapped. "You no longer have a room there. Where do you now live?"

Kirsteen bit her lip. She could just lie and make-up an address. But it would only be putting off the inevitable. "I don't have a room anywhere," she said. "I sleep out anywhere I can find shelter."

"Come here!" He beckoned her with a pudgy finger.   Slowly she moved toward him. "Kneel down," he said when she was in front of him.

A thousand thoughts flashed through her mind as she sank to her knees.

"Liar!" he suddenly screamed again, his hand flashing through the air and smashing the side of her face. She cried out and fell to the floor where she lay as he came to his feet and kicked her in the stomach. "Liar!" he repeated. "You are telling me you are one of the homeless and yet you dress so smartly and go to art galleries?" He kicked her again.

Kirsteen fought for breath. The man wore heavy boots and put force behind his kicks. For a moment she forgot the stinging pain of the slap as she curled up and tried to protect her stomach.

The Master-Sergeant sat down again and studied the papers on the clipboard as though nothing had happened.

"Sit up."

She tried but couldn't

"Sit up!"

Kirsteen managed to kneel again in front of him, partly doubled-over as she still clutched her stomach and tried to get her breath.

"You were apprehended in the apartment of one Gaston Dissart, a Resistant now in custody, at the house on avenue de Villars. There you shot a soldier of the Reich and made your escape. Now you show up again in disguise . . ."

"I - I only cut and dyed my hair," Kirsteen whispered.

"Quiet!" Another brain-rocking blow hit her face. Her head spun but she did not fall over.

"Take off your clothes."

"What? What is it with you . . ?"

"Do as you're told, or it'll be the worse for you," he snarled.

In a daze, she fumbled with her buttons and slowly undressed. Naked, she huddled on the cold floor and looked up at the Nazi with contempt. He hardly glanced at her. Taking up his chair and tucking the clipboard under his arm, he opened the door and kicked all her clothes out into the passageway. He followed them out and slammed the door. She heard the key turn in the lock.

The night was bitter on the cold, cement floor of the room. Kirsteen realized that she had not been made to strip by any lecherous intent of the German, it was purely and simply to make her suffer from the cold. She wrapped her arms about her and rocked herself trying to get some sleep. By the time the gray light of dawn started to filter through the tiny window she had managed no more than a couple of very brief cat-naps. Her face ached from the brutal beatings and her stomach felt as though it was raw. Her buttocks and shoulders were sore from contact with the cement floor and walls and her thoughts went, time and again, to Molly the WRNS Lieutenant to whom Winston Churchill had introduced her. What was it Molly had said?

"It's all part of this damn war."

As near as Kirsteen could guess it was about midday before anyone came to see her again. Her watch had been taken from her, along with her bag, when she was first placed in the room. The door was dragged open and the same SS-Hauptscharführer from the previous afternoon stood there together with the SS-Scharführer she had shot in the leg. This time he was without his crutch, though he limped as he walked. They came in and closed the door behind them. The Master-Sergeant again had his chair with him. He really likes to take it easy, thought Kirsteen as he put it by the wall and slumped down onto it. She noticed that there was no clipboard this time.

"So, Mademoiselle," the seated soldier said. "I trust you slept well. Stand up, please."

Slowly and reluctantly Kirsteen came to her feet, her arms protectively across her body.

"Arms at your sides, head up, like a good soldier," said the wounded Sergeant, chuckling to his companion.

She slowly lowered her arms, feeling incredibly vulnerable in front of the two men. The Sergeant limped slowly around her, studying her body from all angles and muttering to himself. He finished his examination and went to stand beside his colleague.

"Nice body," he said in German, believing that Kirsteen could not understand. "I want her."

"I still don't think we should be doing this," said the seated one. "If it should be found out . . ."

"Oh, come on! She owes me. She shot me, damn it!"

The Master-Sergeant shrugged his shoulders indifferently.

The limping Sergeant moved back to Kirsteen and closely studied her breasts. "Nice!" he said in French. His accent was abominable. He bent his head and went to suck one of her nipples. Instinctively Kirsteen backed away.

"Stand still!" he shrieked, and backhanded her across the face. The blow hurt more than it might because of the previous day's beatings. Tears came to her eyes and she fought to keep them back.

"You will do as you are told! Understand?" he snarled.

"Is this the way Germans treat helpless women?" Kirsteen demanded.

"Helpless? Hah!" He laughed, then pointed down at his leg. "You weren't feeling so helpless when you shot me, were you, bitch? Now you're going to pay for it."

His hand shot out and he grabbed her by the hair, pushing her down on her knees before him. With his other hand he quickly unbuttoned his pants and pulled out his penis.

"Here, French bitch! Try some nice German sausage!"

He tugged back on her hair and at the same time forced his organ against her mouth. Kirsteen opened her mouth, took the end of it in and clamped down her teeth with all her might.

"Aaagh! Aaagh! *Mein Gott!* She's bitten it off! Oh, my God, she's bitten it off!"

Blood spurted all over the place; over Kirsteen's face and down her body. She spat out the end of the penis and felt a certain glow of satisfaction, though she knew she had probably signed her own death warrant.

The Master-Sergeant had come to his feet, knocking over the chair.

"Shit! I said this was a bad idea." he cried.

"Quick! Get me to a doctor! Quick!" screamed the frantic soldier, grabbing up the severed end with one hand while trying to staunch the flow of blood with the other. They pulled open the door and ran out, slamming it behind them. Kirsteen sank to the floor and vomited.

It took a while for it to seep through to her conscious mind, but eventually Kirsteen became aware of a metallic sound coming from somewhere near the ceiling. Gradually it dawned on her that it was Morse code. Someone was sending her a message, tapping it out against a metal pipe that ran across the ceiling.

"Are you alive? Are you alive?" it repeated.

The pipe was too high off the ground for her to reach but, in their excitement, the Germans had left behind the Master-Sergeant's chair. She picked it up and stood it under the pipe. Climbing up she rapped the pipe sharply with her knuckles.

"Yes. I'm alive. Who is this?"

"What was all the shouting?"

For the next few minutes they tapped back and forth. Kirsteen learned that it was another prisoner in a similar room further down the corridor. He had been there for several days, being beaten and interrogated. She told him what she had done to the SS Sergeant. He thought it was wonderful.

"That will teach them some respect," he tapped.

"What is your name?" Kirsteen asked.

"I am known as Stonehenge," came the reply.

22: ROOM SERVICE

Jackboots tramped along the corridor and Kirsteen jumped down from the chair. This is it, she thought, they're coming for me. But the boots marched past her room and on down the passageway. She guessed they were going for Stonehenge and soon heard the sound of his door being opened. She felt miserable that at long last she had found him but she was powerless to do anything to help him.

More boots sounded and suddenly her own door was opened. A short, skinny, SS-Schütze stood there, holding a tin tray with food and drink on it. He came in and placed the tray on the chair. The tin cup held water and there was a mixture of potato and something dark brown on the plate. Kirsteen decided that she didn't care what it was, and wouldn't ask; she was ravenous.

"I think you'll prefer this to German sausage," whispered the soldier, and winked at her. He had a small mustache, not unlike Hitler's -- or Charlie Chaplin's, Kirsteen thought -- and she couldn't help smiling at him. As he turned to go three Gestapo men came into view dragging a man along the corridor past the open door. As they drew level the man -- in scruffy pants and with his shirt hanging in tatters about his waist -- looked directly at Kirsteen and smiled. He nodded slightly and then was dragged on.

"Stonehenge," she murmured to herself. And yet there was something about the man that unsettled her.

"I'll be back later with some water for washing, Fräulein," said the Schütze. "I don't know if I can get you any clothes but I'll try."

"Thank you," Kirsteen murmured, then realized that the man had been speaking in German. But he didn't seem to think anything amiss and went out, closing the door behind him.

Kirsteen ate the mess of food and slowly sipped the water. She went over in her mind what had just happened. She knew that Stonehenge had been transferred from 11 rue des Saussaies to the Hôtel Majestic. She knew this from Molly, back in England. Then she had spoken to him, by way of the iron pipe, and he had said he was Stonehenge . . . but he wasn't!

Churchill had given Kirsteen all the details about the number one agent. She had even studied a photograph of him, though admittedly he was little more than a face in a crowd. But there were certain unalterable facts. Stonehenge was tall and blond. The man claiming to be him was short and dark. He was not Stonehenge so why was he saying that he was?

The SS private did come back later with a bowl of tepid water and a scrap of a wash-rag. Kirsteen thankfully wiped away the blood and grime as well as she was able. Her dress was also returned to her though no underwear, stockings or shoes. The chair was still there so she settled on it, leaning back against the wall, and finally drifted off to sleep.

When she awoke it was dark outside and the washbowl and rag had been removed. She wished she had more drinking water.

Kirsteen moved the chair over to the window wall and stood up on it, on tiptoe, to try to see out. There was little she could make out. It seemed the window looked out on a small vegetable garden, probably at the back of the hôtel, though she couldn't be certain. She climbed down again, sat, and shortly drifted off to sleep again.

She had no idea of the time when she awoke. It was still dark outside, though which side of midnight it was she didn't know. For a moment she wondered what had woken her, then she heard the footsteps coming along the passageway. Who would it be this time, she wondered?

When the door opened it was the stocky SS-Hauptscharführer who this time was wearing his uniform jacket, though unbuttoned. He was accompanied by the friendly Schütze. The Staff-Sergeant's eyes lit on the chair and he muttered "So that's where it got to," in German, then prodded the Private forward. The little man held out a pile of clothing to Kirsteen. It was her underwear, stockings and shoes.

"Put them on," said the Staff-Sergeant. He then busied himself picking up his beloved chair and placing it outside the room, in the corridor, while Kirsteen turned her back and slipped off the dress. The Private tactfully found something interesting to examine on the wall by the door as she quickly got fully dressed and then turned around to them again.

"Hmm. Come!" The SS-Hauptscharführer waggled his finger then turned and marched off down the corridor. Kirsteen followed, with the Schütze bringing up the rear.

They went up the concrete stairs, built around the elevator shaft, for three floors, where the Sergeant signaled a brief halt. He was breathing heavily. Kirsteen could have sworn she heard the Private chuckle, but didn't risk looking back at him. They went on for two more floors then passed through a door and came out in one of the hotel corridors. The Sergeant seemed to hesitate a moment to get his bearings then led them forward, off to the right. At the fourth door down he knocked and listened. There was no response so he opened the door and stuck his head in.

"Come!" he said, again wagging his pudgy finger. He held the door open and Kirsteen went in.

She found herself in one of the small, single rooms of the hotel. There was a bed and night stand, a dressing-table, one armchair and -- thankfully she saw -- a small bathroom. On the night stand was a small tray holding a glass of milk and two sandwiches.

"You will stay in here," said the Sergeant. He closed the door on her and she heard the key turn.

Kirsteen moved forward and scooped up a sandwich then collapsed onto the bed. It felt heavenly. In no time she had finished both sandwiches and the glass of milk and was running a bath. Half an hour later she was in the bed and sound asleep.

Next morning Kirsteen was up by early morning, so far as she could judge. The view from the window was to the rear of the hotel and overlooked a rundown garden and a parking lot. Off in the distance, beyond a row of chestnut trees, she could make out the traffic on rue Galilée. It was an overcast day with light rain falling.

There was a tap on her door and then the key was turned. She braced herself and unnecessarily called "Come in". The door swung open and revealed the Charlie Chaplin-mustached Schütze.

"Good morning, *Fräulein*," he said. He carried a tray with what looked like breakfast on it. Walking briskly into the room he put it down on the night stand and took up the empty tray from the previous evening.

"Please," Kirsteen said. "What's happening? Why have I been moved up here?"

"You don't care for my room service?" the soldier asked, a twinkle in his eyes.

"Oh, I really appreciate all you've done so far," she said. "You've been very kind. As kind as I'm sure you can be under the circumstances."

The Schütze hovered in the doorway. He glanced quickly outside, looking up and down the corridor, and then turned back to Kirsteen. "That bastard sergeant you bit has got himself in a pack of trouble," he volunteered. "And not just from what you did to him. Lucky for you someone's looking out for you."

"What? What do you mean, looking out for me?"

"Sssh! Can't talk now."

He hurried out of the room and closed the door behind himself, remembering to lock it. As Kirsteen listened to his footsteps hurrying away she also heard other more measured footsteps approach and pass by her door. With a sigh, she sat down in the armchair and started in on the breakfast.

An hour or more after she had eaten the door was again opened, this time by a young SS-Unterscharführer. He clicked his heels.

"You will come with me, please."

Kirsteen followed him out and along the corridor. They descended the main staircase to the second floor and then walked along the corridor there.

"Wait in here," he said, opening a door.

She followed him into an austerely furnished outer office. The Corporal went through to the inner office, closing that door behind him. She sat down on the only chair in front of the desk and waited. A few minutes later the Corporal came back into the room.

"He'll see you now," he said.

Not knowing what to expect, Kirsteen got up and went through into the inner office. A Gestapo officer sat at the large oak desk. As she entered he looked up. Her heart gave a slight flutter when she saw it was SS-Brigadeführer Artur Ebernach.

"The delightful schoolteacher, Mademoiselle Marie Nègre, I believe," he said, coming to his feet and extending his hand.

Uncertainly, she took it and was surprised when he bent forward and kissed her hand.

"Please! Sit down."

She sat in the comfortable chair in front of the desk and looked around. It was the same office to which she had been brought on her last visit to the Hôtel Majestic. Behind her was the door out to the large outer office, with the many desks and the loutish SS-Standartenführer who had tried to make her strip in front of everybody. In front of her, behind Artur Ebernach, hung the large picture of Adolf Hitler. She looked at it and quickly glanced away again.

"So we meet again, Marie."

Kirsteen nodded, unsure what to say.

"It seems I am forever finding you in this hôtel in one state or another of undress," he said, a smile hovering around his mouth. She felt herself blush. "Did you get back all your clothes all right?"

"Yes. Yes, thank you. Though not my purse or my watch."

He nodded. On the desk in front of him was a manila folder, which he now opened. "I am sorry to hear of the fate of two of your compatriots. I hear the other one -- Gaston Dissart, is it? -- he has gone for a vacation to Berlin." He looked up from the folder and settled himself more comfortably in his chair. "I did tell you that you were in bad company, did I not, Marie?"

She nodded, mutely. What did he want, she wondered? Why had she been rescued from the abomination of the cell in the basement and installed in a room as though she were a guest in the hôtel? Presumably Artur -- this Gestapo officer -- was the person Charlie Chaplin meant was "looking out for her".

"What were you doing in the art gallery, across the road?" he asked quietly.

"Nothing. I - I was just looking at paintings."

"You said something to the proprietor about a General?"

She smiled at him. "I was just trying to keep him at arm's length. He seemed to be overly attentive."

Ebernach pursed his lips and nodded. "I know the type. But, Marie, it seems you had somehow got into this section of the city without showing your papers to the guard on duty. You had somehow *evaded* him."

His eyes fastened on hers and held them. She felt a little like a schoolchild up in front of the headmaster, having been caught in a prank.

"I - I don't recall being asked . . ."

"This is a restricted zone, you know, Marie."

Kirsteen shook her head. "No. No, I didn't know, sir. As you're aware, I'm from Lyon and unfamiliar . . ."

"Artur."

"I - I beg your pardon?"

"Artur. My name is Artur. You don't have to call me 'sir'."

"Oh! Thank you."

He again studied the folder. "Last time I had the pleasure of your company in my office I relieved you of a Gestapo pass that apparently gave you permission to enter the Forbidden Zone. You remember that?" His eyes again locked onto hers. She nodded. "It seems that the pass was a forgery."

"I - I didn't know. I got it on the black market, I admit," Kirsteen said, thinking desperately. "I didn't know it was forged. I just thought that you could get things like that. As I've told you, I'm . . ."

"Yes, I know. You're from Lyon." He leaned back in his chair and turned his head to look out of the window. "You do remember, though, that you assured me at the time that you had got the pass from the Kommandantur?"

She nodded, her eyes downcast.

"The forgery was not very good," Ebernach continued. There was silence for a moment, then: "Are you a spy, Marie?" he snapped.

Her head came up and she looked him in the eyes.

"No! No, of course not!" She hoped she sounded sincere. To her relief she saw him slowly nod.

"Mmm! Yes, your regular papers seem in order -- unless you are from England? Their forgeries are excellent, I have to admit."

Kirsteen bit her tongue and said nothing. They studied one another for what seemed like a long time.

"I think I prefer you with your normal color hair, as on your papers, Marie. By the way, I hear that last night you bit off rather more than you can chew," Ebernach said, the slight smile again tugging at the corners of his mouth.

Kirsteen couldn't help laughing. "He really asked for it," she said.

"I know. He acted way out of line. You will hear nothing more about that. He is now on his way to the Russian front."

"May I ask . . . how long am I going to be held here?" Kirsteen wasn't sure she wanted to know the answer.

Ebernach shrugged. 'It's difficult to say, Marie. If it was just up to me I'd let you out of here now. But, unfortunately, your file has been seen by others and I have to follow regulations."

"Which say?"

"Which say, that I must keep you in custody for the time being. However," he allowed himself a smile. He should do it more often, Kirsteen thought. He looked very attractive when he smiled. "However, you are not just 'in custody'; you are in my custody. That, I think you'll find, will make a difference."

Kirsteen was puzzled but didn't ask any questions.

"You may go back to your room now," he continued. "I'll have to keep your door locked, for which I apologize. But know that, so far as I'm concerned, you are not really a prisoner. In fact, to show you I mean that I would very much like you to have dinner with me this evening."

Kirsteen was amazed. Yet the idea of dinner -- any dinner -- filled her mind. She almost salivated on the spot. 'Dinner?" she said.

He nodded and looked her up and down. "I think you need some clean clothes. I imagine you've been wearing those for longer than you'd wish."

It was her turn to nod.

"I'll pick you up a little early and we'll do some shopping on the way to the restaurant. For now, I have a lot of work to attend to. I'll look forward to seeing you later, Marie."

He stood up and held out his hand. Kirsteen came to her feet. Again he kissed her hand. "Until this evening."

Kirsteen's bag -- minus her papers -- and her watch were in her room when she got back there. She dug out what small amount of make-up she had and thought about her coming evening out. She was in something of a daze. What exactly was going on, she wondered? She found Artur -- the Brigadeführer -- very attractive, there was no question. But he was a Gestapo officer. She had to keep reminding herself of that.

Yet what harm could there be in becoming friendly with him? If anything, she told herself, it could only be helpful. She needed to be in the Hôtel Majestic to try to help Stonehenge . . . or at least to find out who this man was who was calling himself Stonehenge. Being there as a "guest" rather than as a prisoner should be an advantage.

She decided she'd probably think better after a nap. She had a lot of catching-up to do on her sleep, so she lay down on the bed and in no time was asleep. She was later awakened by the "Charlie Chaplin" private bringing her a light lunch, which she ate as she again went over the events since her arrest in the art gallery.

Outside in the hallway Kirsteen heard a woman cry out. As she listened she made out hushed voices; a man and a woman. They were speaking in French and the woman sounded agitated.

Kirsteen quietly moved over to the door and stood with her ear pressed against the crack, straining to pick up anything she could. The couple was almost right outside her room.

"But you promised!' said the female voice.

The male chuckled. "We all make promises in time of war. Some are -- what shall I say? -- difficult to keep."

"But they're my parents!"

"Of course. That's why you do as we say."

"But - but you can't send them to Germany. Not after what I've done for you."

There was something vaguely familiar about the woman's voice, Kirsteen thought. Where had she heard it before?

"I've told you; they may not be sent. If I can get them out of the consignment I will. That's all I can say. General Schaumburg does not bother himself with petty details. He indicates a section and all within that section are taken. That's all there is to it."

"But, after what I've done for you . . ."

Kirsteen's eyes opened wide. It was Paulette. She would swear to it. It was Paulette's voice she was hearing, talking to someone right here in Gestapo headquarters.

23: DINING OUT

The private escorted Kirsteen to the lobby of the Hôtel Majestic, where Brigadeführer Artur Ebernach was standing talking to his chauffeur. When he saw her approaching the SS officer broke away and hurried to meet her.

"Marie! You look wonderful. I hope you're looking forward to this evening as much as I have been."

"I'm certainly looking forward to a good meal," Kirsteen said, being brutally honest.

Ebernach laughed, his blue eyes bright. "Yes! I can understand that. Come. The car's outside."

They exited through the main doors of the hotel. At the foot of the steps the chauffeur opened the door of a large, black Citroën and waited while they got in.

Kirsteen enjoyed the drive up avenue Kléber and around the Arc de Triomphe. It was a pleasant change from vélo-taxis, she thought. They proceeded down the avenue des Champs

Elysées to the place de la Concorde and then turned left.

"Where are we going?" Kirsteen asked.

"Towards Monmartre," Ebernach answered. "I've been making some discreet inquiries and I understand that the establishment of Mademoiselle Féhner is held in some regard. She makes what I'm told is the finest lingerie in France. I thought we should start you off with the basics and then move on to outer garments. What do you think?"

He smiled and Kirsteen automatically did the same. She really enjoyed Artur Ebernach, she told herself, so for that evening at least she would just forget that he was a Gestapo officer.

"You really have been doing research," she said. "I've heard of Mademoiselle Féhner, though I didn't know she sold other than directly to the top fashion houses."

"Ah! We shall see."

"And from there?" Kirsteen pursued.

"Rue de Faubourg-Monmartre has some excellent dress shops, I hear, and then -- on rue Saint-Augustin -- we can dine at Henri's. Unless you'd prefer the Coq-d'Or?"

"Oh! The Coq-d'Or! I've heard of that. Is that far from where we're shopping?"

"Not at all," he said, obviously enjoying her reactions to his suggestions. "It's right in the same general area. Would you like to eat there, Marie?"

She nodded, hoping not to seem too eager. From what she'd heard the restaurant was quite elegant but, since the Gestapo was paying for it -- or the Gestapo in the form of the SS-Brigadeführer -- why not?

The Brigadeführer spent a lot of money on new clothes for Kirsteen. She didn't object at all. At the last shop they stopped at she changed into all her new finery and they told the proprietor to burn the old clothing she left off. Then they went on to the rue Monmartre and the Coq-d'Or.

The restaurant was very busy and Kirsteen wondered where the people got the money to come there, not to mention how the restaurant was able to provide the food it did. She well knew how desperate most people were becoming for food and how some would lie, cheat, steal, and even collaborate with the occupying forces if it meant getting an extra loaf of bread.

The head waiter, with a fixed smile, led them to a table and seated them. They were not far from the small dais where a quartet played unobtrusive background music for the enjoyment of the customers. As they sat down

Ebernach nodded towards a table on the far side of the band.

"Do you see who that is?" he asked.

Trying not to be too obvious, Kirsteen glanced around to look where he indicated.

"No. Should I?"

"It's Jean Cocteau and Christian Bérard," said her companion. "I understand that one or two celebrities dine here. Last time I was here I sat at the next table to Simone de Beauvois and Jean-Paul Sartre."

The waiter brought them menus and the wine waiter hovered while Ebernach consulted the wine list.

"Is all this thanks to the black market?" Kirsteen couldn't help asking.

"No so loud," murmured the blond officer, leaning in towards her. "Yes. The black market has become an incredibly strong force throughout France, and especially in Paris. It not only controls food, it controls machine tools, stationery, clothing, electric cables, gasoline, cigarettes . . . you name it. And one thing it does prove is that despite German requisitioning there actually are goods available. It's the distribution of those goods that's in the balance."

Kirsteen thought he sounded bitter, which surprised her. She glanced around at the wide variety of German uniforms together with the well-dressed civilians; male and female.

"How on earth does it operate?" she asked.

Ebenarch paused while the waiter served the hors d'oeuvres, then continued.

"Deals are made everywhere; in bistros, on the streets, in back rooms. Do you want chickens or rabbits? Go to the shop on rue such-and-such. Do you want butter? Go and speak to so-and-so. Prices fluctuate at about twice the official rate. Even such a thing as caviar is readily available, from such places as Petrossian's, Hermès, Cartier and Boucheron. You can have your fill of whatever you fancy at Chez Laurent, Ciros, Prè Catalan, the Pavillion de l'Elysée; a dozen top restaurants. Yet cn the open market potatoes have practically disappeared and housewives stand in line for hours to get a few turnips." He took a sip of wine. "Did you know that there's a big black market operated by schoolchildren?"

Kirsteen's eyes widened.

"It's true," he continued. "In the schools the children are given vitamin-enriched candies and cookies. Many of the children pocket these and then sell them at inflated prices or trade them for other things. There's quite a market going on there."

"You've almost made me lose my appetite," Kirsteen said, with a wry smile.

"I'm sorry," he apologized. "That's the last thing I meant to do. Please, Marie, enjoy yourself. If you don't eat this someone else will, and your holding back certainly isn't going to feed anyone out on the street."

Having said that they both tucked into *canard Frédéric* and *asperges sauce hollandaise* and Artur called for a bottle of Château d'Yquem 1921.

Kirsteen felt as though she was in a dream. Two days before she had been suffering from a beating, in a cell in the basement of the Gestapo headquarters, and now here she was dining with a Gestapo officer and surrounded by the upper crust of the occupying forces. Winston Churchill was going to enjoy this one, she thought!

As the evening drew on one or two couples got up and started to move around on the postage-stamp dance-floor in front of the quartet. Artur Ebernach put down his coffee-cup, touched his napkin to his lips, and then looked intensely at Kirsteen.

"Would you care to dance, Marie?"

Her first impulse was to refuse. It just didn't seem right. But then, on reflection, she really couldn't see any sense in not enjoying herself. As Artur had said earlier, denial for herself was not going to benefit anyone else. So why deny, she thought?

"Thank you, Artur. I'd love to."

As he slipped an arm about her and propelled her onto the floor he murmured, "And thank you -- for finally calling me Artur."

It was mid-morning when Charlie Chaplin came into her room. Although she hadn't returned there until after two o'clock in the morning, Kirsteen was up and dressed; wearing a smart wool suit Artur had also bought her the previous evening.

"Congratulations, Fräulein. You've been released."

"What? What d'you mean, I've been released?"

He looked surprised. "I thought you'd be pleased. There's not many people who start out downstairs, like you did, and then get to walk away from it."

Kirsteen tried to cover her confusion.

"No! Oh, I'm sure you're right. Thank you. Yes, thank you. Of course I'm pleased." In her mind she had a thousand questions: had Artur managed to get her released? Yes, of course it was him. But would she see him before she left? If not, then when?

"Do -- do I have to see the, er, the officer before I go?" she asked, as she put her new things into the shopping bags she had acquired.

The private shrugged. "Not so far as I know, Fräulein. I just have to walk you downstairs and see you out the door." He stood to one side of the open doorway and waited.

Downstairs Kirsteen moved out through the hôtel doors. For a second she stood uncertainly on the steps then moved down them to the sidewalk. She glanced up at the hotel windows behind her but didn't know which window she was looking for. She moved off along the street towards the barrier and the avenue Kléber.

At the barrier the guard asked for her papers. Kirsteen had a moment of panic. Her papers hadn't been returned. She looked in her bag and was surprised to see them there. She handed them to the guard.

"Thank you, Mademoiselle," he said, glancing at them. "Oh! I think this is yours." He handed her a folded sheet of paper that had been tucked in with her papers. Her heart pounded.

"Thank you. Thank you very much."

She settled back as comfortably as she could in the bouncing vélo-taxi and breathed deeply. With trembling hands she opened the folded sheet of Gestapo stationery and for the third time read the short message.

"Dearest Marie -- I am still aglow from our enjoyable evening. Take good care of yourself and I will be in touch. Artur."

How could he get in touch with her, she wondered? He had no idea where she was living. Why hadn't he come to see her before she left? Why hadn't he asked her where she would be? Did he *really* want to get in touch, anyway, or was he just being polite?

Her mind was in turmoil and she later had no recollection of the journey back to the Leycurases. She was greeted with open arms and told how worried they had been. Over coffee -- black market, she thought -- Kirsteen told them most of what had happened to her. She didn't elaborate on the evening out with the Brigadeführer, simply saying that they had shared a meal. But she saw Victoire's eyes sweep over the fashionable shopping bags and take in her wool suit.

"You are certain you were not followed here?" Godefrois asked.

"Positive," she said.

But even as she said it, Kirsteen worried that she had not been paying attention to something so fundamental. Back in the hidden room she fretted that she had let them down. Supposing she *was* followed and, because of her, the Leycurases were arrested by the Gestapo and the safe house closed down?

By late morning Kirsteen was seated in the *Rescoe*, hoping that Antoine would show up. She needed to speak to him and let him know that Gaston had been packed off to Germany. But after two hours there had been no sign of him and she felt she couldn't stay sitting there. She made her way over to the church of Saint-Denis and Canon Bizien.

"Marie! How wonderful to see you, my dear." The canon's face lit up when she walked into the church. He was fussing around the altar, placing new candle in the antique holders and arranging some simple flowers. "I haven't seen you for a few days. Is everything all right?"

They sat in the front pew and she brought him up to date on her visit to the Hôtel Majestic. She didn't mention going out with Artur. He was most sympathetic when he heard how she was beaten but joined in her laughter at the fate of the repulsive Sergeant.

"Now you say you actually spoke with Stonehenge and then saw him being taken away?"

She nodded. "Yes. Canon, you've met Stonehenge. What does he ..."

"Marie!"

They both spun around. Hurrying down the aisle toward them were two figures -- Antoine and Gaston. Kirsteen came to her feet and started forward.

"Gaston! Gaston, it's you!"

They met and threw their arms around each other, hugging and laughing. Finally they broke apart.

"Can you hide him, canon?" Antoine asked. The laughter disappeared. "He's on the run from the Gestapo."

"What happened?" Kirsteen asked.

Canon Bizien ushered them all through into the robing room.

"You know I was arrested, along with Norbert and Colette? Well, I was taken to rue des Saussaies and *questioned*." He emphasized the word and looked grim. "After some days of that I was moved to avenue Foch for a few hours and then moved again and put in a cell in some building near the gare de Lyon. I think it was an old barracks, or something. There were a lot of people also locked up there. I never saw Norbert and Colette after the first day. Antoine has told me what happened to them."

"Go on."

"Well, yesterday there was a lot of activity and we were all herded out and packed into the backs of several trucks. They drove us across the city to gare du Nord and there we were held in cattle pens for two or three hours."

The canon had been boiling some water on a small gas ring. He made some weak tea and passed the cups around. Everyone drank thankfully as they continued listening to Gaston's story.

"Two people tried to escape. It wasn't hard to get out of the pens but it was difficult getting away past the guards."

"What happened to them?" Antoine asked.

"They were shot."

There was a moment's silence.

"So how did you manage to get away?" Kirsteen asked.

"It was when they brought in the goods-trains and started loading us into them. They treated us like cattle. We were pushed forward, jabbed with bayonets, beaten with rifle butts. Many people fell and were in danger of being trampled." He swallowed a mouthful of tea. "As we were being driven up the ramp into one of the cattle-cars there was a moment of chaos when an old woman slipped and her son tried to save her. He started beating people out of the way and there was a fight. The Germans climbed in and started swinging. I took the opportunity to slip down the side of the ramp against the wagon and then underneath and out the other side. There was another goods train that had just started to move slowly out of the station. I managed to get under and hang onto the bottom of a wagon. When we were clear of the station I just dropped off, before it really got up speed, and lay flat, letting it run past over me. Then I ran up the embankment and got away."

"We have to get you out of Paris," Kirsteen said. "Why don't we take him to the Leycurases and then they can pass him on down the line?"

"A good idea, Marie," agreed the canon. "Gaston, you can hide up in the bell-tower till dark. Then I'll get Michel to take you across to rue Bièvre."

"No!" Kirsteen instinctively felt that Michel should not do the job. She didn't trust him to get Gaston there safely and she didn't trust him to know the safe house of the Leycurases. "No, I'll come back and get you, Gaston. A man and a woman moving around together will be far less suspicious."

"Agreed."

24: AN INVITATION NORTH

There was a message awaiting Kirsteen when she returned to the Leycurases. Godefrois was in the shop, polishing a silver candelabra that was to be delivered to Standarten-führer Helmut Knochen, commanding officer of the Sicherheitsdienst, responsible for German external security in Paris. It was a beautiful piece, worth at least half of what the good Colonel was paying, according to Godefrois.

"Where did this message come from?" Kirsteen asked, holding the piece of plain white stationery and studying the familiar neat handwriting. *Meet me at the Trocadéro tomorrow at noon -- Artur* it said.

Leycuras paused in his polishing and looked up at her.

"It was dropped off by a Frenchman; a man I know. I didn't ask any questions."

This didn't make any sense, Kirsteen thought. First of all, how did Artur Ebernach know where she could be found and, secondly, how could a Gestapo officer make use of a presumably trusted Frenchman to deliver his messages?

"You say you know this Frenchman?"

"Oh, yes. In fact he's the son of a second cousin of mine. He's all right." He returned to his polishing.

Kirsteen arranged for Gaston to move into the safe house that evening and then left for a neighborhood hairdresser. She told herself that since she was now known by the Gestapo she might just as well return to her original dark hair color and, while she was at it, might as well have it trimmed and styled. It had nothing to do with meeting Artur, she told herself firmly, but was simply a woman's natural need to look good -- for herself!

Later that afternoon she once more made her way to the little church of Saint-Denis.

"Why, Marie! You look beautiful. If I were twenty years younger . . ." Bizien greeted her.

"Oh, stop it, Pierre!" Kirsteen felt herself blush and tried to be business-like. "Is Gaston still safe?"

"Of course, my dear. He's restless, naturally. Would rather be out and about, doing things to the Germans, but he's all right."

She climbed the bell tower and was not happy to find Michel up there with Gaston.

"Marie! Good to see you. My, but you're dressed up! Are you going somewhere?" The Frenchman's brown eyes had their old twinkle.

Kirsteen couldn't help smiling at him. "I have someone I have to see tomorrow, as a matter of fact. How are you doing, Gaston?"

"I was telling him I would take him to this safe house," Michel interrupted. "There's no need for you to put yourself out, Marie."

"I'm not putting myself out. Besides, It will be good to be doing something constructive."

"What's the matter? Don't you trust me?" Michel glowered at her from under lowered eyebrows.

Kirsteen forced herself to laugh. "Don't be absurd, Michel. It's just so long since I've seen Gaston I want to spend some time with him."

"Hey! Don't fight over me," Gaston laughed. "It's all right, Michel. Thanks. I appreciate your offer but, since Marie is staying with the Leycurases anyway, it makes sense for her to take me there. Right?"

The surly, pale-faced man tugged at his small mustache for a moment then made for the ladder.

"Makes no difference to me," he said as he started down.

Kirsteen waited till he was out of earshot.

"I'm sorry but I just don't trust that man," she said.

Gaston nodded. "I know what you mean. I get the same feeling. Why does the canon have him around?"

"I don't know. I think he was the only one who could operate the radio – or claimed that he could. And you know how trusting Pierre can be?"

That evening they made the journey across town to the antique shop with no trouble. When they first left the church Kirsteen had the feeling that they were being followed but, after some fast switching of trains on the *métro*, soon felt secure again. Godefrois and Victoire welcomed Gaston.

"We've made arrangements for you to be passed on down the line, through Orleans, Tours, Limoges and on to Toulouse. That far south you should be fine, though you will still have to be careful," Godefrois said.

"The South should stay relatively free," Victoire added. "We've been hearing lots of rumors about the Germans moving into Midi but I don't think they'll ever be too active in the South."

"I agree," Gaston said. "It'll be hard to leave all my friends here but if I can still continue the fight down there, well, that's better than nothing. And thank goodness Marie got my fake papers from the apartment. I can use those. When do I leave?"

"The pick-up is tomorrow night. You'll stay here, in the back room, all day tomorrow. At ten o'clock one of our people will call for you."

"What about tomorrow night's curfew?" Kirsteen asked.

"Don't worry about it. Everything's taken care of."

The following morning seemed to drag by. Kirsteen sat with Gaston, hidden away in the back room. They talked and they played cards. Kirsteen kept looking at her watch.

"Marie! I'm the one who's being picked up. And it's not till late this evening," Gaston said with a laugh.

"Oh! I know. I'm sorry, Gaston. As I told you, I have to meet someone at noon. I guess I'm just anxious."

"It's a young, handsome man, right?" A wide smile spread across his face.

Kirsteen felt her cheeks flush. She seemed to be doing a lot of that lately, she thought.

"Oh, Gaston!"

"Well, is it?"

She got up and put on her coat. "Maybe it is, and maybe it isn't," she said impishly. She went to the door. "Take care, Gaston. I'm sure I'll be back before you go."

He waved a hand and started dealing out a game of solitaire. "Have fun, Marie. You deserve some."

Kirsteen emerged from the *métro* at the Trocadéro stop. There were a lot of people about, since the sun was shining and it was a beautiful day. She walked between the two curved wings of the palais de Chailot and gazed out at the breath-taking view. At her feet lay the jardins du Trocadéro, centered by fountains. Directly in front, the pont d'Iéna spanned the Seine. And across on the opposite bank stood the magnificent tour d'Eiffel. For a moment she was able to forget all about the war; about her mission to find Stonehenge; even about her attraction to the Gestapo Officer. All her memories of Paris before the war came flooding back. It was truly a beautiful city. A city made for love.

"Beautiful, isn't it?" said a voice at her elbow.

She turned to find herself gazing into the blue eyes of Artur Ebernach. "Yes. Yes, it is," she said.

He took her arm and they turned to look up at the curving arms of the palais.

"This was built for the international exposition of 1878," Artur said. "But did you know that Napolean planned to have his royal palace here?"

"No, I didn't."

"In 1811 he razed the covent of the Visitandines, which was originally Catherine de Médicis' chateau, and cleared the ground for the imperial magnificence with which he intended to surround himself."

"How do you know all this?" Kirsteen asked, fascinated.

"I love Paris," he said, his eyes twinkling as he smiled down at her. "And I love that you've put your hair back to its own color. Thank you. Now we just have to wait for it to grow long again. Look!" They turned again, to gaze down the slopes to the river. "It was down there that Richard Fulton made his first experiments with a power-driven boat. Did you know that?"

They started to stroll through the crowds, Kirsteen noticing that she was not the only young woman on the arm of a uniformed German.

"I wish this war was over," Artur said, after a while.

"And Germany the winner?" Kirsteen couldn't help asking.

He was silent for a moment. "Forget winners and losers for now. That's not what's important. It's life that's important. Life . . . for individuals; for families; for all people."

"That doesn't sound like a Gestapo Bigadier-General to me," she said.

"No. It's not. It's me; Artur Ebernach." They walked on in silence. Then, "Marie. I want you to come with me to the north; to Normandy."

Thoughts of her recent trip to Falaise flashed through Kirsteen's mind. "To Normandy?"

"Yes. I have to go there to look at some fortifications. It's a beautiful part of the country, as I'm sure you know. Won't you come with me?"

"I -- I don't know. For how long?"

"Just a couple of days, then we'll be right back here, in Paris."

His eyes were pleading; his arm held hers tightly. She found it difficult to look away from him.

"All right," she said. In her mind, she immediately tried to justify her reply. Perhaps she could learn something from him? Perhaps there was military activity in Normandy that she could report on, to Churchill? After all, Kirsteen thought, she had been planning to go there originally, so why not now?

"I have to go to Caen. They -- we, that is -- we're building what is called the Atlantic Wall."

He steered her towards an outdoor café set-up near the fountains. They sat and ordered coffees.

"Are you allowed to take a friend with you?" Kirsteen asked, as she sipped the ersatz concoction.

He gave a wry smile. "No one need know," he said. "I'll be taking my car and driving myself. Not even a chauffeur to worry about."

"But what about when we get there. Papers and things?"

"I held onto those forged papers that you had before. I don't know why, except that I didn't want them to get into the wrong hands."

What did he mean by 'the wrong hands', Kirsteen thought. After all, he was Gestapo himself. "I thought you said you recognized them as forgeries," she said. "Doesn't that mean that anyone else will also recognize them?"

He sipped his coffee. "No, not necessarily. If you are with me then this uniform will ensure that no one will look closely at anything presented to them. You'll see. It's amazing what we can get away with." He grinned broadly. "It's really very useful!"

They spent what Kirsteen considered a delightful afternoon together before Artur had to excuse himself. It was necessary to get back to Gestapo headquarters to make final arrangements for the trip, he said. He squeezed her hands and looked hard into her eyes, then turned and was gone. It was only afterwards, on her way back to the Leycurases, that Kirsteen realized she hadn't asked him how he had known where to find her.

With much hugging and well-wishing, Gaston left late that evening. Kirsteen was sorry to see him go but happy to know that he would be safe. He was the first of the Resistants she had met when she had arrived in Paris almost a month before. But now she felt she was getting near the end of the trail. She had seen and spoken to a man who claimed to be Stonehenge -- perhaps he was, and there was some easy explanation for the physical discrepancies -- and she had a good contact in Gestapo headquarters. She felt confident that everything was going to work out well.

The next morning, as arranged with Artur, Kirsteen took the *métro* to the gare St. Lazare and waited at the main entrance. She had only been there five minutes when the big Citroën, with Artur at the wheel, pulled up at the curb. She ran forward and got in beside him. He pulled away again and made for the rue de Rome and the road out of Paris to the north.

It was an easy drive, with so little motorized traffic on the road, and Kirsteen spent much of the time staring at the many landmarks of the ever-beautiful city. As they made their way out through the suburbs she settled back in her seat and looked at the driver.

Artur was watching her out of the corner of his eye. He gave her the smile she was beginning to know so well.

"No regrets?"

"Regrets?"

"Coming away with me."

Kirsteen shook her head. She had made peace with herself on that score. "None at all. I'm determined to enjoy it."

"Good."

"Artur?" She had a sudden idea and thought to pursue it. "When I was, well, in the basement of the Majestic, I made contact with a man held there, in another room."

Her blond companion's eyebrows rose slightly, though he said nothing.

"We got to talking . . ."

"Talking?"

"Well, tapping out messages on a pipe. You know."

"Yes," he said, quietly. "Yes, I suppose I do."

"He said his name was Stonehenge." She pretended not to notice when his head turned sharply towards her, then went back to watching the road. "Do you know the one I mean?"

For the longest while Artur said nothing. Kirsteen was beginning to wonder if she had spoiled the whole relationship. She hadn't meant to but she thought it was an opportunity not to be missed.

"What did this Stonehenge say to you?" Artur said eventually.

"Oh, nothing much. Just that he'd been there a few days." She chuckled. "He heard the commotion when I bit the Sergeant."

A slight smile touched the corners of Artur's mouth.

"So why are you so interested in this man?" he asked.

"I'm not really interested," she protested. "Just curious. What happened to him? I'd hate to think that he might have been executed."

Artur let out a long sigh. Kirsteen waited.

"As a matter of fact," he said, "Your Stonehenge managed to escape."

25: CAEN

The entry into the Forbidden Zone was anticlimactic for Kirsteen. Artur stopped at the barrier which stretched across the road and handed their papers to the guard. As he had predicted, the sentry barely glanced at them before returning them. He stepped back and saluted as Artur put the Citroën in gear and moved on through. They drove through some of the beautiful Normandy countryside until they saw the outskirts of Caen in the distance.

"Now it's my understanding that the 716th Infantry Division is based here," Artur said, as he maneuvered along the road, overtaking a long convoy of army vehicles. "There's the 352nd to the immediate west and the 711th to the east." He looked hard at Kirsteen. "You've got that? The 716th, 352nd, and 711th."

Kirsteen nodded, wondering why he was making such a point of listing the infantry divisions along that part of the coast. Surely that information was secret, she thought? She gave a little gasp. Artur was passing on German secret information to her! What was going on?

"Hold on and sit tight," Artur said as he suddenly pulled in to a gateway entrance to a field and stopped. Up ahead Kirsteen could see there were two Küblerwagens and a staff car parked. Artur got out and walked forward to them. A small group of officers and NCOs were huddled over the hood of the staff car, apparently studying a map. As Artur approached they straightened up and saluted him. She saw him return the salute and then stand talking with them.

A seemingly never-ending line of heavily-laden army trucks trundled past the Citroën while Kirsteen sat there. She noticed that most of them had their cargo well covered with camouflage tarpaulins. Glancing up, Kirsteen saw the group of officers all laughing at something Artur had said, then again salute as he turned and walked back to the car.

"We're doing fine," he said as he got in. "There's a pleasant hôtel on the right, as we go into town, and there's at least one good restaurant." He restarted the car and pulled out. As they passed the group by the roadside they all again saluted him.

"You seem to have a lot of influence here," Kirsteen said.

Artur laughed. "It's not me. It's the uniform. Remember that."

The sight of apple trees reminded Kirsteen of her short visit to Falaise, not too far to the south of Caen.

"I see the anemones are in full bloom," she said. "Oh! And I hope the hôtel does the chicken and duck pie this part of the country's famous for."

"That's what I like," Artur chuckled. "A woman who enjoys her food!"

They both laughed.

"What exactly do you have to do here?" she asked, gazing out of the window at a brilliant display of camellias.

"It's top secret," he said. But then, to Kirsteen's surprise, he went on to tell her. "The Germans are attempting to build what Hitler calls the 'Atlantic Wall'. It's going to stretch along the entire coast, from Amsterdam through Boulogne along to Brest and on down to Bayonne."

"A wall?"

"Not literally a wall," he said. "Although in many sections, yes, it will be a huge length of steel-reinforced concrete. But for most areas it will simply be a wall of defenses; panzer divisions, infantry divisions, sea and beach defenses and the like."

"Will it work?"

Artur shrugged. "If they can stop squabbling amongst themselves as to who's in charge and what should be put where, yes, it might. Hitler seems to think that the most threatened areas are the two west coast peninsulas, Cherbourg and Brest. Other people have other ideas. Many of the smarter generals seem to think they should be concentrating on the Pas-de-Calais."

They were coming into the town now and kept their eyes open for the hôtel.

"There it is!" Kirsteen cried, pointing off to the right. "It looks kind of plain, but at least it's probably clean."

At the desk the elderly proprietor shook his head sadly, scratching his thinning grey hair.

"I don't know, sir. It doesn't look as though we've got much to offer. Things have been keeping pretty busy around here, it seems, what with all the army people and all."

Kirsteen was surprised at a sudden change in Artur. He rapped his knuckles on the desk and spoke in a very harsh tone.

"I've told you, I need two adjoining rooms on the first floor. You will move somebody out if necessary. Do you understand me?"

The man behind the desk paled. "Y-yes, General. Of course, sir. I'll arrange it, don't you worry." He turned quickly to an old woman sitting sorting bills at a desk behind the counter. "Agathe! Move yourself! Get some clean linen for the general and his lady, here."

He hurried her off and Artur and Kirsteen were left alone. She looked at him from under lowered eyelids. He smiled at her.

"Don't get worried. It's still me. Remember what I said about the uniform? I'm just using it to get us some rooms. So some German soldiers have to double up in something smaller for a night? I think they'll survive, don't you?"

He reached out and took her hand, drawing her closer to him. Kirsteen relaxed again at his touch.

"I - I suppose you're right. It was just the sudden change in you that surprised me . . . and kind of frightened me."

"I'm sorry for that. Truly sorry. But it wasn't a real change, Marie, believe me. It was just an act."

They hadn't eaten so they went off in search of a restaurant while their rooms were made up. Soon Kirsteen was tucking into her chicken and duck pie and laughing at Artur's jokes.

"We'll get you settled in your room," he said, "and then I'm going to have to leave you for an hour or two. I have to meet with some officers and do a short tour of inspection. I'll be back for dinner and then we can relax."

"Sounds good to me," Kirsteen said, spooning into a sherbert. "I'll take the opportunity to have a short nap."

As she dressed for dinner, Kirsteen's thoughts were in a turmoil. She couldn't understand what Artur was doing with her. He had brought her into the aptly named Forbidden Zone and had shared some delicate pieces of information with her. When he spoke of the Germans it was almost as though he wasn't one of them. He had made sure she remembered certain things he had said and certainly seemed to have forgotten that she was a French Resistant. Yet he was still very much the German officer and was obviously treated with respect by other ranking Germans. She decided to just go along with things and see what transpired. If nothing else she would have much valuable information to pass on to the British -- supposing that she came out of all this alive, of course.

They dined at a small restaurant in the center of Caen. What it lacked in food quantity and quality it made up for in ambience. They shared a candle-lit booth at the back of the restaurant, away from the traffic of the waiters. There was one lone accordion player who strolled among the tables, playing old French tunes very well and German tunes very badly. Most of the tables were occupied by soldiers, of all ranks. There were few women present, Kirsteen noticed.

As they finished the meal the waiter brought over two glasses of <u>calvados</u>, the local apple brandy, and a plate of sugar cubes.

"What are these for?" Kirsteen asked, indicating the sugar.

"It's another local custom," Artur replied. "Here. I'll show you."

He picked up a sugar cube and dunked it in his brandy, then sucked on it with obvious enjoyment. "Try it," he said.

She found it delicious. As they sucked the sugar and then sipped the brandy, the old musician came to their table and played a number of romantic pieces. Artur picked up a sugar cube, dunked it in his brandy and then held it to Kirsteen's lips. As she gazed into his vivid blue eyes she sucked the liquor from it, laughed, and then did the same to him.

Artur thanked the musician and tucked two hundred francs in his pocket. Beaming, the accordion-player moved on. Artur again leaned forward and took both of Kirsteen's hands in his.

"Marie, I can't tell you how much I'm enjoying having you here with me." She opened her mouth to reply but he shook his head. "No. Let me continue. I'm sure you're finding it strange that a German officer -- a Gestapo officer at that -- should be doing what I'm doing." She nodded. "I'm sure this isn't typical of the Gestapo."

"Not of the popular conception of the Gestapo, anyway," she laughed.

"I know. Ah, Marie!" He looked around him. There was no one at the tables immediate to them and the musician was entertaining the people at the next closest table. "I have to admit that I'm not all that I seem. For now just let me say that I'm not in sympathy with Adolf Hitler. Not now and never have been."

"Artur!" Kirsteen squeezed his hands. "It would be dangerous for anyone to know that, wouldn't it?"

"Oh, don't worry. I don't generally go around announcing it," he laughed. "It's just that, at this moment it's important for me to let you know this. Of course I'm not alone in my feelings about the Führer."

She raised her eyebrows questioningly.

"Even General Karl-Heinrich von Stülpnagel, our esteemed German Military Governor in France, has many reservations, it seems. I've heard rumors that there may be a plot in the offing, somewhere down the line, to assassinate Hitler."

Kirsteen gasped. "Really? When? Any idea?"

He shook his head. "No. If it's true then it's in very early stages yet. But it's amazing that there are some big names involved, along with von Stülpnagel. Colonel Hans Speidel, who was Chief of Staff to the Militärbefehlshaber in Paris until he went to the Russian front in March, is of like mind I know."

"I haven't heard any rumors about a plot."

"I'm not surprised. This is something that could be *extremely* dangerous to a German officer, no matter how high his rank, if there were even the slightest suspicion. No! I think it may be a year or two before it comes to fruition but I'm pretty sure Hitler will eventually rub too many people the wrong way."

He signaled the waiter for some more coffee. Kirsteen joined him. It was real coffee; certainly from the black market. It was delicious.

"We have other things to think about right now," Artur continued. "In a couple of days or so we have another dangerous man arriving."

Kirsteen put down her cup and gave him her full attention. "Who's that?"

"General Karl Oberg. He's being sent to Paris as *Höherer SS und Polizeiführer*. That's Supreme Head of the SS and of the Police."

"And you say he's a dangerous man?"

"He's a vicious anti-Semite. I hear he once dismissed a complaint about the abduction of Jewish orphans by saying that Jews were not human beings!"

"Oh, my God," Kirsteen whispered. She knew that the German's pressure on the Jews was constantly increasing but she had no idea to what extent. She'd heard from the *Réseau* groups about Jews being rounded up by the trainload and sent off to camps in Germany, but she'd taken some of the reports with a pinch of salt. "This is going to make a big difference?"

"To the Jews, of course. But also to the whole state and pace of the war and to the extent of reprisals by Resistants. I don't believe that decent human beings, whether in Britain or in occupied France, are going to sit back and let any atrocities happen. And with Oberg we can expect atrocities."

They discussed the possible path the war might take and the roles of the Resistants until after midnight. By that time the proprietor was standing by the entrance to the restaurant, obviously hoping the last few stragglers would leave. Most of the tables were empty and the musician had long since left. Artur and Kirsteen reluctantly got to their feet and, with a word of thanks to the man at the door, passed out into the night.

They drove back to the hotel in silence, Kirsteen soaking up the initial warm mood of the evening and of the intimacy that had developed between her and Artur. She glanced at him many times; sometimes just at the same moment that he was sneaking a look at her. They'd both laugh but say nothing.

Outside the door to her room they paused and Artur slipped his arms about her.

"Thank you, Marie."

"For what?"

"For everything. For just being. You don't know how much I needed someone like you right now; someone I could talk to."

"You can always talk to me, Artur."

They kissed. It was long and warm. His arms tightened around her and Kirsteen hugged him back. Her head began to spin but she put it down to the brandy. Finally he broke away, though keeping his hands on her hips.

"We -- we do have adjoining rooms, don't we?" she murmured.

He nodded.

"Perhaps you should — I mean, would you like to come through my room . . . to get to yours?"

He never made it to his room.

26: CATASTROPHE

Artur moved around to the passenger side of the car and opened the door. As Kirsteen stepped out of the Citroën, on the Champs-Elysées, she almost bumped into two men.

"Pardon me, Mademoiselle," said one of them as he swung to one side.

"I'm sorry," said Kirsteen, "I . . ."

Her voice stuck in her throat. The two men were Greyhound and Michel.

"I'll be in touch in a couple of days," said Artur, not noticing her shocked state and giving her a quick kiss on the cheek. Then he went back to the driver's side and got into the car. He waved as he drove off and Kirsteen, still numb, half-heartedly waved back.

"So - o - o!" Michel said. "That's the way things are, is it?"

"Wait! No, you don't understand." Kirsteen tried to pull herself together. "Grey--, Claude! I can explain."

Greyhound smiled and nodded. "Don't worry, Marie. I'm not one quick to judge. I'm sure you know what you're doing.'

"I just bet she does," Michel sneered. "Playing both sides, eh, Marie? Pierre will be interested to hear about this.'

"Now just you wait a minute, Michel," snapped Greyhound. "I trust Marie and I'd suggest you do the same. She'll tell us what we need to know when she's good and ready. Until then -- we just keep this to ourselves. Understand?"

Michel said nothing but eyed Kirsteen darkly.

"I said, do you understand?" Greyhound spoke forcefully.

"Sure. Sure I do. I think maybe I'll see you two later." Michel turned on his heel and moved off amongst the people on the boulevard.

"Let's find a café," Kirsteen said.

One of the joys of the avenue des Champs-Elysées was that, even in wartime, you didn't have to walk far to find a sidewalk café. They were soon seated side by side at a little table on the outer edge of a crowded bistro.

"The Gestapo officer I just left is the one who interrogated me at the Hôtel Majestic," Kirsteen started out.

"Ah!" Greyhound said enigmatically.

"He seems somehow -- attracted -- to me, and I've been kind of playing on that." She listened to herself and could hardly believe what she was saying.

"Marie . . . Casey!" He looked her hard in the eyes. "You've got your work to do and I've got mine. Just tell me one thing -- is everything all right?"

"Yes. Yes, Greyhound, it is. It really is!" She reached out and squeezed his hand.

He smiled. "Then that's all that matters. You're a big girl. You know the stakes in this crazy but dangerous war. I've no idea what your assignment is, and don't want to know. But I respect however you decide you need to go about it. Don't worry about Michel. I'll keep an eye on him."

"Thank you. Thank you very much, Claude." She leant forward and kissed the little Gypsy on his cheek. For the first time she saw him blush. "Oh, by the way. I meant to tell you. I think I overheard Paulette speaking to a Gestapo man at the Hôtel Majestic."

"What?"

Quickly she told her friend what she had overheard and how she would swear it was Paulette's voice.

"This make sense," Greyhound said.

"It does?"

He nodded. "Yes. If the Gestapo is holding Paulette's parents then they could be putting pressure on her to act as an agent for them among the Resistants. In return for not harming her parents -- or not shipping them off to a camp in Germany -- she has to provide them with information on our activities. '

"You think she was responsible for turning-in Gaston and the others?"

"It's possible. And for you being picked up in Falaise."

"God! I wouldn't want her conscience after what happened to Norbert and Collette."

"I doubt she's proud of herself, if it *was* her," Greyhound said. "But her parents' safety probably comes before anything else for her."

Kirsteen nodded. She wouldn't have wanted to be put in such a situation, she thought. "Oh! And something else," she said. "Stonehenge has escaped."

"He has? I heard from Pierre about your contact with him, at the Majestic. He's free again?"

"Yes. You've been briefed on Stonehenge, Claude. What does he look like?"

Greyhound looked surprised but asked no questions. "He's tall. Blond. Has a decided 'English public school' accent, though I understand he speaks both French and German like a native, not to mention Spanish and Italian. He's ..."

"That's enough," she said. "That's pretty much what I thought. Claude, the man I spoke to, who claims to be Stonehenge and has now escaped, is nothing like that. I mean, physically. He's dark and on the short side."

"And yet you say he claimed to be Stonehenge?"

She nodded.

"Well, if he's now out and about again we should soon run into him. We'll have to get him to explain himself." He scrambled to his feet. "All right! I was on an errand with that French creep, Michel. *He's* the one I'd never trust. I'd better get on with it. Take care of yourself, Marie."

He dropped some francs on the table and then hurried away. Kirsteen sighed and drained the unpleasant brew in her cup.

"It's a rail depot that's important to the Germans," the canon said. "You all know it, I'm sure. Out at porte de Clichy."

"Marshalling yards, isn't that what they call them?" Hélène asked.

"That's right. We got a message from London asking if we could do anything to disrupt services there."

They all sat around the bell-tower: Canon Bizien, Antoine, Greyhound, Michel, Albert, Hélène, Elise, Lucie and Kirsteen. Kirsteen had roughly filled them in on her trip up to the Forbidden Zone, though without going into any details.

"I'd like to use the radio later tonight, Pierre, if I may? I need to contact someone," she had said.

"Of course, my dear. Of course."

Kirsteen was thankful that Michel had remained silent, though he had fixed her with a baleful stare all evening. She thankfully noticed that Greyhound sat close beside Michel, watching him in turn.

"Tell us exactly what you want to do, Pierre," Albert said to the canon.

"Well, I've given it some thought and I think we should be able to disrupt the whole system if we can blow up the lines north of the yards; that's where they all come together."

"I took a ride out there today," said Greyhound, looking at Kirsteen. "The greatest concentration of lines is at rue Henri, but we need to strike just after the line crosses rue de Neuilly."

"What's security like?" Kirsteen asked.

"Not bad," Greyhound responded. "They're so busy patrolling the yards themselves that they seem to have overlooked the main line that runs into and out of there. If that's broken they're not going anywhere and nothing is coming in."

"Will we all fit into my dad's van?" Lucie asked, uncertainly, looking around and mentally counting them all.

"Don't worry about that," the canon said. "Claude, Michel and myself will travel up separately. We'll rendez-vous at the site."

"You're going too, Pierre?" Kirsteen asked.

"Oh, yes! I'm not going to miss all the fun!"

They discussed the details and set a time for the following night that would still allow them all to get home before curfew. As they broke up Kirsteen noticed that Michel scuttled off down the ladder before anyone else.

"He seems in a hurry," she murmured to Greyhound.

"Running back to his garret and his shrunken head collection," Greyhound chuckled.

Canon Bizien walked with Kirsteen over to the neighboring church of Sainte-Eleanore. There they climbed to its bell-tower and pulled out the radio transmitter.

"You're contacting London, aren't you, Marie?" he asked her, matter-of-factly.

She nodded, saying nothing as she set up the antenna wire.

"I somehow knew you weren't just a schoolteacher from Lyon," he said, happily. "You've obviously been trained in various things. And your name's not really Marie, is it?"

Kirsteen smiled at his friendly face and shook her head. "But it's good enough for now," she said.

"Oh, I agree. I wouldn t dream of asking . . ." his voice trailed off and he settled to watching her lay out her code book and check the time on her watch.

"Is the time important?" he asked.

"Oh, yes. If I'm going to transmit then it should be at either six minutes past the hour or thirty-eight minutes past, so they know it's really me."

"Why those times?"

Kirsteen smiled. "It's a long story, Pierre. But it's to do with the engine number of a railroad locomotive driven by a man named Casey Jones. Engine number 638."

He nodded understandingly, though she knew he had no idea what she was talking about. She placed the headphones over her ears, switched on the power and tested the batteries. They were fine. She ran her finger down the lines of figures in the code book and started tapping the Morse key.

It was raining and Kirsteen turned up her collar as she climbed out of the delivery van. They were parked on rue Baudin, a block away from rue de Neuilly. Once again the six of them tucked flour sacks containing explosives under their coats and hurried along to the rendez-vous point.

They found the three men huddled under a tree in a yard backing onto the railroad lines. Kirsteen dropped down between Greyhound and the canon.

"This weather should help," she said.

"Why's that?" Elise asked. "I think it stinks!" She pulled her beret down over her ears so that her eyes just peeped out from under its edge.

"Guards are apt to be less watchful in bad weather," Kirsteen said.

"You seem to know a lot about it," Hélène commented.

"Just common sense," Greyhound put in. "Who's going to be sticking his head out in the rain if he doesn't have to?"

"So what's the plan, Pierre?" Albert asked.

"We'll blow at three points," the canon said. "Let's break up into three groups. One group -- let's say myself, Marie and Antoine -- will go down to the track about a hundred meters south of here. You, Claude, go with Michel and Elise, right down here, below where we are. And Albert, Lucie and Hélène move about a hundred meters north and go down to the track, just before it crosses rue Victor. We'll set the timers for twenty minutes."

They all moved off through the rain; dark figures blending in with the shadows of the embankment. Kirsteen stuck close behind the cleric with Antoine bringing up the rear. When they felt they'd gone far enough down the line they slipped and slid down to the level of the tracks and cautiously looked up and down the track.

"There should be no traffic at this time of night," Bizien said. "I understand there's an extra-long goods train due out about dawn, but that's going to be out of luck. Come on! Let's get this explosive in place."

Kirsteen and the canon bent to the task of placing the explosive and setting the timer while Antoine stood nervously keeping watch, looking up and down the track. As Kirsteen wiped rain from her face and peered closely at the timer she heard what sounded like a loud crack and then something heavy fell on top of her. It was

Antoine. Suddenly the night came alive with the sound of rifle fire.

"*Mon Dieu!* We've been caught out!" Bizien cried.

"Run, Pierre! Damnit, run!" Kirsteen shouted and, pushing Antoine's body to one side, sprinted as fast as she could up the embankment away from the tracks.

She saw a junction box in the gloom ahead of her and dived down beside it. A bullet ricocheted off the metal of the box. She flung herself up the slope in an erratic line, diving into some bushes at the top. Another bullet whined over her head as she rolled from one set of bushes to another. She half came to her feet and launched herself over a low wooden fence into the back garden of a house. She landed on her knees and felt one of them hit a rock. Limping, she was on her feet and across a vegetable garden, trampling plants and cursing as her feet tangled in string marking rows of vegetables. She flung herself into a tiny, wooden, garden shed and tried to catch her breath.

From the direction of the railroad tracks the shooting died down. There was much shouting in German and she heard someone, probably an NCO, calling the men together. She had no way of knowing if any of the others had escaped and she knew she couldn't stay where she was. She just needed to catch her breath and then get out of there before a search party came up the embankment and along through the houses.

She moved to the door of the shed and carefully eased it open. The hinges on the door squeaked.

"Aha! Now it's my turn!"

The door was yanked open and a small, dark figure leapt in on her, bearing her to the ground. It was obviously not a German soldier and it didn't take Kirsteen long to realize that it was Michel. He had knocked the wind out of her and was laughing asininely. He clamped an arm across her throat, putting all of his weight on it, and thrust the other hand under her coat, groping for her breast. She felt him pressing his body against her, trying hard to force her legs apart with his own. The suddenness of the attack had her at a disadvantage. His breath came in great gasps, blowing in her face, reeking of garlic and cheap wine.

"Oh, no you don't, my lad!"

Another slight figure appeared in the doorway, silhouetted against the faint light of the night sky. Kirsteen had a vague image of a shovel lifting and then being brought down with a dull thud. Michel's body went limp and she was able to push it off.

"Greyhound! Oh, Greyhound! Thank God!"

She burst into tears. The Gypsy knelt and held her briefly.

"I've been watching Master Michel," he said. "I thought it strange that he insisted on keeping watch from up on the embankment, the other side of the tracks. I half expected the bloody Germans to come out of the woodwork so I was one up on them. Obviously he informed on us. I just chased after the runt and saw him dash in here. He must have seen you go to ground and thought his time had come."

"So it has, in a sense," Kirsteen muttered, pulling herself together and getting to her feet. "I owe you, Greyhound."

"No you don't. Come on! We've got to get out of here."

"What about Michel?" It was an idle query. She really didn't care about the nasty little Frenchman.

"I really laid into him with that shovel," Greyhound said. "But if he comes out of it, then we'll meet again, believe me. For now, leave him for the Germans. Come on, let's get going."

27: REPORT AND QUESTIONS

Kirsteen slept soundly, as much from nervous exhaustion as anything else. It was nearly midday when she awoke in her secret room at the Leycurases. She woke to learn, from Victoire, that Greyhound was waiting to see her.

As she got dressed Kirsteen thought of the previous evening's fiasco. It had taken over an hour for Greyhound and her to work their way around to where the van was parked. They had then waited there a further hour to see if any of the others would show up. No one did. Since it was after curfew they drove the van slowly, and without lights, in a circuitous route back toward the antique shop but ran out of gas more than a mile short of their destination.

Greyhound accompanied Kirsteen to the Leycurases, the two of them dodging from doorway to doorway to avoid being seen by any Germans. Then he faded away into the night.

"Good morning, Greyhound. How do you feel this morning?"

"Not too bad, considering, Casey. Have your breakfast and I'll fill you in on what I've learned."

Kirsteen poured herself a cup of tea and buttered a piece of toast. "Have you heard anything of the canon?"

The little man nodded. "Yes. He was wounded but he got away."

"Oh, thank God for that!"

"Mmm. But it seems he was the only one. All of the others were either shot or captured."

"Oh, no! How badly hurt is the canon?" Kirsteen asked.

"He took a bullet in the arm, so he was lucky. But he lost a lot of blood in the time it took him to get out of there. He's at a doctor right now."

Kirsteen looked up from pouring her second cup of tea.

"A doctor? Is that wise? I mean, I know he needs one but..."

"It's all right." Greyhound held up his hand. "Don't worry. This doctor is one that the Resistants have used any number of times. He's safe."

Kirsteen breathed a sigh of relief. "But you say no one else got away?"

"No. I've got people out there trying to find out exactly what the score was; who might still be alive. It's going to take some time."

Kirsteen nodded, her face glum. "And -- Michel?"

Greyhound decided he would also have a cup of tea and busied himself with it so that he didn't have to look Kirsteen in the eyes.

"It seems I got a bit carried away in my feelings about the man . . . he was dead when the Germans found him." He added some sugar and stirred the cup. "That *was* a heavy shovel, you know."

Kirsteen sighed. "Well, I don't think I'll lose any sleep over that. Thank you again, for rescuing me, Greyhound."

He waved away the thanks. "I've got some other news too."

"Oh?"

"I found Paulette and she's connected up with Stonehenge -- as I figured she would when he escaped from the Gestapo."

"Great! Where are they?"

"They're both a bit gun-shy but they've agreed to meet with you whenever you say," he answered. "Though they've both got out of Paris for a while and are lying low in Fontainbleau."

"Fontainbleau? Darn! I don't have time to get there first," Kirsteen said, her brow furrowing.

"What d'you mean?" Greyhound asked.

"I didn't tell you. I've arranged to be picked up tonight. I've got to fly back to London again for a debriefing."

The Gypsy shook his head and chuckled. "Boy, Casey! You go back and forth like a shuttlecock. When will you be back?"

"Two days; three at the most," she said. "It depends on how soon I can see . . . someone."

He nodded, not pressing her. "All right. I'll set up a meeting for four days from now. That should give you enough time. If you can't make it, I'm sure you can get word to the Leycurases somehow."

It was Kirsteen's turn to nod. "But I'll be here, Greyhound. I've waited too long to see Stonehenge. Believe me I'll be here."

The pick-up went well until the take-off. Kirsteen ran out and grabbed the ladder, pulling herself up and into the cockpit as the big Westland Lysander started its run across the field. She had just sat down and slid the cockpit cover forward when the plane bucked and the engine roared. She grabbed hold of the sides of her seat, since she hadn't yet had time to strap herself in, and hung on for dear life. There was a cracking sound and the plane reared up and almost stalled. The pilot -- Wing Commander "Mouse" Fielden again -- quickly pushed the nose down and advanced the throttle. The airplane steadied and roared on up into the night sky.

"Sorry about that, my dear," his voice came over the intercom. "Trifle dodgy there for a moment. Not to worry. Off we go now!"

"What happened?" Kirsteen asked, strapping herself in securely.

"Bloody telephone wires," came the response. "Just clipped them with the gear. Damn short field for a take-off!"

The rest of the journey was uneventful until half way across the English Channel. Suddenly the airplane bucked again as there came a loud report right alongside the pilot's canopy. He threw the airplane into a banked climb and gave it full throttle.

"Hang on!"

The airplane climbed rapidly then did a wing-over and roared seaward. As it flattened out and came around Kirsteen heard the rattle of its guns; one Browning 0.303" machinegun in each of the wheel fairings. Then the plane climbed again, swung to the right and settled down once more to a smooth and steady course.

"What was all that about, Mouse?" Kirsteen asked.

"Bloody cheek!" came back the reply. "Damn U-boat took a pot-shot at us. Made a nasty hole in one of my ailerons. But I soon made him dive down again!"

London never changes, Kirsteen thought as she came out of her flat on Duke Street. She gazed around at the familiar skyline and the people going about their business as if the war wasn't going on. Indeed the only immediate signs of it seemed to be the small, square, cardboard or leather-covered cases hanging from everybody's shoulder, containing a gas mask in case of attack.

When she'd been picked up at Tempsford Kirsteen had been informed that she was to be ready for "an appointment" at ten the next morning. Sure enough, the now familiar black Humber sat at the curb waiting for her. She got in and the chauffeur closed the door. In no time they were turning into Whitehall and running along, past Horse Guards' Parade and the Cenotaph.

George Rance met her as usual and, wearing her Visitor's Pass pinned to her coat lapel, Kirsteen followed him along and down to Winston Churchill's office.

"You've cut your hair, Casey," was the Prime Minister's first comment.

She smiled. "You should have seen me as a blonde," she said.

His eyebrows went up but he said nothing.

"It's all part of a long story, sir," she said.

She sat down to tell it to him. He made copious notes as she progressed, questioning her closely about the army divisions along the coast of Normandy and the convoy she had seen there. She didn't enlighten him as to the exact relationship that had developed between herself and the SS-Brigadeführer but merely hinted that Artur might have a romantic interest in her.

"Be very careful, Casey," was all Churchill said.

"I will, sir. Never fear."

"Now you say this Gestapo officer told you of a plot to assassinate Hitler?"

"He said there were rumors of it, yes sir," she said.

"And he named the German Military Governor, von Stülpnagel, and this other Colonel?"

"Hans Speidel, yes sir. Though he did emphasize that it wasn't going to happen any time soon. I got the impression that everyone was feeling out everyone else on this and that they were all being extremely cautious."

"As well they might be," Churchill said. "This is dynamite, Casey, dynamite!" The pen scribbled away in the notebook.

When Kirsteen had finished her whole story the Prime Minister sat back and studied her thoughtfully.

"You've done very well, Casey," he said. "Even better than I expected. The news of this Oberg's imminent arrival in Paris bodes ill, I'm afraid. We must look into that a little further. But, yes, you've done well! You've been involved in sabotage -- some successful; some not -- you've been a prisoner of the Gestapo . . . and a guest! And you've located Stonehenge and have an appointment to see him when you get back, you say?"

"Correct, sir. But I'm disturbed by the description you gave me and the fact that it doesn't match the person I saw briefly at the Hôtel Majestic."

He put his hands together, making a steeple of his fingers and thrust out his lower lip in what Kirsteen was coming to know as a characteristic pose. For a moment he said nothing. Then he lowered his hands and looked at her.

"This disturbs me, too, Casey, but there's nothing we can do but speculate for now. Better to wait until you meet the man and see what he has to say. It will be interesting to see if he has the true Stonehenge's code book and if he admits to using it to send those suspect messages we received a while back."

"There's no question, I'm sure, sir, that the true Stonehenge is the tall blond one?" she asked.

"No question whatsoever," he replied. "No! If your man is shorter and dark he is *not* Stonehenge. The question, of course, is who is he and why is he claiming to be Stonehenge? Indeed, how does he even know of Stonehenge?"

The Prime Minister picked one of his cigars out of the humidor and held it under his nose, sniffing it. He looked up at the clock on the wall, which showed there was still half an hour to go before noon, and grudgingly returned the cigar to its place.

"Still not smoking before noon, sir?" Kirsteen asked, smiling.

"Ah! You remember? Well, of course you do. You have a mind for details, which is why I wanted you in the first place. Now tell me, my dear, what is the attitude of the people, the regular Parisian, to those who operate the black market?"

It was past one in the afternoon before Kirsteen left Whitehall. She had gone over everything she could think of with the Prime Minister and he had asked many searching questions, scribbling furiously in his notebook as she answered. He seemed very pleased with all that she told him and commended her on her progress.

"This Greyhound has no idea of your connection with me, of course?" he had asked.

"No, sir. But he is an extremely capable man and I did want you to know of his assistance to me."

"Mmm. Mmm." Churchill's head had nodded up and down.

She spent the rest of the day roaming around the shops and stores of London. She didn't spend much money but just absorbed the sights and sounds of the British people she knew and loved. She even took a bus and drove past Queen Charlotte's Hospital, her eyes misting slightly at the thought of all the time she had spent working the floors there, staying long hours and silently cursing Matron. She smiled to herself as the bus moved on along Marylebone Road.

The following evening she was picked up and driven out to Tempsford for the trip back to enemy territory.

28: SOME QUESTIONS ANSWERED

Greyhound had somehow arranged for the use of a small, red, Panhard automobile and he picked up Kirsteen at the Leycurases to drive them both down to Fontainebleau. Only seven thousand cars were licensed in Paris, with the feldgendarmerie supervising traffic and permits (by contrast there were nearly two million bicycles). Greyhound proudly showed her the excellent forged documents he had that would prove to any German who demanded to see them that he was entitled to have the petrol to drive the car. They went out of Paris to the south, by way of the porte d'Orléans.

"It would be so nice if this was just a pleasant excursion out to see the Palace of Fontainebleau," Kirsteen sighed. "It's been years since I've admired the Louis XV staircase, the ballroom and the Napoléonic rooms."

"Not to mention the gardens," Greyhound agreed. "But those days are gone, I'm afraid. Who knows if they'll ever be back."

"Whereabouts are Paulette and this 'Stonehenge'?"

"Apparently they're holed up in a safe house on rue Saint-Honoré, some blocks west of the palace. I've got the address. It's off boulevard de Constance. It's going to be interesting to see this Stonehenge and find out just who he is."

"My contact in London confirmed that the real one is as we said -- tall and fair-haired," Kirsteen said. "So, yes, this will be interesting. I wonder if Paulette's trying to pull something new and she's somehow behind this?"

They arrived without incident and parked the car some distance from the house, walking there while assuring themselves that they were not being followed. Paulette herself opened the door to them.

"Marie! Claude! Come in, come in!"

They entered the small, insignificant house and followed Paulette through into the kitchen, where a young, dark-haired man got up from the table and came to meet them. It was the man Kirsteen had seen at the Hôtel Majestic.

"Greetings!" he said, shaking their hands warmly. "I'm glad we finally get to meet. You're sure you weren't followed?"

"Trust me," Greyhound said. "We're old hands at this game."

"Of course. Of course. Sit down."

Paulette turned and smiled brightly at Kirsteen. She seemed very pleased with herself, Kirsteen thought, as she said "So, Marie, you finally get to meet Stonehenge."

"So it seems," she replied. "Though he and I did have a brief conversation -- if you can call it that -- in the cells of the Hôtel Majestic."

"Of course!" He beamed. "Now I remember where I've seen you before. I was trying to think. So you're Marie?"

"And you're Stonehenge?"

Kirsteen felt Greyhound tapping her foot under the table. She glanced at him and saw him give the very slightest shake of his head. She smiled back at him.

"Tell me, Stonehenge," Greyhound said, "How did you get captured and how long were you held?"

"I told you, everyone was swearing that you were missing," Paulette said to the other man, taking his hand in hers. "Of course, you were a prisoner for a short while, when Marie saw you, but you weren't gone all that long, were you?"

The short man shook his head. "No. I did lie low for a while but I was only in Gestapo hands for about two weeks or so."

"Tell me," Kirsteen said. "When you were 'lying low', did you send any messages to London?"

His eyes flicked to Paulette's then back to meet Kirsteen's.

"Why do you ask?"

"The main reason I was sent over here was to contact you," Kirsteen said. "I understand you sent a message just before I arrived."

"You came to France from England?" Paulette's jaw sagged. "You're not a schoolteacher from Lyons?"

"I told you from the start that it was important I meet Stonehenge," Kirsteen said. "But let's get back to this message. Do you have your code book?" Her eyes locked onto those of the man sitting opposite her. She noticed his waver.

"Of course," he said.

"May I see it?"

"I don't see ..."

"We'd like to see it!" Greyhound said.

"Now see here ..." Paulette got to her feet.

Greyhound slowly came to his feet also, revealing that he was holding a gun. Kirsteen recognized it as a 9mm Beretta model 34; an automatic she had herself been drawn to before deciding on the Walther.

"What the . . . are you Gestapo?" the other man asked, his face grim.

Greyhound shook his head.

"No. Far from it. But we don't happen to believe that you are who you claim to be."

"Let's see that code book," Kirsteen said.

The man moved his hand to his pocket.

"Slowly!" Greyhound snapped.

When the book was dropped on the table Kirsteen pulled it across to her and examined it. She looked up at Greyhound.

"This is Stonehenge's book," she said. Then, to the sham agent, "Where did you get it? Where's the real Stonehenge?"

He looked at Paulette. "We have to tell them," he said.

Reluctantly she nodded and sat down. "All right." She faced Kirsteen and Greyhound. "But we can't tell you where the real Stonehenge is. Even if we knew we couldn't tell you."

"Start talking," Greyhound said, the gun still on them.

"My name is Mathieu. I was Stonehenge's right-hand man. When he had to go underground he passed on his code book to me and asked me to keep going as though I was him. He had set-up a large number of escape routes and safe houses, not to mention *Réseaux*, and it was necessary that no one miss him. They all had to believe that he was still around, running things as usual."

Greyhound slowly sat down again and lowered the gun, but he still kept it on the table in front of him.

"Did you send a coded message to London?" Kirsteen persisted.

Mathieu nodded. "Yes. But I wasn't familiar with the book. I wasn't very good at it. I think I made some error so I haven't used it since. Stonehenge said I only needed to use it in an emergency."

"How did you come to be arrested?" Kirsteen asked. She looked at Paulette. "I know you were giving the Gestapo information. How was it you let your boyfriend get picked up?"

Paulette gasped. "How did you know . . ? Well, it doesn't matter. I was being pressured by the Gestapo. They're holding my parents. They've been promising to do all sorts of terrible things to them if I don't cooperate."

"Yes," Kirsteen said. "I know."

"You - you know? But how?"

"Never mind that. What about our friend here, being picked up?"

"That was just bad luck," Mathieu smiled for the first time. He reached out and took Paulette's hands in his, looking into her eyes.

"Paulette fed the Germans information because she had to, but it wasn't exactly top quality information. She'd tell them of a safe house, but after we'd decided not to use it any more. She'd tell them of a Resistant, but one we were certain was a German informant anyway. Then, when they pushed for something big, she told them where they could find me. But she tried to make sure I left before they got there. Unfortunately her message to me got delayed and I went back to get something from my room, not knowing the Germans had been tipped off. I walked right into their trap."

"At least they then thought that I was really cooperating with them," Paulette said, wryly.

"How did you manage to escape?" Greyhound asked.

"A combination of luck and help from someone on the inside," he replied.

"And where's the real Stonehenge?" Kirsteen asked. "My original mission remains the same. I have to find him."

Mathieu slowly shook his head.

"As we said, we wouldn't tell you if we knew. But in fact we don't know. All we do know is that he went underground."

"What d'you mean by 'underground'?" Greyhound slipped the gun away.

"He found a way to infiltrate the Germans and operate from inside, as a spy," Mathieu said. "But just where he is, and what he's doing, I don't know. He said he'd be in touch when it was time."

Kirsteen and Greyhound got little more information out of the two and finally left them to drive back to Paris.

"I think they're genuine," Kirsteen said. "I really do, finally, believe that Paulette's on our side. I guess Mathieu is doing what Stonehenge wanted him to do, but it doesn't help me much. I suppose I could just go back to London and report that everything's all right after all, but I'd feel a whole lot better to speak directly with Stonehenge first and hear from him that everything is all right."

"I agree with you," Greyhound said. "Any business I had with Stonehenge is pretty much covered by what we've just learned. And I agree with you that they're both on the level. But if I were you, Casey -- though not knowing your precise orders, of course -- yes, I'd want face-to-face contact before going home."

They drove into Paris and agreed to check on Canon Bizien. Greyhound drove up to the Panthéon and then on along the rue Valette Carmes and around to the church of Saint-Denis. He continued on, driving right past the church.

"Did you see that?" he asked.

"No. What?"

"The church doors were closed and there was a chain and padlock on them."

"What do you think that means?"

The Gypsy was grim. "I don't want to jump to any conclusions but I think if we drive on past the doctor's house it may give us a clue."

He turned left onto rue St. Jacques and drove down to boulevard du Montparnasse, where he made a right. Turning up rue Vavin, Greyhound slowed as they approached the doctor's house. There was a German staff car and a *Küblerwagen* parked outside. Once again he drove past without stopping.

"It doesn't look good, does it?" Kirsteen said.

"No. I'm afraid our friend Michel really informed on us before we took care of him."

"Thank God he didn't know where the Leycurases are," Kirsteen murmured. She wiped a tear from her eye and blew her nose as she thought of the loving old canon in Gestapo hands. His age would be no deterrent if they thought they could squeeze any information out of him.

"What do we do now?" she asked.

He shrugged. "I'm out of ideas for the moment. How about you?"

A thought had slowly been working its way into Kirsteen's mind. She decided to try it on her friend.

"Greyhound, what do you think of me speaking to the Brigadeführer; to Artur?"

"You mean, to see if he can help get Pierre out?"

"Yes. I mean -- he can only say no, right?"

Greyhound was silent for a while as he drove. She could see him thinking through the possibilities. Finally he spoke.

"I don't think it can hurt. He already knows you've been connected with the canon, so it's not as though you're making any fresh admissions. And from what you've said, Casey, it sounds as though he does have a heart, which is rare with the Gestapo. Are you going to see if he can get Pierre out or just find out where he is?"

"Get him out. At least I'll try for that to start with. If he can't do that, then perhaps he'll at least let me know where they're keeping him and we can plan from there."

"Go for it! Where do you want me to drop you?"

"It wasn't wise for you to come to me here."

Kirsteen sat in the chair opposite Artur's desk and looked down at her toes.

"I'm sorry, Artur. I felt it was something of an emergency. I just had to see you."

She risked a look up at him. She had talked her way past the guard at the end of the street but he had insisted on calling to have someone escort her into the hôtel and to the SS-Brigadeführer's office. Artur had not seemed pleased to see her.

"I understand, Marie." His eyes finally softened and he smiled. "It's just that it's not easy for me to explain your presence here. If I come to see you it's a whole lot easier because no one knows where I've gone. Here, everyone knows we're together."

"I - I really am sorry, Artur."

He got up and came around the desk. As she came to her feet he took her in his arms and kissed her.

"Don't think I'm not glad to see you. I've really missed you these last few days. But it is dangerous."

"I know. I should have thought."

"No matter."

He kissed her again and then walked back around the desk. They sat.

"I hadn't heard of your canon being arrested but I'm not surprised. There's been a big step-up of arrests. Anyone remotely connected with the Resistants is being pulled-in to be questioned." He looked at her. "I tell you, Marie, it's not been easy for me to keep you free. If I hadn't taken your file out of circulation . . . Well, anyway. Almost certainly the canon is being held here in the hôtel. I'll check on it for you and see what I can come up with."

"Oh, thank you, Artur."

"Don't thank me yet. I'm a high ranking officer but where the Gestapo is concerned rank isn't everything. I do have my enemies. Now, you'd better leave."

"Yes. Yes, of course. And thank you, Artur."

"I'll have someone escort you out and get you a vélo-taxi."

Later that evening Godefrois Leycurases came to Kirsteen's room, the evening newspaper in his hands.

"Marie! What's the name of that German officer of yours?"

Her heart went up into her throat.

"Artur Ebernach. Why, Godefrois?"

He pointed to a headline and brief paragraph in the Stop Press section:

GESTAPO OFFICER FOUND DEAD

SS-Brigadeführer Artur Ebernach's body discovered, shot in the head.

29: DEATH AND RESURRECTION

Kirsteen cried herself to sleep. She hadn't realized just how strong her feelings had been for Artur. Rationally, she knew he was German and a Gestapo officer and she was an English spy in occupied territory. She knew that they were on opposite sides of the war. Yet she also knew that he had awakened in her a spark that she had never known existed. They had spent little time together but every second was ingrained in her memory. She would never forget him.

She was awakened early by Victoire, who told her that Greyhound was waiting to speak to her. Quickly she threw on a robe and went out to him.

"You've seen the papers?" he asked, studying her pale, tear-stained face.

She nodded, mutely.

"Well, don't give up the ghost, Casey. He's alive."

"What?"

The Gypsy took hold of her arms and looked hard into her eyes.

"I don't know what the bit in last night's *Paris-Soir* was all about, or what the Germans are trying to pull, but I can tell you he's alive. He's been arrested but at least he's alive."

Kirsteen sank down on a chair and broke into tears. But they were tears of relief. She quickly pulled herself together and looked up at her friend.

"Greyhound! Oh, thank you! You're sure about this?"

"Don't be silly, Casey. I'd never come to you with half a story knowing how important this is to you."

"I know. Oh, thank you!" She dried her eyes and took several long, deep breaths. "Now, what exactly do you know?"

Greyhound sat down on a chair beside her.

"I, too, have my contacts. It seems that late yesterday evening -- probably three or four hours after you left him -- your Artur Ebernach was arrested and taken away, first to the rue Lauriston Gestapo facilities. He stayed there for a couple of hours and then was moved on to *3-bis*, place des Etats-Unis, the torture annex of the Hôtel Majestic. It's a private house that was taken over from an absent American owner. There was one hell of a lot of activity at the Hôtel Majestic for hours after he left and then a lot of cars going to and fro between the two places. What it's all about I have absolutely no idea but I figured you'd see the newspaper and I wanted you to know he wasn't dead."

"I've got to get to him," Kirsteen said grimly. "I've got to find out what this is all about. Do you think it's to do with my asking him to get Pierre free?"

Greyhound shook his head. "I doubt it. No, I think this is something much more important. There's a real flap going on. Get dressed and we'll see what we can see. I've got the car for one more day so we can run around a bit."

They approached the place des Etat-Unis from avenue d'Iéna; the opposite end from avenue Kléber. It was a white-painted house with a sub-basement and three floors. It was on the corner of the street and surrounded by an unkempt, overgrown garden. Greyhound parked the Panhard across the street and slightly down from the house. They sat and studied the place.

"I'm glad they moved him on here from rue Lauriston," Greyhound said. "That's a similar three-storey private house but they've turned the top-floor servants' quarters into cells and torture chambers. You'd have to get into the house and all the way up to the top floor to make any contact, never mind about trying to get someone out."

"And what's the set-up here?" Kirsteen asked, studying the house.

"See the windows of the sub-basement? They've all had bars fitted on the outside in the past year. That would seem to suggest that any prisoners are kept down there. Much more accessible."

"But still not easy to get anyone out with those bars there," Kirsteen observed.

"Our first move is to find out if he is in one of those cells and, if so, which one," Greyhound said. "Then we can worry about how to get him out. And I suggest we act as soon as possible. They're not going to be keeping him here for too long, I don't think."

"We can't do too much by day," Kirsteen said. "I suggest we come back tonight, as soon as it's dark, and try to make contact with him."

"Agreed. If he's behind one of those sets of bars, I've got the beginnings of an idea on how to get him out."

"We can't cut the bars," Kirsteen said, pensively. "It would take too long and probably be too loud. The ideal would be to break them off with one sharp tug. Too bad we don't have a tank."

"Like I say, I've got some ideas forming," Stonehenge said with a smile. "Let me work on it a while, Casey. Come on, we'd better not sit here too long."

He started the car and they drove back to the Leycuras antique shop.

"I don't know whether or not we can get your Artur out of there," Greyhound said, as Kirsteen got out of the car. "But just in case we get really lucky, get all your things in order so when I pick you up tonight you can leave and not worry about having to come back for anything."

"That won't take long," Kirsteen said, thinking of her code book and gun; her only two true possessions. "I'll see you this evening, Greyhound. And thanks again."

Kirsteen said goodbye to the Leycurases, informing them that there was a good chance she wouldn't be back. She thanked them for all their kindnesses and wished them well with their continued gouging of the Germans and their assistance to allies in need, on their way through Paris. Both Godefrois and Victoire seemed to have a hard time saying farewell, but finally they kissed her and closed the door as Greyhound drove up.

It was a far cry from the pretty little red Panhard that Kirsteen found waiting for her as she turned away from the antique shop.

Greyhound had acquired an old Fiat 1100 van which had had the rear part of it cut off and a flat, wooden, pick-up bed fastened on. On the bed lay a roll of steel cable. There were planks fastened along the sides and across the tailgate, to keep anything on the bed from falling off, but the whole thing looked very primitive to Kirsteen.

"What's the plan?" she asked, as the truck pulled away.

"First we need to find our man," Greyhound said. "Then we'll see how we go from there."

He parked a block away from the house and the two of them walked around to where they could see everything.

"One man on sentry duty out front," Kirsteen said. "He seems not to move around much; just up and down across the front of the property once in a while. No one on the sides or rear."

"That's not too bad," Greyhound agreed. "They must be very complacent. Okay, Casey. Off you go. I'll keep watch."

As they'd planned on the drive over, Kirsteen dropped down into the bushes of the garden and crawled off towards the house. There had once been an ornamental wrought-iron fence around the property but that had long since been taken down and sent off as part of the Germans' scrap metal drive. Their demand for raw materials was working in favor of the two spies.

Crawling under a chestnut tree, Kirsteen took hold of a fallen limb and dragged it with her as she crawled. When she reached the inner edge of the overgrown weeds she pushed the tree branch out ahead of her, towards the nearest barred window. Extending her arm as far as she could, she was able to tap on the window with the end of the limb.

Several taps produced no response and she finally crawled across to the next window, working herself along the side of the house away from the front. A few taps there brought a face to the window, peering out into the near darkness. It was an old man and Kirsteen could see that his face was bloody and many of his teeth were missing. He looked blankly out into the night, while she remained flat on the ground, then he dropped back down again out of view. Kirsteen moved on to the next window.

Of the eight windows along the side of the house only five had seemed to be occupied, and none of them by the face she longed to see. Two of the faces that had peered out had been female; their hair disheveled and noses bloodied. It was quickly obvious to Kirsteen that the occupants of the cells had been badly tortured. What if Artur was in one of them but too weak to come to the window, she thought? Well, she'd try them all first and then consider that possibility.

She moved on around the corner to the first window at the back. She tapped a long time with no response and was about to give up and move on when she saw a hand come up and grip the window sill. Agonizingly slowly the person inside pulled himself up until she saw the face of Artur Ebernach looking out at her. She almost cried. His face was battered and one eye partly closed. It took her a moment to realize that he couldn't see her outside. Just as he was about to turn away she dropped the branch and crawled quickly forward to press her face up between the bars.

There was immediate recognition on his face. He quickly glanced back over his shoulder, as though to be sure no one was approaching his cell from inside the house, then he turned back and smiled at her. Kirsteen put her fingers to her lips, first to blow him a kiss and then to signal silence. He nodded. Then she had to use all her will-power to turn and crawl away from him.

"I've found him!" she cried to Greyhound, as she broke out of the garden and ran quickly across the road to where he was standing in the dim light under a tree. "He's in the rear corner window. Not too bad; away from the sentry at the front of the house."

"Good! We've been lucky. Okay, let's get the truck."

They went back to the old Fiat. Greyhound took the roll of cable from the bed and gave it to Kirsteen then the two of them got into the truck. It took a moment to start.

"God! Don't let it let us down when we need it," Kirsteen whispered.

"It'll be all right," Greyhound said, patting the dashboard. He drove it around the corner and along towards the house with the sentry outside. He drove past the sentry and made a turn down the road along the side of the house, then pumped the clutch pedal so that the truck lurched for a moment before stalling out the engine. He climbed out, loudly cursing and swearing. Meanwhile Kirsteen also slipped out and dropped down once more in the overgrown weeds and bushes of the garden.

As expected, the sentry came around the corner and down the side street to where Greyhound now had the bonnet open on the vehicle.

"Was ist?" demanded the sentry.

Greyhound shrugged at him, pointed at the truck and spat into the road.

"You must move this. You cannot leave it here," the German said, in atrocious French.

"Don't worry, old son," Greyhound said to him. "I've got no intentions of leaving the damn thing here. Wait a minute. I'll get it going."

He went around to the cab and got out the hand crank. Returning to the front of the vehicle he inserted it and gave it a turn. Nothing happened. Greyhound had been careful not to turn on the ignition. He gave the engine several more cranks but to no effect.

"Move it!" the German said.

Greyhound pulled out the crank handle and offered it to the man. "Here! You try!"

The German waved him away.

"All right," Greyhound said. "I'll go and get what I need. I'll be right back."

He threw the crank handle in the back of the truck and started to walk away.

"Wait! Where are you going?" the sentry demanded. "I said you can't leave it here."

"I know!" Greyhound turned and spoke to him slowly and carefully, as though to a child. "I have to go and get the part I need to make it go. I'll only be five minutes. Be right back. You just keep an eye on it for me, all right?"

The German waved his hands in disgust then tapped his watch.

"You be back in five minutes or I will have this thing impounded!"

"No problem, my friend," Greyhound said, smiling. "I'll be right back." He turned and hurried off.

As they had expected, the German sentry gave a last look of disgust at the vehicle then walked back around to the front of the house and resumed his stance in front of the main entrance.

Kirsteen moved forward again and hooked the end of the steel cable around the rear axle of the truck. She then started unwinding the wire as she crawled back through the brush towards the rear corner of the house. At the window she took the other end of the cable and wound it around and between the bars on the outside of the window. She peered closely at the cement as she did so, noting that it had been a recent job badly done. She hoped that consequently it was weak. While she was wrapping the end of the cable around the bars Artur's face appeared once more on the other side. She smiled at him and nodded. When she was satisfied that the cable was well attached, she crawled to one side and looked at her watch. She'd taken less than five minutes.

The timing was good. Greyhound returned to the truck, waving to the guard as he went past the end of the road. He switched on the ignition. When he pressed the starter button the engine started right away and he blipped the gas pedal a few times. Then he put the truck in gear and sharply let out the clutch. The Fiat jumped forward and the cable tightened. Greyhound felt the tug on the truck as the wheels spun. He stopped, backing up again slightly. All the time he tried to keep an eye on the sentry, who seemed to be content that the truck's engine was at least running again and the man was trying to move it away.

Twice more Greyhound jumped the truck forward, each time the cable tugged at the bars on the cell window but each time they held firm. The worn wheels of the old truck spun at an alarming rate and the air was filled with the acrid smell of burning rubber.

"Damn!" Kirsteen cried. "It's *got* to work!"

Greyhound backed up the truck till it was over the sidewalk and into the garden, then he let up the clutch and roared forward. The cable went taut, twanged and, with a crash, the bars ripped out of the cement around the windows and flew up through the air. Kirsteen dashed forward and, with the end of the tree branch, smashed into the glass pane of the window. It broke into pieces. With the heel of her shoe she quickly smashed at jagged edges then grabbed hold of Artur's shoulders. As she was breaking the panes he'd had the presence of mind to throw himself up and now came through the small opening.

Kirsteen tugged while Artur wriggled and pulled until he came out, bleeding freely from both hands but free. Together they ran across the garden towards the truck.

"Achtung! Halt!"

It had finally dawned on the sentry that the noise was more than the reluctant starting of an ancient engine. Swinging his rifle off his shoulder he started running across the unkempt garden, tripping several times on shrubs but managing to keep on his feet. He found his whistle and got it into his mouth, blowing sharp, shrill blasts as he ran.

Kirsteen and Artur ran to the truck, Artur limping badly and leaning heavily on his companion. Greyhound once more backed up into the garden so that they could reach it sooner. The two of them threw themselves flat onto the pick-up bed and Greyhound gunned the engine.

As they roared away Kirsteen glanced back and saw the still-attached cable whip around the legs of the sentry. With a terrible scream he fell to the ground and was dragged behind them. Then the cable and body snagged on a large oak tree and the truck gave a terrible lurch before, with a twang, the cable broke and they were free and on their way again.

It was all Kirsteen could do to hang onto the flat bed of the truck with one hand and keep a good grip on Artur with the other. But she saw his beaten face lying beside her and managed to wriggle forward to kiss it, bracing her legs against the plank sides.

Greyhound had a route mapped out. He made across side streets at full speed and then headed down towards the river. At pointe de l'Alma he crossed the river, swung east and on along the quai d'Orsay. He soon saw what he was looking for. Turning up rue Jean Nicot he pulled into a bakery. There were two bakery vans in the yard and he knew they'd be fully gassed-up ready to start the delivery run at dawn the next morning.

He jumped out of the truck and helped Kirsteen move Artur into one of the vans. In no time they were again on their way, heading south, over the porte de la Plaine and out of Paris.

30: TO THE SOUTH

They by-passed Orleans and drove on down toward the Unoccupied Zone. Artur slept for much of the way but eventually he awoke to find Kirsteen holding him and studying his face.

"Are you all right?" she asked.

"Yes. Yes, I feel quite a bit better after the rest. Sorry to fall asleep on you after all the excitement."

"I'm just glad you could sleep," she said. She tried to make him more comfortable, propping him up with flour sacks, and then leaned back against the side of the van. "How's your leg?" she asked.

"Hurts like a son-of-a-bitch but I don't think it's broken. The bastards kept smashing at it with an oak plank." He tenderly felt the side of his face and his swollen eye and winced. "I must look terrible!"

Kirsteen smiled. "No. You look wonderful!"

"Which is how you looked when I suddenly saw you peering in through that window at me."

"Well, let's cut through all the pleasantries," Greyhound broke in, speaking over his shoulder to them as he drove. "We're all glad everyone's all right but we're also running very low on petrol."

"Where are we?" Artur asked, trying to see out of the window. The sun had started to come up but it was still early and not full light.

"We're heading south, toward the Midi," Greyhound said. "We'll probably have to ditch this van when we get to the River Cher, if we don't run dry before then."

"Tell me," Kirsteen said, taking Artur's hand in hers. "What was that story of you being shot in the head? How did that get started?"

Artur gave a great sigh. "I was afraid you'd hear about that and worry. Actually the story was true."

"What!"

"What do you mean?"

"I'd better back-track. I'm not SS-Brigadeführer Artur Ebernach. At least, not the real one. Some weeks ago the real Ebernach was posted to Paris, by the Gestapo office in Berlin."

"The real one?"

"Yes. He happened to drive through Reims just about the time that I was setting-up a *Réseau* in that area. I was visiting there from Paris, with one of my men."

"You speak as though you're a Resistant yourself," Greyhound said.

"I am. Anyway, this Ebernach happened to run into a spot of sabotage we were working on and he got himself shot."

"In the head?" Kirsteen asked.

"Right."

"And you took his place."

"Right again, Marie. As it happened we're built about the same and had pretty much the same coloring. I thought that if I could pass myself off as him it would be a wonderful opportunity to get into the Gestapo offices in Paris and see what was to be seen. To help matters I do speak pretty good German."

"You really thought you could get away with that?" Greyhound sounded incredulous.

"I didn't know if I could or not, but I was willing to give it a shot."

"But even if you were similar to him in looks, you weren't his double," Kirsteen said, her brow furrowed.

"It didn't matter. I looked close enough. The Germans are more than a little paranoid about paperwork. There are so many forged documents floating around that they look at papers more than they look at faces. The documents I carried, of course, were genuine. The Paris offices were even able to check with Berlin and find that I was indeed posted from Himmler's staff. It was a hell of a lot easier than I ever imagined it would be!"

"So the piece in the newspaper means that they found the real Artur's body," Kirsteen said.

"Right!" He nodded ruefully. "And of course they then dropped on me like a ton of bricks." He chuckled. "You can imagine the panic when they realized I'd been privy to all their documents and actions for the past eight or nine weeks!"

Greyhound chortled. "That's great! I love it! It certainly explains all the panic at Hôtel Majestic when they arrested you."

"No wonder you passed on all that information to me at Caen," Kirsteen said. "So, if you're not Artur Ebernach then who are you?"

"They call me Stonehenge."

The van swerved slightly and they all had to grab hold of something.

"Sorry about that," Greyhound said. "You took me by surprise. Did you say Stonehenge?"

"Uhuh!"

"The *real* Stonehenge -- at last?" Kirsteen asked. "Who was that other man who claimed to be Stonehenge? The one who was in the hôtel cells when I was there?"

"That was Mathieu, my old number one. I had him take over for me. It was a decision we had to make on the spur of the moment. I had to become Artur Ebernach and get on to Paris but of course I didn't want all my connections to know. And I didn't want them to think I'd deserted them. Most of my people had never actually met me face to face; I would organize and advise, rather than personally lead. I made Mathieu into Stonehenge for the time being. I didn't know how long it would be for. I didn't think I'd last as long as I did."

"And you helped Mathieu escape when he got caught," Kirsteen suggested.

"Oh, yes. I helped a lot of people out, indirectly. That was a very useful position. With a rank of Brigadeführer I could do a great deal without being questioned. By the way, I wasn't able to help your canon. Didn't have time. I believe he was being sent to Germany."

The van's engine faltered. Kirsteen and Stonehenge looked to their driver questioningly.

"About to run out of petrol," he said. "I think we'll make the top of this rise and we can coast as far as possible down the other side. Then that's it I'm afraid."

As they topped the rise the engine finally died. In the distance, ahead of them, they could see the morning sun glinting off the waters of the River Cher, as it wound its way across the countryside.

"You'll be able to make it to the river all right," Greyhound said, steering the van into a wood at the side of the road. "We'll push this in here, under the trees a bit more, and then we'll go our separate ways."

"Go our separate ways?" Kirsteen said. "You're not getting out of France with us?"

Greyhound shook his head. "No. I've got other things to get done. Once you're both off into Midi I won't feel so bad. You should be able to make it down to the Forbidden Zone all right, then you've just got to get over the Pyrenees into Spain. That shouldn't be too big a problem for someone like you, Casey."

"'Casey'?" Stonehenge looked at her questioningly.

"Sorry," Greyhound said.

"Oh, that's all right, Greyhound," Kirsteen said. "He has to know sometime. Yes." She smiled at Stonehenge. "It looks as though we've got to get to know each other all over again."

He squeezed her hard. "If it's as much pleasure as the first time, you won't hear me complain. I take it you're not just a school teacher from Lyons? And not just a Resistant either?"

"No," she said, and finally went back to speaking in English. "As a matter of fact I came all the way from London just to find you."

Kirsteen and Greyhound pushed the van in under the trees as far as they could. Although still unsteady on his leg, Stonehenge helped them break off some branches and try to hide the vehicle so it wasn't too obvious. Then the three of them set off along the road, Greyhound and Kirsteen one on either side of Stonehenge, supporting him.

"The river is watched pretty well," Stonehenge said. "I know because I've been across it a few times myself, in the past. It's the dividing line between the Occupied and the Unoccupied Zones so the Germans really keep an eye on it."

"I presume it's best to cross after dark," Greyhound said.

"Not necessarily. Once it gets dark the Jerries sweep the water with high-powered searchlights. And they have patrols going up and down the banks. It's too wide to try to swim across all the way under water and it's not easy to avoid the sweeping beams."

"So you're saying a daytime crossing might be in order?" Kirsteen asked.

Stonehenge nodded. "I've done a daytime crossing more than once. The sentries are fewer and they get careless because they're not expecting anyone to try to cross in broad daylight."

"But surely you're still sticking out like a sore thumb?"

"No. There's a bridge close to the village of Cherville. It has supporting piers going down into the water every hundred feet or so. You can cross in stages, going from pier to pier. And it's possible to duck under and swim under water for short stretches if necessary."

With the village and the bridge in sight they slipped into the woods that had edged the road for some miles. Greyhound reached into the neck of his shirt and pulled out a gold coin on a chain. He slipped it over his head and gave it to Kirsteen.

"Here, Casey. This is for you. It's my lucky talisman."

She looked at it. It was a gold coin in a bezel mounting.

"Greyhound! I can't take this. It's beautiful, and it must be worth something."

"It's a Queen Victoria jubilee sovereign. 1890. Most Roma wear one, though not necessarily a jubilee one. Take it, Casey! Like I say, it's a talisman; it'll keep you safe."

"Oh, thank you, Greyhound. But I'll just keep it for you till we meet again in England."

"That's a deal," he said.

She put her arms around him and kissed him on the cheek.

"Kushti bok, mi pen," he murmured.

"What's that mean?"

"It's Romany. Means 'Good luck, my sister'."

"Then *kushti bok* to you too," she said, tears in her eyes.

Greyhound turned to Stonehenge. "Take good care of her."

"I think she's going to be taking care of me," he chuckled.

The Gypsy turned and disappeared into the trees.

"I think we should at least wait for early evening," Kirsteen said. "When it's not quite so bright but before the sun goes down and it gets dark."

"Good," Stonehenge said. "And also at that time, just before the shift change, the sentries'll probably be getting tired and careless."

They had managed to make their way down to the river bank and crouched in the bushes within easy reach of the old bridge. Kirsteen studied the piers. The bridge was a stone one and the piers were solid legs going down into the fast-moving water. There were three of them spaced out between the end abutments.

There were only two German sentries -- one at each end of the bridge -- at any time throughout the day; the morning pair changing with two fresh ones at noon. They would cross and re-cross at intervals, stopping to chat briefly as they passed one another.

"Greyhound said that at dusk they're supplemented by four others who ride their bicycles up and down the banks on this side," said Stonehenge. "They're the ones with the searchlights."

"Will you be able to swim with your bad leg?" Kirsteen asked.

"I think so. That's the joy of crossing in easy stages. I can rest-up on the foot of a pier if necessary."

"You'll go first," she said, taking charge. "I'll watch the guards from here. Keep an eye on me when you get to each resting place. I'll wave every time they get to the ends of the bridge, then you'll know you've got time to make the next section. When you get across you can watch and wave for me."

"One question, my dear." He leaned forward and kissed her cheek. "What about our clothes? We don't want to be soaking wet for the rest of the journey. And it can get pretty cold at night; it's early in the year yet."

"I'd been thinking about that," Kirsteen replied. "I think we'll have to strip and carry our clothes on our heads."

There was a twinkle in his eyes. "I was hoping you'd say that!"

She gave him a playful jab.

They took turns in napping but by late afternoon it was decided to make the move. Carefully, trying not to cause any great disturbance in the vegetation where they lay, they slipped out of their clothes and made them up into bundles.

"I wish circumstances were otherwise, that we could dally here for a while," Stonehenge said, caressing her body.

"Don't think I don't feel the same way," she said, nuzzling his chest. They kissed and then Stonehenge started the crawl to the bridge.

On Kirsteen's signal, he slipped into the water, making as little noise as he could, and moved across towards the first pier. He found that for half the distance he could walk on the muddy bottom but eventually he had to push off and breast-stroke gently forward. In less than twenty minutes he was safe on the other side. He waited for the guard to move up onto the bridge again and then he slid out from underneath and limped across into a small copse. From there he signaled Kirsteen on her crossing.

They dressed again and turned their backs on the bridge. They were now in the Unoccupied Zone.

"We still need to be careful," Stonehenge admonished. "The Germans may have labeled this the Unoccupied Zone but that doesn't mean they're not active here. It's just that they're not out in the open, that's all."

"I know," Kirsteen said. "We can breathe a little easier but we've still got to be on our toes. And we've got a long way to go."

She unscrewed the cover on her coat button, revealing the compass. She then ripped out the lining of her jacket and turned it over to reveal a map of France printed on the silk.

"Nice equipment," Stonehenge admired. "Government issue, I take it?"

She nodded, smiling. "Oh, yes. They prepared me well. I didn't know if I'd ever have to use this but now I'm glad we have it."

They poured over the map and roughed out a route. They would make their way south to Toulouse, then southwest to cross the Pyrenees at Lourdes.

"Lourdes," Kirsteen said, pensively. "Now that could be useful. With your bad leg, if we're asked we could claim we're brother and sister going to Lourdes looking for a cure for you. What d'you think?"

"I could claim I was in the French Tenth Army and got wounded at the Somme River, or something," Stonehenge said. "Though let's hope we don't get into a situation where we've got to come up with stories."

"Still, it's best to be prepared," Kirsteen said.

They decided to travel by night as much as possible and rest up during the day, at least until they were away from the crossing and well down into the South.

31:   THE FINAL STEP

For three days they made steady progress across country. They slept in barns and under hedgerows. They dug up potatoes, carrots and turnips and stole what other food they could.

Finally their path crossed with that of a railroad line and, following it south, they were able to scramble aboard a slow-moving freight train as it slowed at a sharp curve. The train took them to the outskirts of Toulouse, where they dropped off at the freight yards.

"I know of a safe house in the town," Stonehenge said. "I've used it myself, once, and I've sent many packages down to it. It's the Hôtel de Paris."

Stonehenge had picked up a stick in their travels and had fashioned it into a sturdy walking cane. He leaned on it as they moved into the town along the Allées Jean-Joures and around to rue d'Alsace-Loraine.

"Are there Gestapo here?" Kirsteen asked.

He nodded. "Their headquarters is the Hôtel l'Ours Blanc; a very modern structure. But we need to keep our eyes open. The whole town is crawling with disguised Gestapo looking to make trouble, German agents of all kinds, a swarm of counter-agents, and gendarmes who serve the Germans with varying degrees of loyalty. The trouble is that Resistance just isn't tolerated by the Gestapo here. They've pretty much reverted to mediaeval brutality. They execute the death penalty here by beheading!"

The ancient Hôtel de Paris, at 18, allées Jean-Jaurès, was a striking edifice shaped like a wedding-cake, but its proprietress was even more striking. Madame Mongelard was known as a dragoness. Her countenance was grim and she was a stickler for rules and regulations. She was a good friend of the Resistance but heaven help the person who tried to get into her house without the right password. Not just the password, or series of words, but the correct inflections and the "right" (according to her) attitude. Her many French admirers all used the same word to describe Madame Mongelard. It was _formidable_!

Of tough peasant extraction, Madame always wore a high-necked black dress with a white scarf tied tightly over her steel-gray hair. She sat all day long in the glass cage of the cash-desk at the hôtel, watching the world go by. She said little but apparently thought a great deal.

"Good day, Madame Mongelard!" Stonehenge greeted her. He looked around the lobby, to make sure they were alone, and then leaned forward conspiratorially. "It's early in the year for the swallows to start north."

"Ah, but they did the same thing last year," she replied. Her face was expressionless but her gimlet eyes bored into him before moving on to swiftly appraise Kirsteen.

"You may be right," Stonehenge agreed, giving the final response of the password exchange.

The lady in black got up from her seat and came around to the front of the desk.

"You will come with me."

The hôtel had a dark and gloomy glass-roofed courtyard. No matter how strongly the sun shone outside it remained twilight inside. Beyond it was an even gloomier lounge with a staircase that climbed to a somber interior gallery. Off from the gallery ran a number of passages, like a maze, leading to ancient and decaying rooms of once great splendor.

As they followed the proprietress Stonehenge muttered to Kirsteen out of the side of his mouth.

"Every night the gendarmes come and examine the register," he said. "They ask Madame questions about the few guests that are registered, not knowing that twice that number are tucked safely away in this warren of ancient rooms."

"You require two rooms or just one?" the hostess asked, looking hard into Stonehenge's eyes and daring him to lie to her.

"My wife and I would like to be together," he said, his face a mask.

Kirsteen was happy to be able to relax and, especially, to be able to take a shower and get clean clothes. She had plenty of money secreted in her clothing and pressed some on Madame Mongelard, despite the woman's objections.

"You will need all you have to pay the guides to take you over the mountains," the old woman said. "Don't waste it on me. I have sufficient for my duties here."

"And I have sufficient to contribute to the continuance of this safe house," Kirsteen said, equally insistent. Without thanks, as though she were doing Kirsteen a favor by accepting it, Madame took what was offered and hurried away.

They stayed only one night at the hôtel and left shortly after dawn the following morning. After making love half the night, Kirsteen still felt tired when they left, but she was extremely happy. Arm-in-arm, they went to the railroad station and purchased tickets from the *guichet*, then sat and waited for the train. When it came they climbed in and sat on the hard wooden seats of the third class carriage, typical of the trains in the south of France.

"You never know whether a gendarme, a *garde mobile*, or a disguised Gestapo agent may be in your carriage," Stonehenge said as they found their seats, "so don't talk more than absolutely necessary."

As it happened they had the carriage to themselves after the first hour of the journey. All the other passengers got out at the stops along the way; at Auch and at Tarbes. By the time the train chugged into Lourdes, two and a half hours after leaving Toulouse, they were stiff and hungry. But at least they had been able to catch-up a little on their sleep.

Kirsteen knew that the Germans had a large airfield at Pau, not far away, and also industries including a factory manufacturing optical instruments. In Tarbes, the last stop on the railroad before Lourdes, there were several factories including an arsenal and the car works of Hispano-Suiza. The former made guns and the latter airplane engines. This was an ideal jumping off place for going over the Pyrenees into Spain but also a hotbed of the occupying forces.

Lourdes itself was at the border of the Forbidden Zone. There was a barbed wire fence which ran the length of the town to the south, with sentry-boxes and a barrier across the main road running up into the mountains, to Cauterets.

Kirsteen found Lourdes to be sprawling and untidy, despite the almost "picture-book" quality of most of the houses, with their steep roofs of brownish-red tiles over oak-beamed white walls and lattice windows. It was on the west bank of the Gave de Pau in the beautiful green Pyrenean foothills, surrounded by woods and farm fields. In the middle of the town stood a nondescript castle, for centuries abandoned for military use.

Since the mid-nineteenth century the town had become well-known from the religious experiences of Bernadette Soubirous, who supposedly experienced a series of visions. Subsequently the town had attained a certain notoriety as a healing center, though commercialization appealing to its pilgrims had quickly made the place even more tawdry than before, with souvenir shops lining the main streets of rue de la Grotte and boulevarde de la Grotte.

Kirsteen and Stonehenge found a restaurant and ate a hearty meal. They decided that they would set off to scale the mountains that very evening. Both were anxious to get out of France and back to England.

Near midnight the two of them had moved off to the east of the town, out into the open country, and started the climb into the foothills. It was easy going at first but rapidly grew steeper. With his bad leg, Stonehenge had to lean on his stick all of the time and sometimes also be supported by Kirsteen. Yet slowly and steadily they gained altitude.

At one point the faint track they were following, used mostly by donkeys, crossed a tiny stone bridge and split into two. They chose the left hand path but, after an hour, found that it was curving downhill again. They retraced their steps to the bridge and took the other trail, which kept on climbing steadily.

By dawn they were high up on the mountains. Kirsteen had had the foresight to pack some of the food they had ordered at the restaurant and now she unpacked it and they ate. A nearby stream provided water to drink, though it was icily cold. They found a dense section of undergrowth and, crawling in, slept through most of the day.

"I hope we get over the top and down to civilization by tomorrow," Kirsteen said, as they prepared to set off again that evening. "I've kept a little bread and cheese aside but we're going to need food other than that before long."

Stonehenge was grim. "We haven't got to the snow line yet. I'm afraid the worst is still ahead of us." He gripped Kirsteen's arm and gave it a squeeze. "But we've come this far, my darling -- we'll get through."

"I know it," she said.

They came upon the snow line quickly and unexpectedly. One moment they were dragging themselves up through sparse woods and the next they were floundering through snow and the scant trees had given way to bare rocks.

Stonehenge had a hard time with his leg but refused to give in. He kept apologizing to Kirsteen for holding them back until she sharply told him to "Shut up!" They continued on in silence.

"My God! It's a hut!" Kirsteen cried.

Through the darkness she made out the outline of a ramshackle hut, silhouetted against the snow-covered slope behind it. They dragged themselves toward it.

"Bang on the door," Stonehenge gasped.

"No! Wait," Kirsteen said. "I know this sounds silly but I've got a bad feeling."

"Ridiculous!" he said. "We're miles above where there are any Germans and the place is probably abandoned anyway. Here, let me bang on the door."

Kirsteen didn't argue but she paused long enough to dig her trusty Walther automatic out of her bag and slip it into her pocket. Stonehenge limped forward and beat on the door with the flat of his hand. There was no response. He beat again, this time with his stick, then he tried the door but it was locked. He beat on it again.

Finally there came a shout from inside the house. Then a light glimmered. The door was dragged open and an old man was revealed, holding a lantern. For a moment he stood there, looking at them in surprise.

"Come in! Come in," he eventually said. "What are you doing out here at this time of night?"

Kirsteen hurried forward to join Stonehenge and the two of them passed into the shack. It was warm and dry inside; a fire was banked down in the stone fireplace. They both collapsed on a rickety couch and breathed a sigh of relief. The old man stood studying them, squinting his eyes first at one then the other.

"We're on our way over to Spain," Stonehenge explained. "We need your help. We just want a short rest, if you don't mind . . ."

"Mind? Of course we don't mind, my friends!"

They both jumped as a tall, blond man in a thick, dark gray sweater and corduroy trousers tucked into mountain boots suddenly appeared from the back room. He held a Luger P08 automatic pistol trained on them.

"What the hell . . .?" Stonehenge attempted to get to his feet.

"Sit down!" snapped the man. "I gather you're not aware that we make snap inspections of these sheep-herders huts. These Basque people are smugglers from way back." He spat in the direction of the old man. "Now they try to smuggle human beings -- over the mountains and into Spain. I take it you are two of his clients?"

"No!" Kirsteen protested. "We didn't even know this hut was here."

The man laughed. "Of course you didn't! And you didn't think we knew either! But I know I can always pick up some interesting 'packages' if I take the trouble to climb all the way up here once in a while. Right, old man?"

Again he spat at the silent, bent figure. The saliva hit the old man's chin but he didn't attempt to wipe it off.

"How long have you been here?" Stonehenge asked angrily. "Do you wait here all day and all night just on the off-chance that someone will show up?"

"That's pretty much it, yes," the German replied. "Whenever things are getting slow down in the town I take a hike up here, to one of these hovels along this ridge. Just happened to be this one tonight. Just your luck, right?"

He turned his attention to the old man.

"I guess this is your last job of guiding people over the pass, my friend. I think I'll take them on from here. Though we'll be going down, not up." He swung the Luger around to point it at the frail figure.

A shot rang out. A bright red spot appeared on the German's sweater, at the chest, and he fell to the ground.

"Oh, God! I hate having to do that!" Kirsteen said. "But I had no choice, had I?" She turned her eyes on Stonehenge, who sat there slightly in shock.

"N-no! No, you didn't, my love. But thank God you did it. Who the hell would have expected to find the Gestapo waiting for us up here?"

The old man hung the lantern on a peg on the wall and bent down to examine the German. He looked up at Kirsteen.

"Thank you, lady. He's dead."

He insisted on removing the German's body himself. After taking off the man's sturdy boots and tucking them away he dragged the body out of the hut, exhibiting surprising strength. He was back within half an hour and made some coffee, which they all drank in silence. They slept in front of the fire for the rest of that night.

The next morning the old man gave them food and pointed them on their way, up a scarcely discernible trail to the top of the mountains and over the other side. He advised them to locate another cottage on the far side, where a relative of his lived. He wrote a brief message to be taken to the man.

Kirsteen smelled wild thyme and felt warmer air, as they descended the now obvious path. It was like coming into spring after a particularly long and hard winter. Even Stonehenge seemed to be walking better and rarely used his stick. They found the cottage with no trouble and met a younger man and his wife. They gave him the old man's message and he smiled broadly as he read it.

"You will wait here," he said, in broken English. "I must go down into Barcelona and get for you a *salvoconducto*. This will give you safe passage into Spain. Relax here and my wife will take good care of you."

Kirsteen and Stonehenge sat in two chairs opposite the Prime Minister. Where they thought he couldn't see them, they held hands.

"So, Casey, you have come through with flying colors. I'm not surprised! I knew from the start that I could rely on you, that's why I made you one of my Secret Circle. Well done, my dear!"

"I said I wanted to do something more for my country, in the war effort. I think I should be thanking you, sir, for letting me."

He dipped into his humidor and pulled out a cigar. He glanced at the clock and then at Kirsteen. A smile lit up his face.

"Not yet noon, Kirsteen, but I'm going to have one." He clipped the end and lit up in a cloud of blue smoke. Then he settled back in his chair and beamed at the two of them.

"You have wonderfully vital information for us, young man," he said to Stonehenge. He glanced down at a file on the desk. "Roger, isn't it? Roger Whitehouse?"

"Yes, sir." He glanced at Kirsteen. "Kirsteen?" he mouthed.

She nodded. "So at last we meet officially," she said, and giggled.

"That should excuse your holding hands then," muttered Winston Churchill, examining the end of his cigar.

www.raymondbucklandbooks.com

www.ingramcontent.com/pod-product-compliance
Lightning Source LLC
Chambersburg PA
CBHW030545180626
46816CB00005B/1413